WHEN EARTH SHALL BE NO MORE

PAUL AWAD
KATHRYN O'SULLIVAN

SECANT
PUBLISHING

Secant Publishing, LLC
P.O. Box 4059
Salisbury MD 21803
www.secantpublishing.com

ISBN 978-0-9997503-5-3 (hardcover)
ISBN 978-0-9997503-6-0 (paperback)
ISBN 978-0-9997503-7-7 (ebook)

Library of Congress Control Number: 2022904513

This book is a work of fiction. Names, characters, places, events, and incidents are either the product of the author's imagination or are used fictitiously.

Cover design by MiblArt

"…thou wilt some day, when earth shall be no more, recline and sleep within the realms of space."
 - Gustave Flaubert, *The Dance of Death*

CHAPTER 1: ORB

Constance Roy cupped her hands around her eyes, pressed them against the cold window glass, and peered into the dark vista. She squinted at the sea of stars and spotted the constellations Ursa Major and Minor, Cygnus, and her favorite, the Dog Star, Sirius. She wiped away condensation and focused on the ferocious red eye in the distance. Although she was safe in her cabin, Jupiter's massive storm, the Great Red Spot, gave her pause. She pictured herself tumbling through Jupiter's clouds, her suit ripped away by the three-hundred-mile-per-hour winds, her breath squeezed from her chest by the enormous pressure, gasping for air, for life, as she was wrenched into the planet's cyclone. This terrifying event was only in her imagination—for now. She had survived the nightmare of the migration. She was one of the "lucky" ones. Unless something changed, however, in three days the ship's life-sustaining resources and their luck would run out, and her alarming imaginings would become inevitability.

Constance's father, a well-respected astronomer and mathematics professor, had taught her as a child to identify the constellations during long walks in the West Virginia countryside. He had taken her to the robotic telescope behind the university campus, hoisted her on his shoulders, let her peer into the eyepiece, and regaled her with stories of how ancient mariners had used the stars to navigate back to their countries and families. She had been an eager student—had learned every constellation and planet—and had found comfort in knowing the stars would always guide her home. But with all his knowledge and wisdom, her father could never have conceived of the chain of events that had brought his daughter here, entreating the stars to show her the way and fearing they never would.

She was a seafarer, like the ancient mariners before her, but her old home was gone and her new home was unknown and farther than the early adventurers could have envisioned. The Curators had refused to disclose to the ship's inhabitants what had happened to Earth—only that it no longer was. If Earth still existed, it wouldn't be the glorious planet she had known, but rather remnants, artifacts from a distant past, like her, like Whittaker, like the other forty-nine refugees. They were a living history museum.

She studied Michael Whittaker, fast asleep in the bed across the room with his head buried in a pillow, and listened to his soft, deep breathing. He was her relic and she his. The Curators had assigned them to the same cabin, like college dorm roommates. The refugees had been told the pairings had been created to maximize genetic diversity. While it made sense to Constance on a scientific level, the thought that they had been brought together for breeding purposes offended her. Where were shared interests? Chemistry? Passion?

She couldn't say if she loved Michael. She had always been so sure of her feelings before the transport, but now life was filled with uncertainty even about her own emotions. Still, over the last twelve months, she and Michael had come to understand and trust one another. He was easy to live with, refreshingly forthright, and, beneath the sheets in the darkness of space, he reminded her what it felt like to be alive.

She looked out the porthole and pressed her temple against the cool, smooth surface of the outer wall. Whittaker's breathing sometimes woke her, but she couldn't blame his snoring for her recent insomnia. Her nausea the last few nights was the cause. She had wondered if her queasiness might be due to a problem with the alignment of the gravity generators. She was prone to motion sickness. Random fluctuations in the g-forces were known to wreak havoc on one's equilibrium. She had considered that she was in the family way, but that seemed highly unlikely given what her body had endured during the harrowing transport to the ship.

The more likely—and frightening—explanation for her illness was that it was a side effect of the looming Event, the topic that had dominated the refugees' private conversations for the past three weeks. The Event was the name a crew member had given to the moment the ship's decaying orbit collapsed and the mighty vessel was sucked into the Jovian atmosphere. Some spoke of the Event as the orbit disintegration in combination with the depletion of their food, medicine, oxygen, and other supplies. Either way, it was easier for them to call it the Event than The End.

Whittaker stirred. She felt his eyes on her but didn't turn around. She had caught him staring at her on other occasions, and, when she had asked him what he was looking at, he had commented on how attractive she was. She had never been comfortable with compliments about her looks, perhaps because she had never considered herself a great beauty like her mother, and with the transport's side effects, she was even less at ease when they were directed her way.

"Your hair looks like fire," Whittaker said affectionately.

She imagined it must, given the red-orange light of Jupiter streaming in through the window. What he didn't know was that her hair had once been naturally red before the transport had stripped it of color. Although she was thirty-one, her shoulder-length hair was the color of Colorado snow. The radiation during the migration had caused it to fall out, and what had grown back was a mane of white.

"I thought you were asleep," she said.

Whittaker glanced at the clock beside him. "It's early. You should come back to bed."

"You think the Curators will find a way to save us?" she said. His silence confirmed her fears. "Our orbit is degrading. We're getting closer. See how big it is now?" She pointed at Jupiter. "In three days we're going to hit the atmosphere, the ship's skin will crack, and we'll cook like in a microwave oven."

He threw back the sheet, padded across the room, and put his arm around her waist.

"We're going to be turned into vapor, and all this will have been for nothing," she said.

Whittaker took her by the shoulders and caressed her cheek. "It was not for nothing."

"How can you say that?" she said, unable or unwilling to hide her irritation with his optimism. "There were seven billion of us back home. Seventy-eight of our initial one hundred made it onto this life raft. Now we're down to forty-nine. Soon, the only remaining life in the solar system is going to crash into that gas giant, and there's not a damn thing you or I can do about it."

He returned to bed and whipped the sheet over him. "It was not for nothing," he said.

She caught her reflection in the glass—the mighty red planet a fuzzy background to her image. She hated when they clashed. He was only trying to comfort her.

"Please," he said, this time softer. "Come back to bed."

"In a minute," she said and gazed out the window.

CHAPTER 1: EARTH

C onstance cupped her hands to the window and admired the magnificent swirl of stars twinkling like diamonds sewn across an enormous black velvet cape. She leaned close, her nose touching the glass, and imagined herself lost beyond Earth's atmosphere, deep in space. This was something she had done since childhood whenever she had an unobstructed view of the night sky, and here at the Wallops Flight Facility the view was unhindered by buildings and unpolluted by light.

It had taken her nearly seven hours to drive from Blacksburg, Virginia to the Eastern Shore. Built in 1945 by NASA's predecessor, the National Advisory Committee for Aeronautics, Wallops had become part of NASA when Congress established the agency in 1958. Over ten thousand rockets had been launched from the facility to collect data for science and space missions, atmospheric and astronomical studies, and to support missions of the National Oceanic and Atmospheric Administration, the United States Navy, foreign governments, and, more recently, commercial ventures. It was Wallops' tie with commercial endeavors that had brought Constance to the facility.

She gazed at the water lapping at the property's rocky

shoreline. The idea of launching into space over an ocean horizon had always intrigued her. As a girl, she had considered becoming an astronaut, but after her mother's death, her father had urged her to pursue an Earth-bound profession. At first, she had been hurt by his lack of encouragement. Later, she understood why he had wanted her near him.

She glanced at a rocket on the flight pad, barely discernible in the distance, and stepped back from the window. She assessed her reflection, tugged at her suit jacket, and pushed aside red tendrils that had escaped from the ponytail tied at the nape of her neck. After five years as a professor of environmental science, this was the look she had cultivated for the classroom. She hoped it would be appropriate for tonight's meeting with her benefactor.

"Ms. Roy?" a man said.

Constance spun around, startled. She scanned the room. It was grand in size and outfitted with high-tech monitors. A dozen gray mesh chairs surrounded a glass conference table. The decor was the obvious influence of corporate investors. The stainless steel elevator doors at the end of the conference room were closed. The room was empty.

"Ms. Roy?" the voice said again in a smooth tone that seemed to emanate from the walls.

"Yes?"

"Dr. Malic is finishing his treatment. He will be with you directly. Are you enjoying the view?"

"Yes." She studied the ceiling for hidden speakers. "You mentioned treatment. Is Dr. Malic sick?"

There was a pause before the voice said, "Dr. Malic will be right with you."

She found the lack of specific answers and the mysterious voice's dulcet tone disconcerting. Was the voice human? Or artificial, like Siri?

She had felt off-kilter since she received the invitation to meet the head of the Foundation for Scientific Investigation—

FSI—a week ago. She hadn't wanted to come, but declining the invitation wasn't an option. She had been one of a handful of students in the country who had been given a full scholarship by the organization's education initiative. That meant a lot to a girl from Appalachia.

After college graduation, the foundation had continued sponsorship of her doctoral work on colony collapse disorder in North American honeybees. Skeptical by nature, she had pondered the possible motivations for the foundation's generosity, the strange restrictions it placed on scholarship recipients, and the requirement that she maintain confidentiality about the contract specifics.

It was the foundation's agreement and what would have been her mother's response to its terms that nagged her. "Nothing in life is free, Connie," her mother used to say. Constance's stubborn retort had been, "The stars and trees and everything in nature is," to which her mother would respond, "For now anyway," and then pat Constance's head and change the subject.

From the moment she received the call requesting the Wallops meeting, she had worried that the foundation would pull her funding because she hadn't abided by every condition of their contract. Would they really abandon her simply because she had violated one of its terms?

"You're wondering why we've asked you here."

She jumped. The voice was louder, closer. She turned and discovered a man in a slim gray Italian suit standing a few feet away. The man was skinny, almost gaunt, with willowy limbs and features to match. The gray skin on his face was stretched paper-thin across an angular skull. His white, shoulder-length hair was parted in the center, tucked behind his ears, and framed his face. It was possible the man was in his mid-twenties, but given his odd appearance, Constance found it difficult to assess his true age.

"My apologies," he said. "I didn't mean to alarm you."

She collected herself. "I didn't hear you behind me."

"I hope my appearance doesn't frighten you," he said, bowing his head. "My name is Kylos. I am Dr. Malic's son."

He extended a hand. She held hers out. His long digits wrapped around her petite palm like a spider capturing a fly.

"I wasn't aware Dr. Malic had children," she said. She slid her hand from his cold grasp and gave him a discreet onceover.

He flashed a tiny-toothed grin. "I suffer from a rare condition caused by a gene mutation. The result of that mutation is what you see before you."

She wasn't a medical doctor, but it was difficult for her to conceive of the disease that would cause anyone to look as he did.

He raised his hand and extended an elongated index finger. "I assure you that I'm perfectly healthy." He leaned close and whispered, "Maybe even healthier than you."

She felt a chill and tensed her muscles to keep from shuddering. She didn't want to offend the son of the man who had paid for her entire education.

He motioned toward the table. "Why don't we have a seat?"

She chose a chair on the side of the table. Kylos sat opposite. He folded his bony hands, set them on the table, and caught her staring at them. She felt herself flushing.

"It was decided that, given my condition, it would be best not to let the world know that Dr. Malic had a child. My existence was kept out of the press. This is not difficult when you have the FSI resources at your disposal."

Constance shifted in her seat.

"Does that information make you uncomfortable? It wasn't meant to."

"Forgive me if this offends you," she said. "But that sounds cruel."

Kylos's lips turned up in a sly smile. "How so?"

"I find it distressing that a parent would deny the existence of a child," she said, her voice raised more than she had intended.

His grin widened, stretching to the sides of his face like a scarecrow, and revealed his sharp little teeth. "Really? Do you have any children, Ms. Roy?"

"That would be a breach of the terms of the agreement I have with the foundation."

"Of course it would," he said, smug. "It's quaint of you to feel sympathy and outrage. I can see how coming from where you're from you might view it in a negative light. But you feel pity where none is needed. Being the invisible son of one of the most powerful philanthropists in the world has benefits."

"You're right," she said with force. "I can't imagine the benefits of being hidden away, of being treated like something less than—" She caught herself, but it was too late.

The smile drained from his face like helium escaping a balloon. He straightened in his seat and studied her with the predatory look of the turkey vultures from back home. "Well then," he said. "Shall we talk about the reason you are here?"

"Yes, please," she said, relieved to get the conversation back on track.

"Dr. Malic, my father, is quite sick. He has been unable to govern the foundation like he did in his youth."

She noted a change in his tone, and for an instant his features softened. Then it was gone, replaced by something she couldn't quite identify … arrogance? Self-importance?

"I'm sorry about your father," she said, "but how does this concern me?"

"Surely you are aware of the interest Father has taken in you."

"The foundation has been quite generous in supporting my research."

"Father *is* the foundation. And Father does not care about research. He invests in people."

"I thought I was here about my work," she said, frustrated.

"I've irritated you. I'm truly sorry," he said, feigning remorse. "I don't think you understand what a tremendous compliment this is. Father has done extensive investigation to find the appropriate candidates. Few measured up."

"Candidates? For what?"

Kylos covered his mouth as if he had revealed too much. "I will leave that conversation to Father," he said.

"So I *will* be speaking with Dr. Malic?"

"Of course. You don't think we brought you all this way to talk to me."

"When will I meet him?" she said.

"Soon. But first you must prepare, and, most unfortunately, that means my journey with you tonight must end."

He rose and motioned toward the elevator. She crossed to the stainless steel doors. They opened as she drew near. She turned back at the threshold.

"Mr. Whittaker will show you the rest of the way," he said from across the room.

She stepped inside. The doors to the oval elevator closed, and with that Kylos vanished as mysteriously as he had appeared.

CHAPTER 2: ORB

The sound of running water stirred Constance from slumber. She ran her hand across the empty space on the bed and rolled over. She admired Michael's figure through the smoked glass of the shower capsule adjacent to the sleeping compartment. He had developed the lean musculature of a wide receiver's physique since arriving on their space home. She, too, had developed lean muscle, though more like an Olympic middle distance runner's than a football player's. Their habitat ring spun slightly faster than that of the other refugees' ring, and these fractions of a difference in gravitational pull resulted in those living on the central E ring developing the same body type. The Curators had maintained that this had been an accident—a miscalculation in the g-force— but Constance couldn't help feel it was part of their grand design.

Water ran over Michael's neck and back. Watching him confined in the shower pod reminded her of the first time she had laid eyes on him in the transport cylinder. The memories from the transport to the ship weren't complete … more like rushes of excruciating pain. She had been driving in a pickup on a Saturday morning, listening to the radio, when there was a sudden flash and the rapture that had ripped her on a molecular level from one existence into another.

Her next flash was of waking inside a cylinder, panic-stricken and terrified. She recalled clawing at the glass window with cracked nails. Her blood had felt as if it was boiling and had oozed from her ears, nose, and eyes. She had desperately searched for a way out. That's when she had seen Michael's face—a face that would become so familiar over the next twelve months that she knew every inch even with her eyes closed. Michael's agony had seemed greater than hers. His skin had smoked, and his arteries and veins had throbbed under the epidermis of his neck and face.

The final memory of that monumental day was the clearest. It was the first time she had heard her captor, Kylos's voice. "You're okay. We will take care of you," he had said, and then she had blacked out.

Nearly half of the survivors had made a remarkable recovery given all they had endured. Of the one hundred that had been acquired, sixty-six had withstood the initial entry. Of those sixty-six, nineteen had succumbed to side effects and perished. It was the other ten deaths that Constance found most troubling. These were harder to explain. Whether these individuals had become psychologically unstable due to the trauma of the migration or the confinement on the Orb, nobody knew. The residents never discussed these deaths, fearful they'd meet the same fate.

The thought of ending up like one of them kept Constance up at night. She had lost much in that molecular storm. It was as if a piece of her had been short-circuited or left behind. She felt like a stranger in her own skin. When she was around the animals and those that worked in the menagerie, she felt more deeply connected to other living beings—more like who she sensed she was before the transport to the Orb.

She wondered if Michael experienced the same disconnect. While they enjoyed a physical relationship, at times she found him stoic. She didn't fault him. They had been through an ordeal. Maybe this change in their souls was part of the Curators' strategy to give them the toughness needed to survive on their new planet. Or maybe it was designed to prevent the inhabitants from becoming too attached in any sense beyond biology. Perhaps the emotional distance was aimed to keep the refugees from forming alliances and loyalties.

She arose from bed. The room spun. Again, the vertigo. How much longer would it go on? She was sick of being sick. The Curators had promised to care for the refugees, but the promise seemed more honored in the breach than the observance. She sat on the bed to steady herself.

"You okay?" Michael said, a towel around his waist and dripping water. He sat next to her.

"I despise what the Curators have done to us," she said with such hostility it surprised her.

She stood and paced the cabin, fueled by the adrenalin flooding her body. The anger made her feel alive—like the person she imagined she had been before the migration. So much had been wrong about what had happened to the inhabitants.

She turned to Michael, who had been watching her with concern. "Are you okay?"

"Sure," he said, confused.

She grabbed his hands and locked eyes with him. "I'll ask again. Are–you–okay?"

She noticed the wondrous green and blue marbling of his irises, stared hard into the black hole of his pupils, and willed him to reclaim from deep within what the Curators and their transport had stolen—their ability to connect. The muscles in his jaw twitched, and the artery along his temple pulsed. A long minute passed.

"I hate what has happened to us," he said. "I hate them."

There. Michael had said it. What she had been feeling for weeks and maybe what had been making her sick. Despite the fact that the Curators had saved them from Earth's destruction and were allegedly attempting to find them a new home, she hated their overseers and their secrets and rules.

"It's time things changed," she said.

"Change how?"

It was a good question. How could she change things? They had become lab rats with curious Curator scientists looking on. Where had that got them? Sitting in the middle of space on a ship doomed to crash into Jupiter. Doing nothing was no longer acceptable.

CHAPTER 2: EARTH

The oval tube that functioned as the FSI's private express elevator conducted Constance into the building's belly. After leaving Kylos in the office, the reflective double doors had slid together and the seam that indicated their separation had disappeared. A light on the touch-screen panel that indicated the floor level had faded, and the panel itself blended into the polished container's surface. It was difficult to distinguish the doors from the curved, mirrored walls. Constance imagined the vessel was meant to impress the rider with its high-tech, space-age design, but she found it disorienting and claustrophobic.

The elevator accelerated. Her ears popped. The shiny walls made it challenging to find a fixed point on which to concentrate. She had learned in childhood ballet classes that a clear focal point was a reliable preventative to becoming dizzy and losing one's lunch, so she focused on the one visible subject she could: her reflection. The mirrored surface afforded her an infinite number of Constances to look at. In front, she saw herself staring back. Behind that Constance she saw another reflection of her back and after that another of her front. This pattern repeated forward to back, back to forward, and on and on in a long, continuous line. Her doppelgangers moved in unison, shifting right then left, like a line of Rockettes.

The doors opened with a faint hydraulic hiss, revealing a man positioned directly outside. He was her age or a few years older with dark hair and a tan complexion. Like Kylos, he wore a suit and black tie. But while Kylos's suit fit him like a second skin—or maybe a fungus that had grown up and around him—this man's clothing puckered and gaped like a schoolboy's uniform.

"Dr. Roy," the man said. "My name is Michael Whittaker. Dr. Malic has asked me to escort you."

She stepped from the elevator, glad to be free, and accompanied Whittaker down the corridor. She sensed from the pressure and the heavy silence that absorbed their footsteps that she was underground. The air was cool and damp but in no way musty. The walls were a pleasant eggshell white, and the varnished cement floors gleamed.

She stole a look at her escort in her peripheral vision. His piercing blue-green eyes made her forget for a split second that she was at the FSI for professional reasons. Unlike Kylos, who came across as cruel and alien, Mr. Whittaker seemed kind and familiar.

"You work for the FSI?" she said.

"You sound surprised."

"You don't seem like the corporate type."

He grinned. "Should I be offended?"

"I can see you're not," she said and suppressed a smile. "You're different from..." She thought about the strange Kylos.

"From young Malic?" he said. She nodded. "I only started a few weeks ago. Give it time and I'll be a mini-Kylos."

"I seriously doubt that."

"I'll take that as a compliment," he said with a wink.

She caught herself blushing, straightened her posture, and

attempted a more professional demeanor. "What made you want to work for the foundation?"

"Dr. Malic and the foundation have been quite generous to my family and me. When he made the offer, I accepted."

She was surprised by his candor. "No questions asked?"

"No questions asked."

Kylos had said that the foundation invested in people. Was Michael one of its investments? She was about to ask when they reached a handle-less door at the end of the hall.

"So," Michael said. "You ready?"

She intercepted his hand as he moved to touch a keypad next to the door. "Before I go in," she said. "Anything you'd like to share with me about Dr. Malic, one newbie to another?"

He studied her a moment and leaned close. "In the last twelve months, only Dr. Malic's medical staff and son have seen him in person. He communicates with the rest of us through email and video chat. Some wonder if he's really sick or a little off, like Howard Hughes."

"You mean he's…" She tapped a finger to her temple.

"I can't say. I've never met him," he said and straightened to his full height.

"You've never met Dr. Malic?" she said, stunned.

"Nope."

"Things keep getting curiouser and curiouser. I feel like I'm in Wonderland."

He smiled. "Don't worry, Alice, you'll get used to it. All kidding aside," he said in a reassuring tone, "I suspect the reason for his seclusion is his illness. If what I've heard is true, it's probably best if he didn't expose himself to germs from the outside world. Well, I've kept you long enough. I'm sure Dr. Malic is eager to meet you."

She was sorry her time with Michael was over.

"What's it like in there?" she asked with a glance toward the door.

"Don't know. I've never been invited. You must be one special person, Dr. Roy."

The door slid up. A sudden rush of air pushed her off balance. It had a slight ozone smell. She had expected to see a room, not a chamber with another door identical to the first on the other side. Black fluorescent tubes lined the walls vertically from floor to ceiling and reminded her of lights used to attract insects outside the entrances of houses and dingy restaurants in West Virginia. Innocent bugs would fly toward the lights and be vaporized in a tiny explosion of electrical charge.

"You expect me to go in there?"

"The second door won't open until the first is secure. It's the only way through."

She took a deep breath and a giant step into the chamber. She turned to get a final look at Whittaker, but the door was already closing. "You'll do fine," he said, and then all went dark.

She squinted and raised her hand in front of her face. Complete blackness. She swallowed. She had never been a fan of the dark.

"Keep your eyes closed," said a voice from the void. The voice was male, deep and gravelly—definitely not Kylos's mellifluous one.

Fearing the consequences of ignoring the request, she did as instructed. For good measure, she placed her palms against her eyelids. Seconds later, there was a quiet buzzing. She assumed this was caused by the electricity flowing through the fluorescent tubes. The buzzing increased in volume until it sounded as if she was surrounded by a swarm of bees. She pressed her hands tightly to her face and attempted to keep still so as not to lean near the tubes. She knew what had happened to wayward bugs that got too close to the light.

Her skin warmed and tingled. It was a strange sensation, like a sunburn but different, as if particles were dancing on her epidermis. She wanted to open her eyes … badly. It was all she could do to keep from thrusting her hands away to examine the machinery's inner workings.

She inhaled deeply through her nose and exhaled through her mouth. She repeated the process, trying to calm herself. With each inhale, she smelled the ozone. She separated two fingers but kept her hand tight to her face. A strange purple glow spilled into the sliver of space between her fingers. If the ultraviolet light was able to penetrate through the tiniest opening and her eyelids, she could only imagine the intensity she would experience with her eyes unprotected.

The buzzing increased to an almost deafening level. She considered moving her hands from her eyes to her ears, but then came a sudden change in pressure and it was over. The chamber fell silent, and the darkness returned. A cool breeze filled the compartment. She hesitated before removing her hands from her face. She stretched her fingers, trying to work out the cramps that had developed from squeezing them so tight. She peered into the black and waited.

The door slid up. Another rush of air. She blinked as her eyes adjusted to the brightness.

"Come in, Dr. Roy," said the gravelly voice. "It's so lovely to see you again."

CHAPTER 3: ORB

C onstance lingered in the doorway that connected her residence cabin to the main corridor of E ring. Today's experiment would be a simple one: to see how the Curators would react to a minor act of rebellion. She would deviate from her assigned schedule and see what happened. Her plan was born from her anger at the Curators and the inhabitants' seemingly helpless situation. She had decided to keep her activity a secret from Michael until she had collected data to share with him. Plus, if there were consequences for her disobedience, it was better she bore the Curators' wrath alone.

She stepped into the hall and set out for the menagerie. It had been twelve months since the ship had been placed in geostationary orbit over the gas giant Jupiter, when the nine interconnecting rings began rotating in alternating directions and power began flowing through the station. From a short distance in space, the high-tech ark looked like an oversized volleyball that had been sliced into nine sections and then reattached by a spike driven through its core. From farther away, the Orb might be mistaken for an insignificant mete-oroid or space debris.

The central or E ring where she, Michael, and some of the

other refugees lived was the most massive of the nine centrifuges, measuring 269 meters in diameter with the ring itself twenty-eight meters wide. Three evenly spaced struts connected each ring to the central axle, with the largest spoke functioning as a passageway to the axle that housed the elevator that took residents to the other rings.

On either side of the central E ring were four smaller rings in descending diameter. Each of these rings had its own function and ecosystem. E and F rings housed the humans and the generators. The three outer rings on one side of the Orb—G, H, and I—contained the greenhouse and dining hall, exercise training facility, and the disposition chamber and garbage shoot. The opposite rings—D, C, B, and A—contained the menagerie, two supply rings, and on the outermost belt, the Curators' ring—the only area off-limits to the inhabitants. D ring, where Constance was heading now, was her favorite and housed the sixty-seven animal species from Earth that the Curators had deemed essential to rebuilding their civilization.

The Orb's intricacies were still a mystery to the inhabitants. The Curators had not provided them any details about the ship's design, construction, or operation. The technology that had brought the inhabitants to the Orb was clearly advanced, but parts of the ship were remarkably functional and rudimentary. This led some crew members to speculate that the Orb might have been a joint venture between humans and the Curators who now ran it.

Constance strode down the empty corridor, passing doors that led to other cabins. Half of the cabins were empty, and half had residents preparing for their shift. The Curators had arranged for two work shifts. Since day and night within the ship could be manipulated, everyone had the sensation of working the day shift and nobody the graveyard one.

She noted with sorrow the cabins that were permanently empty and their doors forever closed. It was a reminder of those who had perished during the migration—and after. She had come to terms with the deaths that had been due to the side effects of the transport. It was the ten others that troubled her. The Curators had reported discovering these ten individuals deceased in various areas of the ship, had given no explanation as to the causes or manner of death, and had recommended the crew not dwell on their loss.

She reached the end of the cabins and picked up her pace. The passageway curved toward the connecting strut that would take her to the central axle elevator. In the early weeks on the ship, she had found the corridors beautiful and calming. The recessed lighting panels cast a cool indigo-violet glow over the gleaming white walls that reminded her of foggy early morning winter walks on snow-covered mountains. Now she felt the lighting lacked warmth.

She arrived at the opening to the strut that connected the E ring to the central axle. The network of conduits that served as the ship's veins and arteries became visible, and the flooring changed from the smooth white surface that blended with the corridor walls to an industrial metal. This environment had not been created for the residents' comfort but for practicality.

She entered the connecting spoke and climbed up the narrow steel stairs that ran in a spiral along the wall of the hollow tube to the central axle. Occasionally two residents met on the staircase and were forced to turn sideways in order to squeeze by one another.

At the top of the stairs was the alignment stall. She entered the stall, grabbed the safety bars, and pressed her back against the hard mesh cage. Two seconds passed and then, like a carnival ride, the stall shifted her from an x-axis to a y-axis position and reoriented her to line up with the elevator inside the central axle. The shift in the stall always made Constance feel like she had stepped into the topsy-turvy world of an Escher drawing.

She stepped from the alignment cage onto a landing to wait for the elevator. Within the central axle, the elevator plat-

forms ran in a continuous loop—like dumbwaiter compartments— and transported residents from one ring to another.
Each compartment was large enough for two. The inhabitants
had learned to carefully time their steps on and off the
compartments. One misstep and a person could be hit on the
head by the floor above them or trap a foot in the space
between landings and the elevator. Constance eyed an
approaching empty compartment and hopped on with practiced ease.

Residents waiting on platforms nodded or waved as she
passed. She approached the landing to the ring where she
was expected. She had been assigned to the environmental
and agricultural ring to maintain and monitor the bees, as
well as corn, soybean, and other crops. She watched as the
landing to her ring drew closer and then disappeared. Her
heart skipped a beat. Up until this moment, she had
adhered to the Curators' precisely prescribed routine. Now
she was no longer following protocol. Her experiment had
begun.

The landing for the menagerie habitat ring approached.
How soon after she stepped onto the ring would it take for her
presence to be noticed? She exited the elevator, entered the
alignment cage, shifted orientation, and descended the stairs.
She scanned the corridor. All clear. She took a breath and
strolled down the hall toward the menagerie.

"Ms. Roy?" came a voice from behind her.

She stopped. The Curators were the only creatures she
knew who could travel as if barely moving the molecules of
air. "Yes?" she said but did not turn around.

The voice belonged to the Curator the refugees called Fifi.
Nobody could remember who had come up with the nick-
name, but it had made everyone laugh and stuck. Like the
other Curators, Fifi's features were angular, thin, and asexual.
It was only because of her smaller stature, slightly puckered
lips, and short, softly curling hair that she had been given a

female gender. She was the opposite of everything Constance thought a Fifi might be.

"You are not scheduled to be on this ring today," Fifi said.

"No," Constance said, turning around. "I needed to stretch my legs."

Fifi cocked her head like a befuddled Golden Retriever and scanned Constance's legs. Constance knew how literal the Curators could be, particularly Fifi, and she imagined what must have been running through Fifi's mind as she tried to contemplate the stretching of legs. For all their sophistication, the Curators seemed incapable of understanding metaphors or similes or the subtleties of human emotion. She had studied the Curators when they attempted some representation of feeling. They never endeavored to show anything other than the six universally recognized feelings of happiness, sadness, fear, disgust, surprise, and anger. And when they did, at no time did it seem genuine—like a smile that involved upturned corners of the mouth but not the eyes. Their mimicked facial expressions were an attempt to put the refugees at ease, not a reflection of limbic system activity in their brains. Constance wondered if they could feel at all.

"Did Kylos tell you to stretch your legs?" Fifi asked.

"No one tells you to stretch your legs," Constance said. "You just do."

Fifi took a moment to process her response and tried again. "Did Kylos tell you to work on this ring today?"

"Yes."

Her lie was a test. Did Kylos withhold information from his fellow Curators like he did with the ship's human residents? Constance detected the slightest widening of Fifi's eyes. Had Fifi felt honest surprise? As interesting as she found that possibility, she wasn't going to stick around to find out.

"If there's nothing further," Constance said, "I have work to do." And with that she strode away toward the menagerie.

It was everything she could do to keep from sprinting

toward the animal habitat to safety. She reached the thick door to the menagerie, pulled the lever, and entered. The door closed behind her with a gust of air designed to keep the animal smells inside. She inhaled the earthy air and sighed with relief. The animal smells were repugnant to the Curators, but to Constance they were heaven and reminded her of home. She'd be safe from questions here.

She crept along the deck lined with the pens that housed the animals. There were seventy pens in all, each grouped and divided into nine sections along the inner wall. Each of the nine sections represented a distinct habitat. Sixty-seven of the seventy animal species had survived the migration. *A better rate than us humans*, she thought.

Nature sounds piped in over ceiling speakers filled the air. The Curators had thought that recordings from the animals' natural habitats would help soothe them in their captivity. The sounds, as well as the lighting, were synchronized with the individual animal's biorhythms and created day, night, and the seasons. She detected the chirp of a cricket, the hush of a breeze, and the faint croak of a toad. It was night.

She slowed her pace, found the pen she had been looking for, and opened the door.

CHAPTER 3: EARTH

Constance squinted as her eyes adjusted to the light streaming from Dr. Malic's subterranean Wallops office into the decontamination chamber. Beyond the door, books were stacked from floor to ceiling in columns that resembled cave stalagmites, and every surface was covered with a variety of objects—some antiques, some contemporary items still wrapped in their original manufacturer's packaging. A small stone tablet with ancient hieroglyphics leaned against a pile of computer hard drives. A cracked porcelain doll dressed in a tattered sailor's outfit slumped over a Segway handlebar. A drone perched atop a rusty manual typewriter. The room looked more like the domain of a hoarder than that of a world-famous inventor and philanthropist.

She stepped inside, almost knocking an old *Time* magazine from one of the piles, and cautiously worked her way through a winding maze of boxes and rubbish that led away from the door and deeper into the world of what Constance thought must be a deranged mind.

It's so nice to see you again. What could Dr. Malic have meant by that? She was certain their paths had never crossed. She reached a fork in the box forest and tried to ascertain which way to go. She stood on tiptoe to see over a shorter pile. The room was quite large, with a twelve-foot-high ceiling, yet it still felt suffocating.

She detected a faint clicking. She tucked a strand of hair behind her ear and listened. There it was ... rhythmic and repetitive, like the ticking of a clock but different. She chose the path to the right and inched past a six-foot-high stack of books, fearful that the slightest contact would cause an avalanche. If the clicking sound got louder, she continued; if it faded, she backtracked and took a new route. Finally, she had a solid fix on the location of the noise. She proceeded with more confidence, rounded a corner, and discovered ... a tiny galloping horse automaton beneath a glass sphere sitting atop a simple card table.

The figure moved wild and free as it raced over a mechanical treadmill, the gears visible below the base. Constance edged forward, mesmerized by the movement of the delicate hinged legs. Each leg repeatedly touched down on the rotating track and popped up again while the body remained fixed by a single screw through its middle that was attached to a post running up the side of the treadmill. With each bounce, the horse rocked forward and back, seesawing like a real horse at a full sprint.

She watched with her face inches from the protective glass sphere. The creative side of her brain found the near perfect representation of the movement compelling, and the scientific side wanted to crack the glass and study the inner workings more closely. There was something familiar about the object. She was overcome by a feeling of déjà vu.

"Do you like it?" a frail voice said.

"Very much," she said, so entranced by the machine that she almost failed to notice the figure moving on the other side of the table.

"I am pleased," Malic said.

She peered across the table at the diminutive man

standing before her. Despite having been told of Dr. Malic's illness, she had expected the powerful head of the FSI to be more robust. He looked fifteen years older than his documented age of sixty-five, and the skin on his face was in a losing war with gravity. A suit several sizes too large hung on his frame like a hanger. Malic clung to an IV stand from which hung a full clear bag of liquid. The fluid drained down a tube into a needle inserted into the back of his left hand.

There was little confirmed public information about Dr. Malic, which had prompted conspiracy theorists and fringy geeky sects to post wild speculations about him on social media and in underground online discussion forums. Many suspected Malic was fast at work on a hyper supercharged ion collider and voiced fears he would create micro black holes and strange matter that would destroy Earth.

"Dr. Malic?" she said.

A knowing smiled formed across his shrunken face. "Not what you were expecting," he said.

No, she thought.

"No need to answer," he said, raising his free hand. "I'm sure Kylos told you I'm not well."

"He didn't get into specifics."

"I was exposed to radiation years ago. The particulars aren't important. It's only the result you see here that is." He gestured to his withered body. "Metastatic cancer." He wheeled the IV stand to a stack of crates and sat. "You know what my treatment is?"

She shook her head.

"More radiation," he said, amused. "A vicious cycle, wouldn't you say?"

She smiled sympathetically.

"And there's this. My magic elixir." He indicated the IV bag.

She looked at her feet, uncomfortable with the personal nature of the conversation.

Malic turned his attention to the horse still running under the glass. "It's remarkable, isn't it?"

"It's an amazing automaton," she said, relieved to have a change in topic.

"From the seventeen hundreds. I have a collection. This is my favorite. I thought maybe you'd like to see it." He waved for her to help him from the crate. "Walk with me."

She extended her arm. He slipped his hand around her bicep and pulled himself to a standing position. Constance was surprised at how light he was—as if his bones were as hollow as a bird's. They made their way around the mountains of belongings. She was impressed by how he managed to maneuver his IV stand without toppling a single item. She wasn't sure if they were traveling toward a destination or if he merely needed to move. She had made similar walks with her father years ago.

"You know who developed the first automata?" he said as they reached the end of the room and turned.

"No."

"The Ancient Greeks … a remarkable people."

"Yes. They provided us the foundations for literature, philosophy, and teaching."

"And miraculous machines. Machines run by water, air pumps, and steam. They were this close," he said, holding up his thumb and index finger, "to an industrial revolution. Two thousand years before modern man developed mechanization. Imagine the automata we would have now if they had. How civilization would have evolved over two millennia."

"Why didn't that happen?"

"Maybe it did in another life," he said with a twinkle in his eye. "Or maybe they were smarter than us. Maybe they knew the damage man could do. Think about the chaos we've created since industrialization. If that's what we can do in over two hundred years, can you imagine what we could do in two thousand?" He halted and turned to her. "Your environmental research on the colony collapse of bees is most impressive."

"Is that why you brought me here?" she asked, thankful they were getting to the purpose of her visit. "To discuss my research?"

"At this point in my life I'm more interested in people."

"Kylos mentioned that. But I don't understand. Is this about my research grant or a job offer?" She wanted to be polite, but she had spent the entire day traveling to Wallops and was, after dealing with Kylos and the bug zapper machine, tired.

"Come. I have a gift for you," he said and shuffled away.

She followed him through the box and book forest, trying not to be angry with a man so clearly at the end of his life. She noted mechanical hinges, joints, and gears among the junk and spotted a pair of mechanical eyes frozen open in an eerie stare. She caught up to Malic. They had come full circle and were back where they had begun with the horse automaton.

He removed a key from the winding mechanism. The horse stopped. He placed the key in a small drawer in the base and motioned to the automaton. "I want you to have it."

Constance didn't know what to make of this. At the end of his life, her father had given away cherished items to people he loved, but she was a stranger to Dr. Malic. "I'm afraid I can't—"

"I insist," he said, cutting her off.

There was no point in protesting. He was a man who had gotten his way his entire life. Even in his feeble state, she could sense he'd fight her. "Thank you," she said. "You've been quite generous to me."

"Generosity has nothing to do with it, Dr. Roy. I need you to save humanity."

"What?"

"The Greeks made a choice—sacrificed their own

advancement in order to buy us time. Now you must do the same."

And there it was. Whether it had happened because he had been locked away from people and the world for too long or because the cancer had spread to his brain, he had clearly lost his mind. She had come all this way to satisfy the delusion of a madman.

CHAPTER 4: ORB

Constance crept through the deep synthetic straw toward the bay mare sleeping at the far end of the stall. She placed her hand on the withers and glided it over the freckled hide, the patches of beige a result of the transport. She caressed the horse's mane. The mare's eyelids fluttered.

"Hey there, Patches," she whispered. She put her cheek to the horse's neck and stroked between its eyes.

The horse exhaled. She imagined it dreaming of grazing on the slopes of Montana or Wyoming or strolling on the sandy shores of Assateague or Hatteras Islands on the east coast of the United States. She closed her eyes and tried to disappear into the horse's dream world. Being with the animals eased her feelings of helplessness and isolation.

She heard rustling and discovered Grace watching from the entranceway.

"I thought I heard you in here," the woman said.

Constance ran her fingers down the horse's mane, quietly made her way through the hay, and closed the stall door. "How long were you standing there?"

"Not long," Grace said. "Care to help me feed the chickens?"

"I'd love to."

Grace Yoholo was the oldest inhabitant and the only surviving Indigenous American aboard the Orb. She had white hair that hung loose to her waist and striking coal-black eyes. Constance would normally have guessed Grace's age at about sixty, but given how the migration had transformed and prematurely aged almost everyone on the ship, it was more likely that she was in her early to mid fifties. She had a wicked sense of humor, a blunt manner of speaking, and an unwavering optimism that had instantly drawn Constance to her. It was not lost on Constance that Grace was the age her mother would have been if she had lived that long.

They made their way down the passageway. "Aren't you supposed to be on D ring?" Grace said.

"The less you know, the better," Constance said.

Grace stole a look at Constance in her peripheral vision. "That sounds cryptic."

Constance stared at the floor.

"Fine. Don't tell me. I'll find out. You know I'm good at puzzles," Grace teased.

Constance smiled.

When they reached their destination, Grace grabbed the lever handle and swung open the metal door. "Welcome to paradise."

She handed Constance a bucket of feed from a hook. The chickens and goats ran to the fence that separated the entrance area from their dirt-floor living quarters. Grace leaned forward, her necklace clanging on the fencing and temporarily scaring the animals. "I always forget to tuck this in," she said, touching the jewelry.

Constance had always admired the necklace. The pendant was a thin metal disc approximately eight centimeters in diameter, with holes of various sizes poked through the circle on one side and the image of a dove on the other. Grace had looped straw around the perimeter to soften the pendant's metal edge and had attached it to a braided straw chain. Constance had watched Grace make the jewelry over the course of a week and had figured the ritual of fashioning the piece and the piece itself was of significance to Grace's Cherokee-Algonquian heritage. She had secretly hoped that Grace would make her one too, but had never asked. It seemed presumptuous.

Grace pulled the pendant by the braided straw and tucked it under her shirt.

The chickens scurried, scratched, and pecked at the ground in a game of follow-the-leader. One of the goats rubbed its horns on the wall.

Constance leaned against the fence. "You mind if I ask you something?" she said.

"Don't know if I'll have an answer, but shoot."

"Why are you here on the Orb?"

"You mean how did I get so lucky when I clearly can't help in the procreation department?" Grace said with a twinkle in her eye.

Constance turned to her. "I'm serious."

Grace studied Constance. "The Curators need me to assist them in identifying and assessing our Goldilocks planet."

"I would have thought the sensors and processors on the ship could do that. It's just data."

"Sure," Grace said. "But would you trust the survival of the human race to just data? A processor can calculate survivability numbers. Tell you if we could live a day, week, maybe even a year. But they lack imagination, experience. They don't know what goes on here." She pointed to her head. "Or here," she said and pointed to her heart.

"What about the Curators? Can't they find our Goldilocks?"

Grace shook her head. "The Curators are worse than computers. They're linear, sequential thinkers. They analyze data in order. What's needed to find our special new world is someone that can see everything at once, a simultaneous thinker."

"And that's you?" Constance said.

"You're looking at one of the best. It was hell for me in school until I went to MIT. You know how sequentially oriented our world is? When this life raft crosses with the right planet, I'll know. Then my work will be done and yours will begin."

"*If* we find the right planet," Constance said.

"We'll find it."

"How can you be so confident?"

"We're still here, aren't we? As long as I have that, I have hope. Giving up without a fight isn't in my nature."

"Speaking of fighting," Constance said. "I had a run-in with Fifi."

Grace raised a brow. "What type of run-in?"

"She confronted me about being here. I told her Kylos sent me."

"You lied?"

Constance nodded.

"Be careful," Grace said in a hushed voice. "Those creatures aren't to be trifled with. Don't forget they're the same things that yanked us from our homes, allegedly because they like us. Imagine what they'd do if their feelings turned negative."

The woman's distrust of the Curators and anyone who claimed to be helping people while putting those same people through hell ran deep. She didn't blame Grace. The native tribes had been repeatedly mistreated and betrayed by the European settlers in America. The distrust was rightfully in her DNA.

"You think that's what happened with the ten others?"

"Why is it that we don't use their names?" Grace said, anger bubbling to the surface. "They were people, just like us. Isaac and Vinnie and Finn and—"

Constance gave Grace's hand a sympathetic squeeze.

"Their names are important," Grace said, tapping the fence with her finger for emphasis. "They should be remembered. Ten people have mysteriously died on this ship, and nobody knows how or why."

"Perhaps it's time you and I found out," Constance said.

Grace looked at her with surprise. But before she could respond, the lunch bell chimed.

"Has that much time passed?" Constance said. It seemed early for their meal break.

"I still have the cows to feed," Grace said.

"I'll help you."

"No. You go. If Fifi said something to Kylos, you're probably already in enough trouble. I'll meet you there."

"Are you sure?" Constance said, not wanting to leave her friend or the safety of the menagerie.

"Go on. I'll be along shortly."

Constance had been dreading leaving. There would undoubtedly be consequences for her lie. She crossed to the door.

"Hey," Grace said. "Keep your guard up."

Constance left Grace with the chickens and goats and made her way to the menagerie exit. She hesitated when she reached the door. She had chosen to deviate from protocol and intensify that deviation by lying to Fifi. This was her social experiment within the Orb petri dish. If there would be a response to her introduction of abnormal behavior into the dish, it would be quick.

She yanked open the door and stepped into the corridor. As she had anticipated, Kylos and Fifi were waiting.

"There you are, Ms. Roy," Kylos said, flashing his pointy-toothed grin.

"Kylos didn't tell you to work on this ring today," Fifi said.

Fifi's eyes looked dead and glassy as always, but her face seemed different. The musculature under her thin, pale skin appeared to twitch involuntarily. Was this what a Curator looked like when it was angry?

"No, he didn't," Constance said matter-of-factly.

"I'm assuming you have an explanation for this behavior, Ms. Roy," Kylos said.

"As I told Fi—" She caught herself. "As I said earlier, I needed to stretch my legs."

He nodded. "Are you requesting more time for physical exercise and training?"

She studied Kylos, unsure if he was truly misinterpreting her actions or if he was playing a game. Her experiment had yielded results, but what they were was still up to interpretation.

"Yes," she said, aiming her response at Fifi. "I would appreciate it if my schedule could be adjusted so as to accommodate more exercise time."

"You should have come to me," Kylos said. "I'm afraid my colleague thought you were being deceitful. Even after all this time, we're still unaccustomed to your use of figurative language."

"She doesn't want to exercise," Fifi said, her voice rising slightly in pitch.

Kylos raised his hand in a dismissive gesture. "That is all."

"But—" Fifi said.

"That will be all," he said with more force.

Fifi hesitated, looked at Constance one last time, and then turned on her heels. Constance watched with interest as Fifi retreated around the bend. It seemed the Curators were not as united as she had thought.

Kylos stepped to within inches of Constance. "Now we are alone," he said. His breath was an odd mixture of electrical discharge and freezer burn. "Ms. Roy, we are friends, no?"

Constance had never been good at poker, but right now she was using every bit of her power to hide her revulsion. She forced a smile and nodded.

"Good. I think of us as friends, too. As a friend, I'd like to be honest with you. We, my colleagues and I, have gone to a great deal of trouble for you. We bent time and space to ensure that the human species survives. Like it or not, we have become your caretakers. And what do we get for our efforts? How do you show your appreciation? By lying like a silly little child."

"I didn't lie to—"

"Fifi?" Kylos interrupted. Constance paled. "Oh, yes. I know about your little nicknames for us." He grinned. "Very amusing."

Here it comes, Constance thought, the consequence—the result—of her experiment.

"Walk with me," he said.

Constance eyed him with suspicion as they walked from the menagerie toward the central axle. Where was he taking her?

"What we have here," he said, motioning in a grand gesture, "is a colony, and the Orb is its hive …. much like the honeybees you've worked so hard to study and protect. The Orb is a delicate system, and that system must be maintained. When you violate the rules, Ms. Roy, you risk causing the colony to collapse. What a shame it would be for that to happen before we find you a new home."

Constance spun to face him. She squared her shoulders, rolled onto the balls of her feet to meet him eye-to-eye, and peered into the glassy dark spheres. "In three days, our orbit will decay and my behavior won't make a damn bit of difference. You say you're our caretaker, and yet we don't have a clue as to what you're doing to find us a new home. We've been sitting here like some anchored ship, just waiting, for as long as I can remember. What are you planning to do if we don't find a new home?"

Kylos leaned back, appearing stunned. "If that unfortunate scenario plays out," he said, "Then we try again."

It was her turn to be surprised. What could he mean by that?

"This conversation has been most enlightening," he said. "But I'm afraid I've kept you from lunch."

She gave him a slight nod and then hurried away. She had poked a stick at the hive and managed not to get stung. She half walked, half jogged toward the central axle, eager to get to the dining ring and share what had happened with Fifi and Kylos with Michael. She rounded the bend to the connecting strut and discovered Fifi waiting at its entrance. Neither said a word as Constance passed, but what she saw on Fifi's face was unmistakable. It was decidedly an emotion, and that emotion was hate.

CHAPTER 4: EARTH

I need you to save humanity. Dr. Malic's words echoed in Constance's mind. The trip to Wallops had been a whirlwind of emotions and ultimately a waste. She was thankful the experience was over and that she would be returning home to the safety of the Blue Ridge Mountains.

She had made several bizarre discoveries on this trip, but the one that surprised her most was that one of the world's most influential and brilliant men had gone mad. She wasn't certain if his madness was a symptom of his illness or if he had always been a little off. Her scholarship and grant funding from the FSI had filled her with pride, a sign that her research was scientifically important and relevant. Now she wondered if the money had more to do with a man's obsession with a girl saving the world and less about her academic prowess and achievements. *It's good to see you again*, he had said. Constance was certain she and Malic had never met. His idea that their paths had crossed was delusional.

She watched the FSI building diminish in her rear-view mirror, rounded a bend, and passed the rocket on the launch pad. The rocket was small by NASA standards, but to Constance it was enormous, rising fifty feet above the sandy shore. Maybe it would take supplies to the astronauts on the space station or put a new communication satellite into orbit. Whatever its mission, she wasn't sticking around long enough to find out.

She pulled her Honda Civic to the Wallops exit security checkpoint. A young soldier gave her a friendly salute, and the gate opened.

I need you to save humanity. The weight of his words had seemed to exhaust Malic. He had waved for her to take the automaton, excused himself without any further explanation as to how she could help humankind, and disappeared into his maze. That had been the abrupt end of their meeting.

She scanned the two-lane road for traffic and turned right onto Route 175, the main road that ran along the perimeter of the Wallops Flight Facility on the left and the US Fish and Wildlife Service's Wallops Island National Wildlife Refuge on the right. In the distance on the left, past the high chain-link fence that prevented intruders from trespassing onto the rolling hills of the flight facility's main campus, sat a cluster of nondescript buildings and the enormous radio telescope dishes that listened to space.

There was something otherworldly and yet logical about the facility being located at a place where water and land meet … the extension of life moving from the ocean to land to the heavens. She glanced at the lightening sky, rolled down her window to let in the spring air, and had a sudden vision of Whittaker. He had been the bright spot in an otherwise gloomy visit. She imagined they could have been friends— maybe more—in another lifetime, but it was unlikely they would meet again. And besides, she had other obligations.

Seagulls and terns swooped low over the causeway that connected the mainland to Chincoteague Island. Reeds swayed in the gentle breeze. Morning broke, and Constance marveled at the beauty of the orange sky. She passed small billboards planted deep into the marsh mud advertising Etta's

Channel Side restaurant; the Refuge and Waterside inns; Island Creamery; Tom's Cove; and—of course—where to see the famous Chincoteague ponies. Her parents would have loved this place.

The glass sphere with the horse automaton wobbled on the passenger seat. She tugged on the seat belt to make sure the machine was secure. After everything she had been through, she'd hate for a bump in the road to jostle the sphere loose and send it crashing to the floor. That would ruin the surprise.

She left the causeway, drove past the bright blue-and-white sign that welcomed visitors, crossed over Main Street, and continued onto Maddox Boulevard. Beach shops and cottages with potted flowers lined the street. She stopped to let a sturdy black cat cross the road and disappear into the foggy high grass in search of breakfast.

She circled past the campground and gas station to Woodland Drive, turned, and then turned again onto Pine Drive, where her motel was located. It wasn't as nice as the other island lodgings, but the plain two-story structure was clean and well situated. While the motel's front was rather unimpressive, the back offered an unparalleled view of the channel that divided Chincoteague from the protected Assateague refuge. Assateague was known for its undeveloped, pristine beaches and the wild ponies made famous by Marguerite Henry's *Misty of Chincoteague*. Constance had been intrigued by the idea of sitting on the second-story balcony, looking across the water, and, perhaps, if she was lucky, catching a glimpse of the ponies.

She parked and retrieved the automaton from the passenger seat. She held the machine with two hands as she walked across the lot toward the stairs leading to the second floor. A mist rolled from the water over the lot, and she half expected to see ghosts of the native Chincoteague tribe.

She climbed the stairs and tiptoed along the wooden

landing toward her room. It had never been her aim to deceive the FSI. Years ago, when she had signed the paperwork outlining the terms of her college scholarship, she had intended to honor the conditions, even if they were a bit strange. Like many young people, however, she hadn't anticipated the surprising twists and turns of life. After college, when the foundation had offered to fund her graduate and post-doctoral studies, she had signed a new agreement knowing that she had already violated its explicit requirements. But what choice did she have? With her parents gone, she was alone, without any other means of support. Maybe things would have been different if she only had to think of herself. She had lived with the guilt of her deception and had become paranoid over the years about the foundation discovering her secret. Given Malic's physical and mental condition, she wondered if it mattered anymore.

She reached room forty-nine, unlocked the door, and slipped inside. She remained still as her eyes adjusted to the dark. A sliver of light streamed in through the slit in the curtain and stretched across the carpet over a queen-sized bed and its occupant. She slipped out of her shoes and set the globe down on the desk.

The sheets rustled. She sat on the edge of the bed and gazed at the sleepy face of her fair-skinned ten-year-old son.

CHAPTER 5: ORB

Constance pushed the food around on her plate and anxiously watched the commissary door. Where was Michael? She shoved a forkful of beige food in her mouth. The Curators had provided them with everything ... except a tasty diet. In an attempt to give their meals flavor, she had secretly removed seeds from the ship's stocks, grown thyme, basil, and oregano, and given the plants to the kitchen staff to use. Unfortunately, they had quickly depleted the herbs and, before she had a chance to grow more plants, someone—she suspected the Curators—had locked the seed storage.

She surveyed the room and the dozen or so crew members who shared her lunch schedule. The dining facility was small given the one hundred inhabitants that had originally been antic-ipated. At one end was the food-dispenser area and at the other the conveyor belt on which the dishes would be washed with recycled water and dried with a powerful fan. Between the two ends were gray molded tables with matching molded chairs. In some respects the room reminded her of a high-school cafeteria.

Hashim and Dru, two crew assigned to assist the Curators with the Orb's massive generators, huddled close with worried expressions and scribbled notes and diagrams on scratch paper. Like Constance, they had voiced alarm regarding the looming Event.

At a nearby table, Muhammad, a member of the maintenance crew, tinkered with what appeared to be a makeshift oud constructed from discarded supply parts. The lute-like creation reminded her of the instruments constructed by junkyard luthiers. He gave the instrument a quick tuning and began playing.

Michael entered the commissary and greeted others as he made his way to her table.

"Where have you been?" she said before he had a chance to sit.

He held up his hands as if in surrender. "On my shift," he said, defensive. "How many places are there to be?"

"I need to talk to you," she said.

"Can you give me a sec? I just got here."

"But I—"

Michael covered her lips with his finger. "Listen," he said and watched Muhammad.

Muhammad sang in Arabic, and the room fell silent. The song reminded Constance of a lullaby.

"We should dance," Michael said.

"What?" she said. "I don't feel like dancing."

"It's not for us. It's for them." He indicated the crew.

She surveyed the room and noted the worried expressions on her colleagues' faces.

Michael offered his hand. She reluctantly took it. As they danced, Muhammad picked up the tempo, and the mood lightened. Soon others joined them on the floor, weaving their way around the tables.

"I need to talk to you about something I did," she said.

Before she could continue, the door to the dining ward flew open. The music stopped. The dancers stumbled to a halt; the laughter faded; and all eyes focused on Kylos and Fifi in the entrance.

Constance's heart skipped a beat. Were they here to announce her violation? To make an example of her?

"We have some rather unfortunate news," Kylos said.

The air grew heavy.

"It seems Dr. Yoholo met with an unfortunate accident in the menagerie," Kylos said.

"No," Dru said and clutched Hashim.

"Is she okay?" someone asked.

Michael put his hand on Constance's shoulder, but she didn't look at him. Her eyes were fixed on Kylos.

"We believe one of the horses attacked her," Kylos said. "Dr. Yoholo has perished."

CHAPTER 5: EARTH

C onstance stroked the platinum-blond hair from her son's eyes. He stirred and blinked.

"Is it time to get up, Mommy?" he said.

She kissed him on the forehead. "I'm afraid it is."

"Ten more minutes," Nicolas said, turning on his side and pulling the blanket over his head.

"We have a long ride back. You can sleep in the car."

He didn't move. She grinned. Okay, she'd play along. "Nicolas? Nicolas, are you asleep?"

A fake snore was the reply. She went to the desk and turned on the small light next to the horse automaton. "Well, that's too bad. I guess you can't see your gift."

The sheet flew back. "I'm awake!"

"Ta-da," she said and pointed to the automaton in the glass globe.

He crawled from bed. "Whoa," he said with awe. "How does it work?"

She twisted and removed the glass from above the automaton. She slid open a little drawer at the bottom and found a key with the shape of a horse at the end. She inserted and cranked the key and then pressed a button on the side.

The horse's legs galloped over the treadmill and filled the room with a gentle clicking.

"Cool," Nicolas said. He bounced onto the bed, held his arms in front of him as if grasping the horse's reins, and rocked back and forth, mimicking each of the automaton's movements.

She felt tremendous guilt about having left him alone while she attended the late-night meeting at the FSI. It would take her a long time to forgive herself, even if Nicolas had already done so. She hadn't set out to deny her son's existence. Nicolas was the one person that had brought her joy after her father's death. She had lost her mother when she was young, but when her father died from cancer, the loss was felt tenfold. It made her sad knowing Nicolas would never meet his grandparents.

Her son's actuality made her dealings with the FSI complicated. She had signed a contract and accepted money on the condition she live a life free of entanglements—no romantic partner, no children. In exchange for their funding, she was to devote herself fully to her research. She had signed the contract despite already having violated the terms. She hadn't had a choice. If lying meant she had enough to provide her son with a warm home, plenty of food, and a shot at a good future, then she'd do that and more. There was no way she'd let him feel less-than because of her youthful passions. She wasn't proud of her actions, but she didn't regret them either. She was a hypocrite for lecturing Kylos about Dr. Malic hiding he had a son.

Her shame about lying had been eased by the thought that, in the age of the Internet, the FSI had undoubtedly learned of the boy's existence and had chosen to turn a blind eye. Nicolas had a birth certificate, attended public school, and was included in census data. Finding out the truth would have been easy.

When she got the call to come to Wallops, she was sure

that the FSI would confront her about her son and her breach of contract. At best, they'd discontinue her funding and at worst they'd demand a refund of the monies they had given her over the years—something she'd never be able to do. She had thought that hiding Nicolas at the motel would allow her to plead her case. If that failed, she'd present her son to them. If they had any heart at all, once they met him, they'd see that having a child had in no way distracted her from her work. Now she understood that Nicolas was the last thing on Malic's mind.

"Can we see the real horses?" the boy asked.

"They're ponies," she said.

"Can we see the ponies then?" He gazed at her with wide-eyed anticipation.

She hadn't slept in more than a day, and the events of the last twenty-four hours were taking a toll on her mind and body. "I'm afraid we're not going to have time." The enthusiasm drained from his face. He turned away and began packing his bag. "Okay," she said. "We can see the ponies as soon as you get dressed."

Suddenly, his energy was back. He grabbed clothes and jammed them into a kid-sized duffel bag.

"But you need to wash up before we go. Ready?"

He gave her a quick nod.

She held up one finger. "Tick…" she said.

"Tac…" he said, holding up two fingers.

They both threw up three fingers and said, "Go!"

Nicolas pulled off his T-shirt, grabbed clean clothes, and ran into the bathroom.

"And don't forget to brush your teeth," she said.

"Yes, ma'am," he said and slammed the door closed behind him.

Maybe it was because she was his mother, but Constance thought Nicolas was the most special child in the world. She wondered what she had done to be blessed with the boy—how empty her life would have been without him. He had taught her to live in the moment, to appreciate that research wasn't worth anything unless it was about bettering people and the world, and so many little things she couldn't name. He filled her life with love. She might have been as successful without Nicolas, but definitely not as happy.

The shower started. She sank onto the bed, shifted to her side, fluffed the pillow, and gazed through heavy lids at the mechanical horse galloping on the desk. Each footstep sounded like a metronome click, and every click lulled her deeper and deeper into unconsciousness.

Her body surrendered to sleep, and her brain defragged the previous night's events. Images flashed through her mind: Kylos with his grin stretched across his bony face; Malic hobbling through his junk maze, his words about her saving humanity echoing off the high ceilings; and the Wallops rocket reflecting the Chincoteague sunrise.

She felt things, too: the decontamination chamber's electrical charge dancing across her skin; the slight pain of the bright ultraviolet light penetrating through her closed lids; the cool window of the FSI meeting room against her nose as she gazed at the stars.

Then there was a new sensation. It felt like a memory, but one that wasn't hers—more like a broadcast signal from a distant radio station. As the signal faded in and out, she felt as if she was spinning. Unfamiliar faces whirred by. Spinning with her was Michael Whittaker. He looked as he had when she had met him but leaner, older. She heard a voice. It was distorted, as if under water. "Are you ready?"

Her eyes snapped open. Nicolas stood beside the bed, gently shaking her shoulder.

"Can we see the ponies now?" he said.

She nodded and pushed the bizarre dream from her thoughts.

CHAPTER 6: ORB

Constance felt the Orb's dining room spin, and it wasn't because of the centripetal force. How could Grace be dead? Her friend was fine when she saw her in the menagerie. She caught Fifi staring and detected a hint of satisfaction on the Curator's face. Constance moved toward Fifi with a clenched fist.

Michael grabbed her wrist. "Don't," he whispered. "There's nothing we can do."

"I don't believe them," she said. "Do you?"

He studied her face and let go of her arm. She marched to Kylos. Michael followed.

"I want to see Grace," Constance said.

"That's really not—"

"I want to see her," she almost shouted.

Kylos cocked his head with interest. "Very well."

"Whittaker comes with me. And *she* stays," Constance said, indicating Fifi.

Kylos's mouth turned up in a slight grin. "Of course," he said and withdrew.

Constance glared at Fifi before exiting. It was everything she could do to keep from punching the Curator.

She hurried after Kylos—amazed at how quickly he moved—and caught up to him as they reached the spiral stairs to the central axle. "Who found her?" she called to him as he sailed up the steps.

"Ms. Belkin, I believe," he said, not slowing down.

Maria Belkin was one of the least-liked inhabitants. In their twelve months on the ship, she and Maria had only exchanged a few words.

"And where is Maria?" Constance said, taking the steps two at a time.

Kylos glided into the adjustment stall. "In her quarters, resting," he said as he shifted to become level with the dumb-waiter landing.

Constance waited for the stall to return, stepped in, swung around, and joined Kylos on the tiny platform. "What horse was it?"

Kylos hopped onto the elevator without answering and disappeared up the shaft. Constance waited impatiently for the next compartment and then sprang in as Michael was stepping onto the platform. He spotted Constance, took a giant leap, and stumbled into the elevator compartment.

"What the hell is going on?" he said.

Constance recounted lying to Fifi and her conversations with Grace and Kylos.

"You should have told me what you were up to," he said as they reached the menagerie ring and exited onto the landing.

She slipped into the adjustment stall, and it shifted to align with the stairs.

Michael followed and grabbed Constance on the stairwell. "What you did was dangerous and reckless."

"It was an experiment," she said.

"I'm serious, Roy. We don't know who these people are, where they came from, how they got us here, or what they want with us. You really thought it would be a good idea to piss them off?"

What if her misbehavior had caused Grace's death? *No.* She refused to believe Grace was gone. She spun on her heels and ran down the stairs to the menagerie ring, where Kylos was waiting.

"Where is she?" Constance said.

"Just outside the stall … or at least that's where Ms. Belkin said she left her. You'll excuse me if I don't accompany you in. The smell is most unpleasant to us."

She grabbed the lever and entered the menagerie. Fourteen meters down the hall was a body. Constance forced herself to move forward. She gazed at Grace's lifeless body in disbelief. She looked away from the woman's face and focused on the legs stretched straight on the floor. She scanned up the legs to the torso and noted the crooked arms. Constance lifted the tunic sleeves and discovered that both arms were broken and bruised. She re-covered the arms and lifted the material over Grace's midsection. Her stomach was covered in welts. Constance forced herself once again to look at her friend's face. Hair was matted to a bloody gash on her forehead. The nose had been broken. One eye was swollen closed. The other stared blankly at the ceiling.

Michael knelt beside her. "I'm sorry."

Her lip quivered. She shook her head, took a deep breath, and stood. Now was no time to fall apart. Grace needed her. She moved to the stall where Patches lived.

"You think that's a good idea?" Michael said with concern.

"I'll be fine."

She swung open the door and stepped inside.

"If you need me, I'm right here," he said.

She advanced toward the horse. Constance knew the damage an agitated horse could inflict, but Patches in no way looked agitated. In fact, she had never known the mare to be anything but good-natured and even-tempered. Patches blinked at Constance several times, her usual greeting. She touched the horse's withers. "Hey there, lady," she said. The horse affectionately leaned into her.

Constance inspected the horse's legs and the straw for any sign of a violent incident. "Was Grace in the stall with you?" The horse's ears twitched, perhaps recognizing Grace's name, but the animal in no way appeared as if it was or had been distressed enough to kick a person to death.

"Look at this," Michael said.

He pointed to blood smeared on the doorjamb. She checked the wall and hay. If Grace had been attacked by Patches, then there should be evidence of that. She brushed straw aside to be sure she wasn't missing anything, but there were no signs of a struggle or injury. She checked the wall outside the door. It, too, was clean. Yet here on the doorjamb was blood.

"What do you make of that?" he said.

Her jaw clenched. Grace had been attacked, either when she was entering or exiting the stall, but it wasn't by a horse. Her injuries revealed she had put up a fight. She wondered if the ten others who had mysteriously died aboard the ship had met with a similar fate.

She kneeled by Grace, closed her open eye, and smoothed her locks. She wanted to cry out and throw something but knew it wouldn't bring her friend back. She caressed Grace's cheek. Her finger caught on the braided rope of her necklace. Constance pulled the jewelry from where Grace had tucked it under her tunic, gazed at the disc, and replayed their last conversation: Grace's reproductive jokes, her warning about the Curators, her anger over what had happened to the others, and her simultaneous thinking. Constance's eyes widened with a sudden realization. Earth's survivors had lost the one person capable of helping the Curators find their Goldilocks planet, the one person who could help save them from extinction.

CHAPTER 6: EARTH

Constance gazed at the sign for Sundial Books, a shop on Chincoteague's historic Main Street, and studied its smiling sun surrounded by blue. Roman numerals for the hours of the day ran around the sun's perimeter, but the numbers one, six, seven, and twelve had not been drawn into the design. She imagined the decision had been made for an aesthetic purpose, but her mind, always attracted to numbers, couldn't help running through various combinations of the missing digits to see if there was any significance to their absence.

She sipped the coffee she had purchased to help her stay awake. Seeing the ponies earlier at the lookout had been a treat for Nicolas and had helped wipe the strange FSI visit from her brain. The seven-hour trip to Chincoteague and the meetings at Wallops, however, were finally taking a toll. She had promised Nicolas a final stop at the local bookstore after lunch, but after that they would need to be on their way back to Blacksburg.

"Mom, you coming?" Nicolas asked from the store's doorway.

The boy had inherited her love of books, and his bedroom

bookcases were overflowing. What was the harm in buying him one more? She nodded, and he yanked open the door. A bell tinkled against the glass as they entered.

The bookstore was cheerful, with white shelves, Persian rugs, and comfy chairs. In addition to selling books, it carried a variety of unique jewelry pieces and paintings by local artists. It was early for the summer tourist crowd, but there was already a handful of customers milling about.

Nicolas ran to the shelves in the front, where an array of children's books lined several cases. Many of the covers featured illustrations of the famous ponies.

A man with glasses behind the counter glanced at Constance and whispered to an attractive woman with him. The woman nodded and disappeared into the back.

"How many can I get?" Nicolas said from the children's section.

"Only one today," Constance said. "So choose wisely."

The boy's brow furrowed as if the fate of the world hung on his decision. He folded his arms and tapped a finger on his chin. It was a gesture his father had often made in the class-room when listening to students and—because Nicolas had never met his father to learn the behavior—was likely hard-wired in her son's DNA. "Hmm," Nicolas said. He inspected each book's cover and description. "This might take a while." He retrieved a book from the top shelf, sat on a nearby stool, and turned to page one.

"Is there anything I can help you find?" the man behind the counter said.

"I think we're good," Constance said.

A brown-and-tan tabby sitting on the counter meowed at her. She had always loved cats and couldn't resist the feline's plea.

She crossed to the counter and rubbed the cat's cheek. "Who's your friend?" she asked.

"Truffaut," the man said. He watched Constance with the cat and smiled. "Are you sure I can't help you find anything?"

She glanced at Nicolas with his head in the book and then at the man. The man had an easy way about him that drew her in and made her want to stay for a while. "On second thought," she said, "do you have any nonfiction?"

"For him or you?"

"Me. Maybe something in the sciences."

He motioned to the second-floor balcony. "Upstairs we have an entire section of used and out-of-print books. Are you looking for anything in particular?"

"No," she said and returned the man's friendly smile. "But thank you." She glanced at Nicolas reading on the stool. "Nick," she said. "I'm going upstairs. Okay?"

The boy nodded without looking up.

"How do I get there?" she said and pointed to the gallery.

"Go to the back. The stairs are on the left. Let me know if you need help."

Constance walked to the back and found a staircase leading to the second floor.

The woman she had seen earlier behind the counter nodded as she descended the stairs. "Let us know if you can't find what you're looking for," the woman said.

Constance made her way up the narrow passage, emerged on the second floor, and peeked over the railing. From this vantage point she could keep an eye on Nicolas. Satisfied that he was safe, she scanned the shelves, located the one with the science books, and began the ritual she practiced every time she found a bookstore that carried used or rare books.

She started at the top of the shelf and worked her way from left to right and top to bottom, searching for the long out-of-print text she remembered from her childhood. She never allowed herself to go straight to the Rs for fear that her hopes would be dashed too quickly. Instead, she'd start with the beginning of the alphabet and work her way through to Z. As was her ritual, she pressed her finger to the spines and slowly traced her progress. She stooped to scan the lower shelves. Her finger stopped.

She had searched so often without success that she had to blink to be certain her tired mind wasn't playing tricks on her. There it was, the book she had read so many times as a child: *A Map to the Galaxy* by Dr. Nick Roy. She slid the book from the shelf and flipped to the dedication page. *For my darling girls, Barbara and Constance.*

She sat on the floor and leaned against the shelf. Her father's book had been a limited edition and impossible to find. Constance had come to believe that the copy her father had given her had been the only one in existence. When she couldn't find it after going through his belongings after his death, she was convinced that the book had been lost forever. But here it was, like the one she remembered as a child, only better. This one had the original dust jacket.

She caressed the artist's rendering of the Milky Way on the cover. It was beautiful, all swirls of blue and green and stars reaching beyond the ends of the paper. As a kid she would have loved the book that much more if hers had had this cover. She peered over the railing, saw Nicolas deep into the book he had chosen, and smiled. They had both found a treasure.

She stroked the cover once more and opened to the first chapter: "Near Earth." The book was different from the astronomy and astrophysics texts of its time. Rather than treat the subject of space as a hard science, her father had written the book in the style of a glorious travel log. The reader would start their journey near Earth then head out on a sojourn through the solar system and the Milky Way. Along the way, voyager readers would be treated to vivid descriptions of the stars and planetary bodies, accompanied by notes about places to visit and sights to see while in the area.

Constance flipped through the chapters, briefly pausing on

the pages for Mercury, Mars, and Venus. These pages contained some of her favorite illustrations. She paused again when she reached Jupiter. This destination, her father suggested in the book, was inhospitable, with freezing temperatures, unbreathable air, and oppressive gravity. The planet and its unique beauty were best appreciated from afar. The book suggested visitors be sure to see the Great Red Spot, the enormous three-hundred-year-old storm that had become Jupiter's most distinct feature, and recommended that if one were to plan an interstellar journey, one might want to anchor just within Jupiter's orbit before making the next leg of an extended trip. Dr. Roy reasoned that since this planet was located in the middle of the system, it would be a perfect launching point. If properly calibrated, its gravity and enormous orbit would enable star travelers to slingshot their ships to the outer reaches of the galaxy.

She skipped ahead to where the reader left the solar system. The book became more speculative as less was known about this region. The discussion shifted to Goldilocks planets and the necessary elements needed for humans to survive and flourish. The book suggested possible locations for these ideal terminuses, if one were adventurous enough to make a trip beyond the known system. Constance remembered thinking how excited her dad would have been when NASA launched the Kepler space observatory to find other Earth-like planets in the Milky Way. Unfortunately, he hadn't lived long enough to learn about the discovery of the habitable Kepler exoplanets.

She turned to the back of the book and was delighted to see the familiar circular star charts. The pages in this section mapped most of the known stars and systems. These were the same stars that her father had pointed out on their walks. She spread the pages wide in her lap, closed her eyes, held up a finger, and brought it down on a random spot. This was the game she had played with her father. Once she had touched the paper, she would open her eyes and her father would ask her to name the constellation based on its position in the sky. If she guessed correctly, he would ask her if she wanted to live there. Most often she responded with an enthusiastic yes, sending her father into a fit of laughter.

She opened her eyes, eager to see what she had selected. The chart was as she remembered, but upon closer inspection, she was surprised to discover that many of the star clusters had been circled in pencil, with lines leading from the circles to notes in the margins. Her finger covered one of these circled areas. She removed her digit, followed the line from the circle, and read the scribble in the margin: *Goldilocks?*

She scrutinized the cursive handwriting—small, precise, and sometimes curling around the text. She fanned the pages and noticed other pages had been annotated in the same scrawl. There were question marks, mathematical formulas, and doodles. She didn't like that someone had written in the book but took some comfort in knowing that the pencil scribbling was only on a few pages. Thank goodness the book hadn't been marked in pen or with a highlighter. If she was careful when she erased, the book would be like new.

The randomness of the markings reminded her of Malic's crazy Wallops office. That had disturbed her, but something about the notes in her father's book bothered her more. Its perfectness should not have been marred by the handwriting of a college student or amateur astronomer.

She flipped to her father's biography and picture on the inside of the dust jacket. She lingered on his face and smiled, amused by his hairstyle from the time. She noted the shoulder of another person had been cropped out. Rather than use a headshot, he had given the publisher a photo he already had. So wonderfully practical and typical of Dad, she thought.

Her attention was drawn to something tucked under the back flap. She lifted the dust jacket and discovered a small photograph. Two women and two men were squeezed on a bench at what looked like the back of a house. She held the picture close. Was she seeing what she thought? Despite the 1980s hairstyles, two faces were unmistakable. They were her parents.

Her father's arm was wrapped around his mother's shoulder. She compared the picture of her father with the cropped headshot on the book jacket. They were a match. She marveled at how young and happy her parents seemed. The other couple looked about her parents' age, but she didn't recognize the man or the woman. She turned the picture over to see if someone had noted who was in the picture or when it was taken. Written in block print across the bottom was *THE DEVIL'S BACK PORCH.*

She examined the book's front page to see if she could find the name of the book's former owner, but it was blank. How had the book ended up on the shelf? And how long had it been there? What if she hadn't acquiesced to Nicolas's request to come to the bookstore? She might never have found it and the mysterious picture.

She tucked the picture into her purse, closed the book, stood, and gazed down at the children's section. "Nick," she said. Her son was nowhere in sight. Perhaps he was concealed by the bookshelf. "Nick," she said again, this time a little louder.

She squeezed the book tight under her arm, bolted down the stairs, and scanned the first floor. No Nicolas. She hurried to the store owner, who was helping another customer. "Excuse me," she said, trying to keep her voice calm. "I don't mean to interrupt, but have you seen my son?"

"He's out back looking at the boats with his father," the man said.

Constance's eyes widened in shock. Nick's father?

CHAPTER 7: ORB

"We're doomed," Constance said and paced the interior of the menagerie a short distance from Grace's body. Normally, the piped-in sounds of chirping birds, crickets, and frogs would have soothed her, but there was nothing that could ease her fear that they were destined to die on the Orb now that Grace was gone.

"You don't really believe Grace is the only one who could find our home," Michael said.

"She explained it to me. Something about the Curators not being simultaneous thinkers."

"I'm sure the ship is equipped to do that analysis, even if they can't."

She pulled Michael away from Grace's body and the outer door where Kylos was waiting and lowered her voice. "What if the Curators didn't bring us here to help us?"

The piped-in sounds ceased. "Ms. Roy, Mr. Whittaker, it's time you joined us," Kylos said over the speakers.

She waited for the nature sounds to return. They didn't.

"We should go," Michael said.

She folded her arms. "I'm not going out there."

"You can't stay in here forever."

"Watch me," she said and walked away. She knew she was being childish, but she didn't care. She wasn't ready to look at Kylos again.

Michael chased after her. "I'm sorry about Grace. I know how much you liked her. But hiding in the menagerie isn't going to bring her back. And if what you say is true about the Curators not being able to locate a new planet, Grace would want you doing everything in your power to do so."

She stopped. "You're right," she said.

"What's that?" he said, cupping his hand to his ear as if he hadn't heard her.

She rolled her eyes. "I said you're right."

"Ms. Roy, Mr. Whittaker, we're waiting," Kylos said, this time more insistent. "Please bring Dr. Yoholo with you."

"What do they want with Grace?" she said.

Michael gave her a knowing look.

"No," she said.

He touched her on the shoulder. "You know we can't keep her on the ship."

The ship had no place to store dead bodies. Like deceased sailors on the ocean, humans and animals had been jettisoned into space after they perished on the Orb. She had attended the ceremonies. She understood the rationale. But this was different. This was Grace.

"You okay?" Michael said.

She gave him a curt nod and approached Grace's body. This would be her last moment with her friend. She kissed Grace on the cheek. "We'll find that planet for you," she said.

Michael lifted Grace into his arms. Constance made sure her friend's head was tucked toward his chest to hide her face and, for as long as possible, preserve Grace's dignity. The entire menagerie was silent as they proceeded to the door, as if the animals, too, were in mourning.

"Wait," she said. She removed Grace's necklace, put it over her own head, and tucked it under her clothes. "The Curators will just think it's trash," she said to Michael by way of explanation. "They don't have a clue about sentimental value."

She opened the menagerie door. Twelve Curators stood along the walls in two perfectly straight lines. Kylos stood to the side, his hands behind his back, staring—or was it glaring —at Fifi in one of the lines. Constance studied the others, and it struck her that it was only on occasions such as this that she saw the Curators together. They were virtually indistinguishable from one another. Some were more familiar to the inhabitants and had earned nicknames based on their slight variations in appearance. She spotted Dumbo with his large ears and Lemon Drop with her pursed lips. She wondered about the activity of the less recognizable Curators. What did they do on the Orb? The humans were prohibited from visiting the Curators' ring and cabins. Did these foreign Curators spend time there? She scanned their faces. It became more apparent when they were in a group how cold and distant they were.

One row lifted a makeshift stretcher, and the other row took the opposite side. They were ready to receive Grace's body. Constance was grateful that nobody spoke as Michael lowered Grace onto the stretcher. For once she was glad the Curators had no feelings. Anything they said would have made her angry.

The Curators carried Grace's body away.

Kylos lingered as if he had something on his mind. "My condolences to you and the other inhabitants," he said. "Dr. Yoholo's death is most unfortunate."

Was he attempting to be empathetic, or was he concerned because he knew that with Grace gone they might never find their new Earth? Or was this feigned sympathy to cover up a more sinister event? She forced a nod but said nothing.

"The disposition ceremony will begin in one hour," he said and then followed the other Curators down the hall.

She sighed as Grace disappeared from sight, already feeling the loss.

CHAPTER 7: EARTH

"Did you say my son was with his father?" Constance said to the bookstore owner, almost choking on the words.

"Yes. I just assumed—" the man began, but she was already running out the door.

She raced outside, the screen slamming behind her, and spotted Nicolas with a stranger watching the boats from the walkway across the parking lot. "Nick!" She sprinted across the lot and halted when both the boy and man turned around.

"You," she said.

"This is Mr. Whittaker," Nicolas said.

"Yes, I know." She took the boy's hand and pulled him to her. "Why would you take my son away from the store?" she said, trying to keep her voice calm.

"Your son?" Whittaker said, surprised.

Nicolas tugged on her sleeve. "He didn't take me," he said. "I was looking for you. To show you the book I picked out." He held up his book. The cover featured an illustration of a horse bucking in anger against a swirling red background. The title read *King of the Wind: The Story of the Godolphin Arabian.*

"I told you I was going upstairs," Constance said.

"I'm sorry. I guess I didn't hear you."

"I was asking where his parents were when you arrived," Whittaker said. "I didn't mean to frighten you."

She exhaled and brushed her son's hair from his eyes. "It's all okay now."

Nicolas tucked his book under his arm. "Mr. Whittaker was telling me about the island. Did you know those boats bring in clams and oysters?" he said, pointing to several vessels making their way along the channel.

"No, I didn't," she said, not taking her eyes off of Whittaker.

Whittaker smiled. "Your son's a real smart kid. Maybe he'll grow up to be a scientist someday like his mother."

"I want to be an astronaut," Nicolas said.

"Wouldn't you be afraid of shooting into space?" Whittaker said and winked at Constance.

"Nah," Nicolas said with a dismissive wave of a hand.

"It's true," she said to Whittaker. "He's not afraid of anything."

"I guess you've raised him with a lot of confidence."

She shifted her weight. She didn't want to get into a conversation with Whittaker about how she had raised her son or why his father wasn't around.

"Well," she said, turning to her son. "We should pay for these books and get going. We have a long ride ahead of us."

Nicolas spotted the book under her arm. "Is that your book, Mom?"

"Yes it is. Now say goodbye to Mr. Whittaker."

Whittaker cocked his head and tried to read the spine of Constance's book. "Do you mind if I take a look?"

She tightened her grip. She had finally found her father's book after searching so many years. The thought of handing it over to a stranger, even for a moment, filled her with dread.

"I promise I'll return it," he said.

Even though they had just met, there was something reassuring about him that made her feel silly for the way she was acting. She handed him the book.

He flipped to an early chapter. "I remember this," he said with delight.

"You know it?" she said.

He gazed at the cover. "*A Map to the Galaxy* by Dr. Nick Roy." He looked at Constance. "Is Dr. Roy your..."

"Father? Yes."

"Of course. I suspected as much."

"That's Grandpa's book?" Nicolas said.

"I don't understand," she said to Whittaker. "You knew my father?"

"I know *of* your father. I had the book when I was a kid... A lot of us did."

"How is that possible?"

Whittaker lowered himself to Nicolas's level and handed him Constance's astronomy book, along with a fifty-dollar bill. "How about you take the books inside and give them to the man behind the counter, along with this money, and you can get any other book you want, my treat."

"Any book?" the boy said, wide-eyed.

"Any book," Whittaker said. "If it's okay with your mom."

"Can I, Mom?"

Constance nodded. "What do you say, Nicolas?"

"Thank you," her son said with enthusiasm, saluted, and ran toward the store.

"Nick," Whittaker called. The boy stopped. "Don't run off. You don't want to scare your mom again, do you?"

"No, sir," Nicolas said, slowed his run to a fast walk, and disappeared inside the store.

"You didn't need to buy him anything," she said.

Whittaker's demeanor turned serious. "I needed to talk to you—alone."

She gazed at the boats. "It isn't a coincidence we ran into one another, is it, Mr. Whittaker?"

"Please. Call me Michael."

Whittaker hadn't been anything but kind, but her fatigue left little patience for small talk. "What do you want?"

"Why don't we have a seat," he said, motioning to the bench on the store's back porch.

She accompanied him to the bench. They sat a moment in silence, listening to the gulls squawk and the wind chimes hanging above them tinkling in the breeze.

"You said you wanted to talk," she said.

He inhaled deeply. "When I was about ten months old, I was diagnosed with a disease called SCID."

"That's an immune disorder," she said, remembering an article she had read years ago.

"Correct. Those who have the disorder are extremely susceptible to infections. As you can imagine, my parents were quite protective. I spent a lot of time in isolation growing up. Then a family friend gave me your father's book. I spent months confined to a sterile chamber, but when I read *A Map to the Galaxy* I could imagine life outside the walls, an entire universe with stars and planets. Your dad's book saved my life."

She had always known her father's book was exceptional but had assumed that its magic was special only to her—an exclusive bond between father and daughter. She was pleased that his text had touched others. "That's a lovely thing to say, but I imagine your treatment is what saved your life. You're well now?"

"Yes, the treatment cured me, but it wasn't easy going. A bone marrow transplant is the usual course of therapy, but my parents weren't a match, and I didn't have siblings. Even if they had found a donor, we didn't have the money. When my health declined further, doctors told my parents to prepare for the worst."

She knew what was coming next. "That's when the FSI came into your life," she said.

He nodded. "They moved us to Virginia, paid for everything, and began an experimental treatment developed in their lab here at Wallops."

"What kind of experimental treatment?" she said, the curious scientist taking over.

"Gene therapy."

She raised her brows in surprise. "Gene therapy would have been cutting-edge when you were young."

"The treatment completely reversed my immune deficiency. I played baseball in high school and earned a college scholarship. I owe my life to the FSI."

"I'm happy for you," she said with sincerity. "But I'm not sure why you're telling me this."

"I sensed when we met that your meeting with Kylos didn't go well and suspect your encounter with Dr. Malic was not what you expected."

"Why would you think that?" she said, feeling defensive.

"Kylos, the elevator, the decontamination chamber, the way Dr. Malic communicates with the rest of the world … they're all, well…"

"Nuts?" she said.

"Unusual," he said. "Dr. Malic wants nothing but the best for people."

"I'm happy Dr. Malic was able to help you, but I'm sure I don't need to tell you that his generosity comes with a price."

"That's true."

"Doesn't that make you the least bit suspicious about his motivations?"

He hesitated. "Yes."

"Then why do you trust him?"

Whittaker looked her in the eyes. "Because your father did."

CHAPTER 8: ORB

Constance peered through the cabin porthole at Jupiter in the distance. Tears streaked her cheeks. Death had visited the Orb before, but now that it had claimed Grace, the weight of the previous losses and the futility of the inhabitants' quest for a new home came crashing down. Any minute, the Curators would begin the disposition ceremony, and Grace, like the other inhabitants and animals that had perished before her, would be expelled from the ship and become a permanent part of space.

After the death of the first crew member months earlier, the Curators had ejected the body into space without a word of prayer, a moment of silence, or notice to the rest of the inhabitants until after the deed had been done. This unceremonious removal had so outraged the crew that the Curators had quickly—and with suggestions from the refugees—created the formal procedure that was occurring now. Everyone knew the Curators had invented the ritual to appease them and not out of any desire to honor the deceased's sacrifice, but that didn't matter ... so long as those left behind had a chance to say goodbye and those who had perished weren't tossed from the ship like rubbish.

Michael had tried to convince Constance to attend Grace's ceremony, that everyone would expect her to say a few words since she had known Grace best, but she had declined. How could she put into words everything she felt about her friend while the Curators watched coldly from the sidelines? Michael hadn't understood her refusal, but she knew Grace would have. No. She preferred to honor her friend alone.

The lights in her cabin—like those around the rest of the ship—dimmed. This signaled that the initial prayers were over and permitted those unable to attend the ceremony to participate in a moment of silence before the body was loaded into the disposition chamber. Constance hung her head and tried not to think about Grace wrapped in a Mylar shroud and encased in a metal cylinder. She preferred to remember her in the menagerie.

The lights flickered. The ceremony had concluded. It was time. Constance gazed out the window. Grace's body floated from the Orb toward Jupiter's Great Red Spot. She watched Grace become a speck in the distance and thought about her faith—not in religion, but in science. The first law of thermodynamics stated that energy cannot be destroyed, that it could only be transformed from one state to another. This was the law that gave her comfort. Maybe Grace's energy—her spirit—was altered but not lost. Maybe it was still with them on the ship. She held her breath, barely able to detect the dot making its way toward the eye of Jupiter's storm, and then, finally, her friend was gone.

She rubbed Grace's necklace. Constance had loved the jewelry—had wished that she possessed it when Grace was alive—but would gladly give it and much more up if it meant bringing Grace back. Despite how much her heart wished it, she knew Grace couldn't return. Even the Curators hadn't figured out how to cheat death.

How could the Curators have let this happen? The refugees had not only lost a friend, but also their best hope of survival. Didn't the Curators' survival also depend on Grace? Weren't all of their fates linked together? How could Kylos have let a murderer exist on the ship? Or was that the real plan? Was what happened to Grace what had happened to the others? And if so, did that mean that the Curators weren't interested in seeing Earth's refugees survive after all? But then why go to all the trouble of saving them in the first place? Had their plans changed? Time to find Kylos and demand the truth.

She spun on her heels and froze. Sitting cross-legged in the open doorway was something nobody had ever seen on the Orb ... a child. The boy was young, maybe nine or ten years old, and was hunched over a book. He glanced up from reading, an impish grin on his face, and looked at—or rather through—her. Was this vision an effect of her nights of insomnia, or had a boy actually been transported onto the ship? The lack of pigment in his hair would seem to indicate that he, too, had survived a migration. She shook her head. *What are you thinking, Roy? Get it together. That boy isn't real. He's a hallucination born from your grief—an imaginary friend—and you're too old for an imaginary friend.*

The boy tucked the book under his arm and disappeared down the corridor. Constance raced after him. As the boy traveled, the hall's recessed indigo lights changed from blue to orange and then back to blue once he had passed, as if he was surrounded by a force that could change the wavelength of light. He entered the connecting strut. She broke into a run and flew up the staircase to the alignment stall. She caught sight of his legs as he withdrew up the dumbwaiter.

She hopped into the alignment stall, rotated to the platform, and sprang into an elevator compartment. Each time she reached an entrance opening, she peered up the shaft to catch sight of the boy and then swiftly brought her head back inside before she was decapitated. She repeated the dangerous move several times but didn't see the boy again. She kicked the floor in frustration. She had lost him … if he had been there in the first place.

The elevator approached the entrance to G ring that contained the dining facility. Grace's wake would be in full progress with food and music, as was the custom they had established. She reluctantly stepped onto the landing for the ring and leaned against the metal piping. So much had happened since she ventured out this morning to perform her experiment. By breaking protocol had she, as Kylos had warned, upset the delicate balance on the ship?

That's ridiculous. There's a logical explanation for what has occurred. Someone obviously attacked and maliciously killed Grace. There was nothing supernatural about it. But how did she explain the boy? She was in mourning, yes, but even when her parents died she hadn't hallucinated. Maybe Grace's energy hadn't left the ship. Was it possible her energy had transformed into the boy? Why a boy and not a girl or woman or even herself? Maybe Michael was right. Maybe she shouldn't have spent time grieving alone. Now was the time to be with the crew, celebrating Grace's life, not chasing an imaginary little boy.

CHAPTER 8: EARTH

"My father trusted Dr. Malic?" Constance said to Whittaker. "I doubt he even knew him." She rose from the bench on the bookstore's back porch and paced.

"The FSI paid for your education. Malic is head of the FSI. Of course your father knew him."

"So they met because of my scholarship," she said. "That doesn't mean they were friends."

"It's quite possible, since they worked together."

"My father was a professor of mathematics in West Virginia. Dr. Malic never taught at my father's university."

"This was work outside of what your father was doing at the university."

She peered through the screen door to check on Nicolas and saw him sorting through a pile of books. She crossed to Whittaker and lowered her voice. "What do you know about my father's work?"

"Just what I've read in the FSI logs."

"My father's name is in the logs?"

He nodded. She wrung her hands. Could her father really have worked with Malic? If so, on what? Was that why she had been given the scholarships—because she was the daughter of a colleague? The thought of her dear father being friends with Malic was preposterous. Why was she listening to this man? But Constance was too much of a scientist not to consider this new information. Whittaker had succeeded in planting a seed of doubt.

"I'm sorry you're upset," he said. "I thought you knew. This probably means you didn't know about your mother either."

Her eyes darted to him. "What about her?"

"She knew Malic too."

"This is crazy." She spotted Nicolas at the counter with the books and Whittaker's fifty-dollar bill. "Nick," she said through the screen. "Hurry up. We have to get home."

Nicolas smiled and waved at her with the bill.

Whittaker approached. "Everything I've told you is true, Constance."

"Don't call me that. You don't know me well enough to call me that."

"I don't know why your father didn't tell you," he said, "but he did work with the FSI. He did research on Wallops. I've seen the pictures."

She remembered the picture she had found in her father's book, pulled it from her purse, and held it in his face. "You've seen pictures of this man at Wallops?"

He examined the image. "Yes, that's Dr. Roy … with your mother."

"Look at it closer," she said, moving it toward him.

He gently pushed the photograph toward her. "Why don't *you* look at it closer? Recognize anyone else?"

She squinted at her parents seated next to the other couple. Her anger dissipated, lost in the memory of them. "I don't see anything," she said.

"Not your parents. Look at the man next to them."

She shifted her focus to the man on the bench with her father. He and the other woman looked to be the same age as her parents. The man was handsome in a nerdy way, and the woman was quite striking. She shrugged.

"Doesn't that man look familiar?" he said.

The man was lean, with thin fingers and slight features. Compared to her father, he looked rather fragile. Then, all at once, she realized everything Whittaker had been telling her was true.

She met his gaze. "That's Dr. Malic."

"Yes."

"Who's the woman?" she said, wondering if she, too, had worked with her parents.

"She's the original owner of this bookstore."

"The woman in the picture knew my parents," she said. "She must have lived in the area, perhaps on the island."

"She did," he said. "And still does."

Her heart skipped a beat. "Are you sure?"

He nodded.

Could this woman explain how her father had come to know Malic and what work he had done at Wallops? More importantly, could she fill in the details of her mother's death? Her father had never fully explained the circumstances of her mother's disappearance and death, and she had always dreaded why. Perhaps, at last, she'd learn the truth.

"Looks like my trip home is going to be delayed," she said to Michael and entered the bookstore to retrieve Nicolas.

CHAPTER 9: ORB

Constance rounded the bend in the corridor that led to the commissary and heard Muhammad singing. Grace would have been pleased. Her friend had remarked on more than one occasion how beautiful Muhammad sounded singing in his native Arabic. In fact, it had been Grace's idea that, following the melancholic disposition ceremonies, the wakes of their lost companions be a celebration of the deceased. Constance wasn't sure she was ready to see people partying with Grace forever lost in the eye of Jupiter, but she took a deep breath and opened the door anyway.

Several of the crew smiled at her sympathetically as she wound her way through the congregation. She found Michael waiting for her at their usual table.

"Thought you could use something strong," Michael said and handed her a metal cup.

"You have no idea." She looked at the liquid. "What is it?"

"Don't ask. Just know that it's potent." He raised his cup. "To Grace."

She touched her cup to his and took a sip. The liquid burned as it touched her tongue and got worse as it made its way down her throat. Her eyes watered. Even her nostrils stung. "Tastes like corn mash," she said, trying to catch her breath.

"Best white lightning this side of Jupiter," Michael said and finished his cup without a twitch.

She smelled his cup to be sure he was drinking the same liquid and shook her head in awe. "I'm impressed."

"One of my many talents," he said.

She surveyed the room. "You haven't seen Kylos, have you?"

"Clearly knowing how to relax at a party isn't your forte."

"I can't believe she's gone," she said and was tempted to take another swig of the poison in her cup. "Don't you wonder what her last words were?"

"Would it change anything? Besides, aren't we here to honor Grace by celebrating her life?"

He was right. Nothing had annoyed Grace more than a person who didn't know how to have a good time. Constance marveled that she and Grace had become friends, given their different personalities. Michael held out his hand for a dance. She took it. *This is for you, Grace*, she thought.

Michael spun her in a circle. The faces in the room whirred by—faces of people laughing and kissing and making toasts to Grace and then … Kylos's face. She grabbed Michael's arm to stop. He gave her a puzzled look, and she nodded toward Kylos lurking in the doorway.

She pushed her way through the crowd. "I want to talk to you," she said to the Curator.

"Dr. Yoholo would be quite pleased by this gathering," Kylos said, gazing about the room.

"You don't know anything about her," Constance said.

Kylos cocked his head.

"I'm afraid she's had too much to drink," Michael said and put his arm around her shoulders.

Constance shrugged him off. "I'm fine," she said but felt

her ears burning from the corn mash. "Grace told me. I know we're doomed," she said.

People nearby stopped to listen.

"What exactly do you think you know?" Kylos said with an expression of mild amusement on his face.

"That you and the other Curators don't know how to find us a new home," she said, her voice getting louder. "That Grace was the only one that could help us."

The room fell silent.

"Go ahead," she said. "Tell everyone how we're going to crash into Jupiter in three days because you let someone kill the one person who could help us."

"Did she say kill?" someone said.

Constance and Kylos locked eyes. Murmurs of concern rippled over the group.

"Congratulations, Roy," Michael said. "You've finally succeeded in being the universe's biggest party pooper." He turned to the others. "No more whiskey for Roy, you hear?" Crew members laughed nervously. Michael leaned close and lowered his voice, "Watch yourself."

"Get Fifi," Constance said to Kylos, ignoring Michael's warning.

Several people snickered at Fifi's name.

"Human entertainment is so … fatuous," Kylos said, smug.

"What's that—fatuous?" someone whispered.

"He just called us stupid," Michael said and squared his shoulders.

"Fifi," Constance demanded.

"Even if I desired to do so, I'm afraid I cannot grant your request. Please carry on as you were," Kylos said and exited.

No you don't, Constance thought and raced after Kylos. Someone said, "What's going on?" as she left with Michael.

"Kylos," she yelled after him, her voice echoing down the corridor.

The Curator glanced over his shoulder and then darted into the connecting strut. She and Michael raced after him into the stairwell. She leaned over the railing and spotted Kylos.

"You owe us an explanation," she called up the stairs.

They followed Kylos, flipped in the alignment chamber, and jumped into the dumbwaiter.

"He's retreating to A ring," Michael said.

The living quarters for the Curators on A ring were off limits to the inhabitants. Constance pounded her foot on the metal floor several times, shaking the conveyor unit.

"I know you can hear me," she yelled toward where she imagined Kylos was in a compartment above them. "I want to know why. You owe us that much."

The soft hum of the gears was the only reply.

"He's not going to answer," Michael said, watching ring platforms go by.

"Doesn't that bother you?"

His jaw clenched. "I want to snap his scrawny little neck."

She had never seen evidence of a violent side to Michael, but observing the tension in his face and muscles, she now appreciated for the first time how easily he could kill Kylos and how much self-control her companion was exercising.

They approached the platform for A ring. Standing sideways in the topsy-turvy, Escher-like world of the stairwell connecting strut and safely on the other side of the alignment stall was Kylos. They hopped from the dumbwaiter. She darted into the alignment cage.

"I'm afraid this is as far as you'll get," Kylos said. "No humans are granted access to this ring. The alignment chamber won't work for you."

She lowered herself to his level and tilted her head sideways so she could face him straight on. "Grace was telling the truth, wasn't she?"

"I'm afraid so," Kylos said without malice.

"You don't seem concerned," Michael said. "Why is that?"

Every species fights for its survival, Constance thought, *so why aren't the Curators?* She had a sudden realization. "You're not going to die with us, are you?"

"Dr. Yoholo's death was not part of the plan," he said. To her surprise, Kylos looked genuinely sorry for the way things had transpired. "I'm afraid the fact that you can experience emotion will only bring you misery. Try to keep the morale of the rest of the inhabitants up. There's no point in them knowing the experiment is over," he said and then disappeared down the stairwell.

"What experiment?" she yelled down the stairwell, "Kylos!" but he was already gone.

CHAPTER 9: EARTH

"Her name is Dr. Grace Yoholo," Michael said from the driver's seat of his sedan. "She owned the bookstore—mostly antiquarian books, as I understand it—until she sold it in the nineties lock, stock, and barrel."

"Yoholo," Constance said thoughtfully and stared out the windshield. "Never heard my parents mention her."

After discovering that the former bookstore owner had known her parents and still lived on the island, Constance had insisted Michael take her to meet the woman. Since the trip was a short one, she had agreed to leave her car at the store and ride with him. Nicolas sat in the back seat, engrossed in her father's book and looking much like she imagined she must have when she had first discovered its wonders. The automaton was secured on the seat next to him.

"Here's the turn," Michael said and nodded to the left.

A large blue sign read *Tom's Cove Park*. An arrow pointed to a narrow paved road. They approached Tom's Cove Park. Trailers and RVs, permanent and temporary, lined the street. Constance suspected the year-round residents lived in the double-wide trailers with the fences, porches, and well-maintained yards while the temporary residents—there for a week, month or the season—lived in the recreation vehicles.

Michael passed the entrance.

"You missed the turn," she said and watched it disappear behind them.

"It's up ahead." He drove deeper into a neighborhood of neat mobile homes and cottages.

As they made their way through the winding streets, she had second thoughts about their journey. What exactly was she hoping to discover from this Dr. Yoholo? Insight into what her father had been working on at Wallops and what had motivated him to work with Malic? Yes. But also the key to the riddle of her mother's life and death. Constance lived with the pain of her mother's loss and the fear that she had somehow been partially responsible. Would Dr. Yoholo have the answers she sought?

The road forked. Michael took the left and drove along a small waterway. He slowed, turned onto a one-lane street, and stopped before a cream-colored trailer. White wooden ginger-bread lattice hid the cinderblock foundation and ran the length of the structure. A welcoming stone walk led past a gazebo, between two small gardens, to the porch where yellow metal chairs sat surrounded by potted flowers. Clear glass spheres containing feathers hung on fishing line from the roofs of the gazebo and porch and swung freely in the wind. A blue mailbox stood at the end of the property. *G. YOHOLO* was stenciled in white letters on its side.

"This is it," Michael said and cut the engine.

The home was secluded yet warm and inviting. Would they find Grace to be the same?

"Thanks for bringing me," she said.

"You have a lot of questions about the FSI," Michael said. "Maybe she'll have answers."

Nicolas leaned forward. "Where are we?"

"The woman that lives here was a friend of your grandma and grandpa," she said.

"Can I meet her?"

"We haven't been invited," she said. "Maybe it's best if you wait here while we talk to her first."

He sighed and flumped back in disappointment.

"Ready?" Michael said.

She nodded and exited.

"When was the last time you saw her?" Constance said as they passed several rows of flint corn growing behind a chicken-wire fence.

"I was a kid. When I found out she lived here, I asked around and discovered her address. Drove by a few times with the intention of introducing myself but never did."

"Why not?"

"Never felt I had a reason to disturb her. From what I understand, she's fairly reclusive. I'm not sure she would even know who I am."

They reached the porch, climbed three steps, and approached the door. "Want me to knock?" he said.

"No, I got it." She raised her hand.

"Can I help you?" said someone from behind them.

A woman dressed in worn jeans, a T-shirt, and a floppy straw hat emerged from the garden. She held shears in one hand and a basket with weeds and trimmings in the other. Her skin was tan and dotted with a smattering of freckles, and her long brown hair was streaked with white. A gray cat with green eyes, white mustache, and tuxedo markings rubbed against her legs.

Constance had a sudden vision of the woman—older with white hair feeding chickens and goats—and an overwhelming feeling of sadness. The sensation was like what she experienced concerning her mother ... yet different.

"You look like you've seen a ghost," the woman said.

Constance descended the porch steps. "Are you Dr. Yoholo?"

"I haven't been called doctor in a while, but yes, I'm Grace Yoholo."

"Dr. Yoholo," Michael said. "My name is Michael Whittaker. I don't know if you remember—"

"Whittaker," Grace interrupted. "Of course. You must be little Michael."

"Yes, ma'am."

Grace gave him the once-over and shook her head in amazement. "You were quite the sick boy. I'm glad to see you looking so robust."

He blushed, and Constance grinned.

"And who's this attractive young woman?" Grace said.

"Dr. Constance Roy," he said.

"Constance is fine," she said.

"Connie Roy," Grace said reflectively, and then her eyes widened. "You're Nick and Barbara's girl."

"Yes," Constance said. It had been decades since anyone called her Connie.

Grace grabbed Constance in a bear hug. Constance froze, stunned by the sudden show of affection. The embrace was warm and soft and familiar. Constance involuntarily wrapped her arms around the woman. She had so missed her mother's embrace that for a moment she forgot she was hugging a stranger.

"I've worried about you," Grace said. "About you both."

Constance pulled away. "Why?"

"The transposons. Isn't that why you two are here?"

Constance and Michael exchanged puzzled looks.

"I don't know anything about transposons," Constance said. She reached into her purse and retrieved the photograph of her parents with Malic and Grace. "I found a copy of my father's book at Sundial Books, and this was inside."

Grace took the picture and traced an outline of the figures

with her finger. "This was a long time ago," she said with a sigh and returned the photo.

"Michael thought you might be able to answer some questions about my parents and what they were doing at Wallops."

"You said you found the picture in your father's book."

"*A Map to the Galaxy*," Michael said, pointing at Grace. "You gave me the book when I was sick."

Grace nodded. "Do you have the book with you?"

"My son has it in the car." Constance pointed to Nicolas sitting in Michael's vehicle.

Grace paled. "Your son?" she said.

"Nick, come over here," Constance said. "I'd like you to meet someone."

The door was flung open, and Nicolas jumped out, the book under his arm. Grace's cat bounded to Nicolas. The boy rubbed the cat on the head. "Hey there, kitty," he said.

Grace stared at Nicolas. He cocked his head and looked at her curiously. Constance and Michael watched the woman and boy studying one another, puzzled by the almost palpable energy that existed between them. Grace gently touched Nicolas's platinum locks.

The cat rolled over and meowed. "I think he likes me," Nicolas said with a giggle and rubbed the cat's belly. "What's his name?"

"Schrodi," Grace said.

"You have a soft belly, Schrodi," Nicolas said and then rose and examined the nearby corn. "Mommy, that corn is weird," he said.

"Nicolas, don't be rude," Constance said.

"The corn isn't weird," Grace said. "It's special."

"Does it taste good?" he said.

"If you stay for dinner, you'll find out." Grace turned to Constance and Michael. "I have a lot to discuss with your mother and Mr. Whittaker."

CHAPTER 10: ORB

Constance and Michael retreated to their cabin. They walked in silence. They didn't want the others overhearing them discuss what they had learned from Kylos.

"You think Grace knew where our Goldilocks planet is?" Constance asked as soon as Michael closed the cabin door.

"If she had, wouldn't she have told the Curators and we'd be on our way?"

Constance paced. "What if Grace did tell them and they don't care?"

"Why would the Curators go to all the effort of building us a ship and transporting us here just to let us die?"

"You heard Kylos. He said we were an experiment."

"No ... he said the experiment is over."

She stared out the window. Jupiter's red eye—Grace's final resting place—came into view. She gazed into the dark sea of stars and thought of her father. If there was a Goldilocks planet out there, he would have helped them find it.

Even if they could find their new planet, how would they get to it? The ability to move the Orb fell strictly under the Curators' domain. During the initial orientation session to the ship, the Curators had warned the refugees of the destructive force that could be unleashed when repositioning an object as immense as the Orb. It was for their own protection that the Curators alone possessed the knowledge and power to move the vessel. She wondered if Kylos ever had any intention of shifting the ship's trajectory. Perhaps they had been in a floating crypt from the beginning.

"Why didn't you tell me?" she said, unconsciously speaking aloud the question she longed to ask Grace.

"Why didn't I tell you what?" Michael said.

"I meant Grace," she said. "Why didn't she tell me how to find our Goldilocks?"

He opened his mouth to say something then thought better of it.

"What?" she said.

"Maybe Grace didn't find the planet," he said. "Maybe she was doing as Kylos instructed us—keeping up morale."

She shook her head. "Grace was confident she would find our new home. It was like she already had."

"Then why didn't she tell you of all people?" he said. "When you two spoke in the menagerie."

The menagerie. Where Grace had taken her last breath. She wished she had been the one with Grace instead of Maria. Then it struck her. "What if Grace was still alive when Maria found her?" Constance said. "What if Grace told Maria?"

"If that were the case, don't you think Maria would have told the Curators?"

"Maybe Maria was afraid to tell them," Constance said with newfound energy.

"That doesn't sound like the Maria Belkin I know," he said with displeasure.

"We need to talk to Maria," she said.

"You go," he said and folded his arms.

She didn't blame him for his reaction. Maria Belkin had offended nearly everyone with her refusal to cooperate with the rest of the crew. If the task wasn't a Curator-assigned duty, she didn't do it. Even when her cabinmate had been sick, Maria had refused to do extra work unless she got something out of it. Collaboration, negotiation, and compromise were not in her. On more than one occasion, inhabitants had threatened to put her in the disposition chamber and expel her from the Orb. It wasn't because she was petty that her shipmates disliked her; it was because, on the ship, Maria's pettiness had life-and-death consequences.

If Grace had said anything to Maria about whether or not she had found their Goldilocks planet, it would be a challenge convincing Maria she should reveal that information. It would take two of them exerting pressure on the woman if they had any chance of learning what Maria knew. Without Michael's help, Constance had little chance of success.

"You're right," Constance said sarcastically. "There's no point in talking to Maria. Just because she might have information that could save the human race. Let's sit here and wait to die."

"For crying out loud," he said, throwing his hands in the air. "Let's hear what Princess Belkin has to say."

She suppressed a victorious grin. He growled at her as they entered the corridor. Maria's cabin was on the opposite side of the ring. As they walked, Constance recalled seeing the boy and the hallway's indigo lights changing colors as he had passed. She hadn't told Michael about her imaginary friend. She didn't want a lecture about needing sleep or the dangers of stress.

They approached Maria's cabin, different from most in that it was a single-occupant dwelling. Maria had been paired with a male refugee, like the other couples on the ship, but Angus fell ill and died shortly after they recovered from the migration, leaving Maria to live alone.

Constance rapped on Maria's door. "Maria," she said.

"It's Constance and Michael. We wanted to check on you to make sure you're okay."

Michael grimaced. Constance gave him a warning look. They waited.

"I guess that's that," he said.

She pounded on the door. "Maria, we need to talk to you."

"She's not in," Michael said and walked away.

"What if she's hurt? We should check," she said, knowing how flimsy the excuse was. Right now, finding out what had happened to Grace and if she had had any final words to Maria was more important than the inhabitants' honor code. She grabbed the handle.

"Damn it, Roy," he said, marching back and taking her arm. "Let's get outta here before someone sees you."

The refugees had arrived on the Orb without possessions, so there was no need for security to protect their belongings. The things the inhabitants did have were those given to them since their arrival or those they had made for themselves. However, in the interest of harmony, the refugees had agreed on strict respect for the personal space of others. No one was to enter another's cabin unless invited or remove another's property unless expressly asked to do so by the owner. The policy had never been enforced because it had never been violated. Constance was taking a risk entering Maria's cabin. The sooner she looked around and got out, the better.

"I'll just be a minute," she said, flung open the door, and gasped.

Sitting in a gray metal chair with her feet flat on the floor, back straight and hands folded in her lap, was Fifi.

"Now you've done it," Michael muttered.

"Your disregard for protocol continues," the Curator said. "I see you've recruited Mr. Whittaker."

Michael took Constance by the elbow. "We were just leaving," he said.

"We're looking for Maria," Constance said, holding her ground.

"She's not here," Fifi said. "I'm sure she'd find it interesting that you entered her cabin without her permission. And before you lie to me again, I am aware that Ms. Belkin has no knowledge of your presence here."

Constance's eyes narrowed. Fifi had wised up since their earlier encounter.

"Perhaps you could tell us where to find Maria," Michael said.

Fifi rose from the chair, crossed to them, studied Michael for a brief moment, and then turned her full attention to Constance. "Why do you wish to see Ms. Belkin?"

Constance cocked her head, realizing this was the first time she had seen a Curator on E ring. "Does Maria know *you* are here?"

A slight smile formed at the corners of Fifi's mouth. "She does."

"Okay, that answers that," Michael said and tightened his grip on Constance's arm. "Nice talking to you," he said over his shoulder as he dragged Constance away.

"Ms. Roy," Fifi called after them. Constance tugged against Michael, forcing him to stop. "I'd encourage you to rethink your recent rule-breaking impulse. Mr. Whittaker might not always be there to save you from yourself."

Constance made a move to charge back down the hall at Fifi, but Michael wrapped an arm around her shoulders and forced her down the corridor. She stole a look over her shoulder and could swear she saw Fifi grinning.

"Let go of me," Constance said, trying to break Michael's iron grip.

Michael released her and stormed away.

She caught up to him. "Do you think Maria knew Fifi was in her cabin?"

"Why don't you ask her?" Michael said through gritted teeth, heading toward the connecting staircase.

"Don't you think that's a little suspicious?" she said.

He stopped. "I think if Maria doesn't kill you, I might," he said. "It's one thing to break the Curators' rules. It's another to disregard your fellow crew members'."

"You're really mad I went into Maria's cabin?"

"It's about honor, Roy. Everyone agreed to it, including you. Next time you want to violate another crew member's personal space, leave me out of it."

"Fine," she said and pushed past him. She headed up the connecting spoke stairwell.

"Where are you going?" he said.

"To talk to Maria. With or without your help," she said. "You can tell Fifi if you'd like."

She stormed up the stairs. Seconds later she heard Michael's footsteps behind her.

"You're lucky I like you," he said.

She grinned. She knew it was the stress of their situation that had caused them to snap at one another. In all the time they had been together, they had only had a handful of disagreements. She was relieved he was with her. Now, more than ever, they needed to be on the same side.

CHAPTER 10: EARTH

"Don't chew with your mouth open," Constance said, pointing at the napkin sitting on the dining room table next to her son.

"Sorry," Nicolas said and wiped his cheeks. "It's just so good." He smiled, bits of buttery corn dotting his lips, and sank his teeth deep into the cob for another bite. Schrodi purred loudly at his feet.

"I'm glad you like it," Grace said, seated next to him.

Constance and Michael sat across from Grace, each with a plate of partially eaten food. The woman had insisted they stay for dinner. At first, having a meal had seemed like a good idea—a way of easing into the conversation about her parents. But they had been at the woman's house for nearly an hour, with no answers. Her patience was wearing thin.

"The corn isn't sweet," Nicolas said between bites.

"Nick," Constance reproached.

"It's okay," Grace said with an easy smile. "It's flint corn. It's not supposed to be sweet."

Nicolas cocked his head. "Flint corn?"

"Some people call it Indian corn because a long time ago

tribes like mine used to grow it all over this country," Grace said.

Nicolas held his corn in midair. "You're an Indian?"

"Nick, that isn't polite," Constance said.

"Algonquian and Cherokee, to be specific," Grace said. "My ancestors lived here, on Chincoteague, before being driven off our land."

Nicolas set down the now stripped cob, wiped his face, leaned toward Grace, and whispered, "I'm sorry the settlers weren't nice to your people."

Grace whispered back, "Me too."

Constance observed Nicolas and Grace regarding one another, their faces inches apart. From the moment her son and the former bookstore owner had met, it seemed there was a connection between them, like two old friends meeting again after years of separation, and something about that troubled her. She had considered that what she was feeling was jealousy —she and Nicolas had a tight mother-child bond—but soon realized that the way Nicolas responded to Grace was nothing like the love he showed her. His connection with the woman seemed to be on a more intellectual or otherworldly level.

Michael exhaled loudly, breaking the spell between Nicolas and Grace. "I'm sorry," he said, pushing his plate away. "I don't mean to be abrupt, but it's getting late and Ms. Roy still has a long ride home."

"Don't you like your corn, Michael?" Grace said.

"It was delicious," Constance said. "But Mr. Whittaker's right. I had hoped I'd find out about my parents before we left town."

Grace smiled and passed the plate of corn to Nicolas, who eagerly grabbed the final ear. "You want to know why the kernels are different colors?" she said to Nicolas. The boy nodded. "It has to do with the genetic information contained inside the corn's cells. Do you know what genes are?"

"It's the information that tells us who we are," he said, pleased with his own knowledge.

"That's right," Grace said. "A long time ago, people believed that a genetic code was a fixed thing, hardwired into your being."

Nicolas's brows furrowed. "It's not?"

"No. Years ago, in the 1930s, there was a smart lady scientist—"

"Like my mom," the boy said with pride.

Grace looked pointedly at Constance. "She was a lot like your mother. Her name was Barbara McClintock, and she studied the pattern of corn kernels like the kind you are eating."

Michael sighed, frustrated. Constance shot him a look to be quiet, sensing that Grace was talking about more than corn kernels.

"McClintock discovered that genes aren't fixed but are able to jump from one position to another."

"Like duck duck goose?"

Grace chuckled. "Very much like duck duck goose. Only before they move, they make a copy of their characteristics so that now there are two or three or more of them." Grace eyed Constance. "Sometimes they pass on these characteristics to their offspring."

Constance leaned forward.

"Do you know what they call these genes that change positions?" Grace said.

Nicolas shook his head.

"Transposons," Constance said softly.

The boy looked thoughtfully at the corn in his hands. "The lady scientist learned about genes from looking at corn," he said. "Hm."

Grace pointed to the kernels. "The pattern is a genetic marker. If we study the pattern, we can understand the genes."

"Do I have genetic markers?" he said.

Grace ran her hand through the boy's silvery blond mane. "I think you may have a few."

"Nicolas," Constance said. "I think it's time you let Mommy talk to Grace alone."

"Aw," he said. "I was learning about genes."

"Your mom's right," Michael said. "Why don't you and I go outside and check out the sky? You know, on a clear night in Chincoteague you can see virtually all the stars and even some planets."

"Really?" the boy said, his eyes lighting up. "Which ones?"

"Let's see if we can find out." Michael rose from his seat.

"I have a telescope out back you can use," Grace said.

"Can we take Schrodi with us?" Nicolas said.

"I'm sure he'd be delighted to go with you."

Nicolas slid his chair back and lifted the cat. "Schrodi's certainly a weird name for a kitty," he said. He crossed to the door. "Come on, Mr. Whittaker."

"I'll fill you in on everything," Constance said to Michael.

"Let's go find some planets, little man," Michael said. He let Nicolas and Schrodi out and stole a final look at Constance before exiting and closing the door behind him.

"Michael's a handsome man, don't you think?" Grace said.

Constance resisted the urge to roll her eyes. "Schrodi. Is that short for Erwin Schrödinger?" she said, changing the subject.

Grace smiled. "Too much?"

"No," Constance said. "It's funny." She ran a finger along the edge of her plate. "I noticed how you were with Nicolas," she said, surprised to hear her voice quiver. She took a breath and started again. "Do you know something about my son?"

Grace grabbed the plates, crossed to the kitchen, and set the dishes in the sink. "Would you like something to drink?" Constance shook her head. Grace nodded. "You weren't supposed to have children," she said. "Edward promised me none of the candidates would have children."

"Who's Edward?"

"Malic," Grace said.

"Dr. Malic doesn't know about Nicolas," Constance said. Her cheeks flushed with her confession.

Grace pushed back the curtain and watched Nicolas and Michael through the window over the sink. "Does Kylos know?" she said without looking at Constance.

"I don't think so," Constance said.

Grace turned from the window. "You can't let that creature discover Nicolas. It would be dangerous for everyone. Promise me he'll never know."

"What's really going on at the FSI?" Constance said. "Why did you tell Nicolas that story about the genes?"

Grace returned to the table and opened *A Map to the Galaxy* to one of the star charts. "Have you ever thought about traveling through the universe?"

"Of course. How could I not after reading Dad's book?"

Grace caressed the page. "There may be ten billion Earthlike planets in the galaxy. Your father would have been amazed at what we've learned since he…"

Constance was struck by how sad the woman appeared to be about her father's death.

Grace turned the book to face Constance and placed her finger on an area that had been circled. "There's a planet somewhere in this area, orbiting this star," she said, tapping her finger on the page. "If the theory is correct, this planet is like our own, only better. Like Earth was before humans abused her … and one another."

"Whose theory is this?" Constance said.

"Mine, Edward's, your parents'."

Her mind was awhirl. Transposons, Earth-like planets, the warning about Kylos … it was all too much. She wanted to retreat to a quiet place to process everything Grace had told her and organize her thoughts.

"What do you think it would take to get there?" Grace said and pointed to the area where the theorized Goldilocks planet existed.

"A rocket?"

Grace shook her head. "It's five hundred light years away. Humans would never survive. Try again."

"I don't know," Constance said, feeling like a kid being given a pop quiz.

"Think," Grace said. "How would we need to change to get here?" She pointed to the circled area again.

"You're talking in riddles," Constance said, frustrated. "I want to talk about my mother."

"We *are* talking about your mother."

What was the woman trying to tell her? Perhaps Grace was as crazy as Malic. She pushed herself away from the table. She felt lightheaded. She needed fresh air. She stumbled to the kitchen window, sucked in the breeze coming in through the small opening, and observed Nicolas and Michael. Nicolas peered through the telescope and motioned for Michael to redirect the instrument's focus. Michael did as instructed until Nicolas gave him a thumbs-up. Seeing them happily stargazing steadied her.

She turned back to Grace. "Transposons, space travel … I want answers about my parents, what happened to my mother, and you're giving me nothing."

"It wasn't nothing to your parents. They thought it was of the utmost importance. They knew the truth."

"Which is what exactly?"

"Eventually our planet is going to die. Your parents, Edward, and I wanted to figure out how to ensure the survival of the human species."

"You're saying you all were trying to find a way to get us off Earth to that other planet?"

"Not at first. At first it was conjecture, theory, and hypothesis, an intellectual exercise. That was before he arrived."

"Who?"

"The one that calls himself Kylos."

"You mean Dr. Malic's son?"

Grace chuckled. "Is that what he told you?"

"He gave me a speech about how Dr. Malic and he had decided to keep his presence a secret due to his medical condition."

Grace lowered her voice. "Edward doesn't have any children, so Kylos is most definitely not his son. He's something quite different. A corrupter … and treacherous."

"Treacherous how?"

"He made a deal with Edward and your parents—a deal I couldn't abide. It was the last time I saw any of them."

Constance was all too familiar with deals with the FSI and how difficult they were to adhere to. What could it be that had caused Grace to turn away from her friends? Had her parents done something terrible? "Are you saying my parents were working with Kylos?" she said, skeptical.

"If you don't believe what I've told you so far, why should I tell you more?" Grace said.

Constance's hope of discovering information about her mother was vanishing, and her heart ached all over again. "Please," she said, her voice shaking. "I deserve to know what happened to my mother. Was it something I did?"

Grace's face softened. "Look at your father's book again," she said in a gentler tone. "When you see it, you'll know what I'm saying is true. Then we'll talk."

Grace squeezed Constance's hand and joined Michael and Nicolas. Nicolas invited Grace to look through the eyepiece. Constance sat at the table and tapped her father's book. What secrets did Grace think it contained? She had a feeling that it hadn't been an accident she had discovered the book at the store … that she had been meant to find it.

She studied the pencil circle on the star guide where Grace had indicated there might be an Earth-like planet. As she had done before, she followed the line that connected it to the note in the margin that read: *Goldilocks?* She thought about what Grace had said about the planet being five hundred light years away and what it would take to get there. She had spent her entire career studying Earth's environment; trying to understand another world made her temples throb.

Her eyes moved up the margin. She read the notes. They didn't make sense. She stared at the page and, like a hidden three-dimensional image in a stereogram picture book, she suddenly saw it. The way the letters L and T were capitalized when they shouldn't be and the tight spacing between words. It wasn't a stranger who had written in her father's book; it was her father.

The air pressure changed. She heard ringing and became short of breath. She looked about the room and had the sensation of being in a foreign place surrounded by a crowd. She pushed herself up against the table. The book fell to the floor with a thud. She stumbled toward the kitchen, bracing herself against the wall. The room slipped in and out of focus. She grabbed the kitchen counter. Voices whispered behind her. She whipped around. The room was empty and still again, the strange people only a mirage. She heard giggling from outside and saw Michael, Nicolas, and Grace looking at the night sky. What was happening to her?

She smoothed her hair and retrieved the book from the floor in an attempt to regain her composure and focus. The back half of the dust jacket had come free and flapped loosely. There was something on the blank side of the cover. She set it on the table under the light. She studied the handwriting on the book cover's back. It wasn't her father's. The schematics were precisely drawn, like an architect's blueprints. The image seemed to come alive in three dimensions. She had the sensation of being both inside and outside of the drawing and heard the echo of machinery, as if on a ship. She traced the curved shape with her finger and stopped. Under the image and written in neat block letters were the words *THE ORB*.

CHAPTER 11: ORB

Constance and Michael entered H ring, otherwise known as the training ring, and made their way toward what the Curators had quaintly termed the gymnasium. After becoming acquainted with the gym in their first weeks in recovery, the crew had renamed it the crucible. The crucible had been designed so the residents could exercise their bodies in a variety of environments in the event their future planet did not have an atmosphere that precisely matched Earth's. Gravity, oxygen levels, air pressure, temperature, and wind could all be manipulated inside a series of chambers. Some chambers contained equipment resembling treadmill and stair-climbing machines, while others were empty. The empty chambers were used for sparring and endurance tests in extreme atmospheric conditions. It was in one of the empty chambers that Constance and Michael had been told they could find Maria.

They approached Lina, Zhang Yong, and Garcia peering in through a chamber window. The trio worked side by side on the supply rings tracking inventory, rationing supplies, and refurbishing ship parts. Unbeknownst to the Curators, they also ran an underground trading post.

"Have you seen Maria?" Constance said to the group.

Zhang Yong pointed at the window. "She's setting a new record. I don't know what's got into her."

Constance glanced at the panel next to the door that displayed the atmospheric conditions within the chamber. Gravity was Earth-normed, but the oxygen level had been reduced from Earth's usual 20.9 percent to 18.4 percent, and the temperature had been raised to thirty-seven degrees Celsius. The clock indicated that Maria had been running in the crucible under these strenuous conditions for nearly fourteen minutes.

"How's she still moving?" Michael said, watching Maria circling the silo-like compartment.

Constance inched to the window and felt the heat through the layers of glass. Maria jogged the perimeter, punching the air like a boxer. The woman's cheeks were flushed and her shirt soaked with sweat, but otherwise she didn't appear to be feeling the stress of the conditions. Like professional athletes, dancers, and others who had superior physical abilities, Maria had high bodily kinesthetic intelligence. Constance wished the woman had interpersonal intelligence, too.

Constance pushed the intercom button located next to the panel. "Maria," she said. Maria glanced at her. "I need to talk to you." She watched Maria curve away from them and then approach as she finished making another loop. "Maria, please."

Maria jogged to the window and hit the intercom button inside the chamber. "What do you want?" she said between heavy breaths.

"To talk to you about Grace."

"What about her?"

"She's dead, that's what," Michael said.

"What's it to me?"

"Bitch," Lina mumbled under her breath.

Constance resisted the urge to call Maria a few names of

her own, but she needed to find out if Grace had shared anything before she died. "I want to talk to you about anything Grace might have said to you in her final moments."

Maria rolled her eyes and spat.

"...and about Fifi," Constance added. It was a gamble, but Constance thought that by mentioning Fifi, Maria might think she knew more than she did about whatever relationship the woman had with the Curator.

Maria's eyes darted to the faces watching her on the other side of the glass. "What about her?"

"I think you know," Constance said, bluffing.

Maria gave her the once-over and then hit the button that unlocked the chamber. "You wanna talk?" she said. "Come on in."

"You should take a break. Let's talk out here."

"Come in or leave me alone," Maria said and jogged away.

Constance released the intercom button.

"She's playing you," Michael said. "She doesn't know anything."

Constance yanked open the door and quickly locked it behind her before she had a chance to change her mind. The heat enveloped her ... much like the warm blankets Kylos had placed on her when he had nurtured her back to health after the brutal migration and arrival on the ship. She gazed up the curved walls made of white interlocking thermal protective tiles to the two-story ceiling and the fan that controlled the wind. She could use a little breeze right now. She inhaled deeply. Her breathing felt normal ... but for how long?

Maria trotted by. "You gonna stand there gawking or join me?" she said.

"I'm not dressed for a workout," Constance said, already sweating.

"This isn't a fashion show," Maria said. "You wanna talk? Then you have to keep up ... if you can."

The comment was meant to push Constance's buttons, and it worked. She stripped off her long-sleeved shirt, grateful she had worn a T-shirt underneath, and waited for Maria to come by again before joining her. She fell in stride. She was a strong runner, and Maria had already been in the chamber for quite some time, so she figured she'd only have to go a few laps before they would stop.

"So tell me about finding Grace," Constance said.

"Not much to say. I found her, end of story."

"I heard you were pretty shook up," Constance lied.

Maria faltered. "Who said that?"

"Kylos and Fifi."

"Oh," she said and relaxed.

Constance eyed Maria in her peripheral vision. "When you found Grace, was she still alive?"

"How do you mean?"

"You know," Constance said, feeling irritable. "With a pulse ... breathing." On her last word, she sucked in air and sensed the oxygen deficiency.

Maria's breathing, too, grew labored. "Yeah, I don't know, I guess so."

Constance jumped in front of Maria. The woman stumbled to a stop. "Why don't we talk in the corridor?" Constance said. She wanted out of the crucible before her judgment or mental alertness was impacted.

"What's the matter, Roy? Can't take the heat?" Maria swatted at Constance, her fingers brushing Constance's nose. Maria had always been aggressive, but this was even much for her.

Constance hit Maria's hand away, trying to control her own feeling of hostility—a symptom of the crucible conditions. Maria laughed and threw a jab, this time intending to make full contact with Constance's face. Constance deftly evaded the punch and redirected Maria's energy, sending her lurching past her. Maria regained her footing and whirled around furious.

"I don't want to fight you," Constance said, feeling wobbly.

A blurry Maria charged. Before Constance could focus, she felt Maria's shoulders hit her in the gut. They landed hard on the metal floor. A thud echoed in the chamber. Constance gasped for air but felt as if she were drowning. She heard pounding, turned, and saw Michael and the others hitting the glass. They were yelling, but everything sounded like it was underwater.

Maria sat on top of her, hit a button on her wrist remote that controlled the conditions, grinned, and wrapped her hands around Constance's throat. The fan kicked on. They shifted and slid in a circle on the floor as the wind picked up. Everything grew dark as Maria's fingers pressed on her carotid artery. Was Maria's angry and grotesque mug the last face Grace had seen?

The thought that Grace may have died at Maria's hands had the effect of smelling salts and sent a jolt of adrenalin through Constance's veins. Maria's fingers tightened. Constance's vision diminished to two pinpoints of light. She threw a hand between Maria's arms and slammed her palm into Maria's chin. Maria lost her grip. Constance's vision returned. She grabbed Maria's arm and twisted it behind her back. Maria cried out in pain.

"I'm willing to die here with you if you don't tell me what I want to know," Constance said.

The wind whipped around them. The group outside the window pounded harder, but Constance ignored them. The crucible conditions and fight had finally taken their toll on Maria. Constance felt the woman's strength diminish and her resistance weaken.

"Was Grace alive when you found her?" she said between gasps.

Maria nodded.

"Did she say anything … anything about finding our new planet?"

Maria shook her head. Constance stripped the control from Maria's wrist and crawled away, exhausted. Constance attempted to hit the kill switch on her wrist control but couldn't get her fingers to work and kept missing the screen. She needed to get to the control panel on the wall or release the door lock before she passed out. She attempted to stand, but her legs gave out. It felt like she had run a marathon.

The wind thrashed her hair across her face, and the room seemed to spin. The laughing faces of Michael, Grace, and the mysterious little boy who had appeared to her on the ship whirled by. She heard pounding and blinked. People at the window were yelling and pointing. She cocked her head, trying to figure out what they were saying, but everything sounded and looked as if it was caught in a tornado. She squinted at the group. What were they pointing at? Something behind her?

A hand grabbed her by the hair and lifted her to her knees. Maria tripped above her, but she was on her feet. "You're not going to die here," the woman hissed in her ear. "But you are going to die… You all are."

Constance tried to grab Maria's hands but couldn't lift her arms. Her strength was gone. She hung by her hair like a doll in a demonic child's hands. "Then I guess we all die together," she said.

Maria swayed but held on to Constance. "You think I'll be on this ship with you weaklings when Jupiter claims it?"

Constance felt nauseated. How easy it would be to let herself sink into oblivion. "What are you gonna do, teleport?" she said.

"Exactly."

"You're delusional," Constance said, feeling herself slipping away.

"We'll see how delusional I am when the Event comes...
See if you can find me or the Curators then."

Maria released Constance, sending her to the floor face-
first. Constance felt the hot metal against her cheek. She
mustered the strength to keep her eyes open long enough to
watch Maria stagger away toward the door ... and then the
world went black.

CHAPTER 11: EARTH

Constance felt as if she had been drugged. Hazy images of people hovered nearby. She tried to make out faces, but the figures evaporated like clouds. Voices grew louder. She squeezed an object in her hand and discovered she was clutching the top of a dining room chair. A door slammed. She felt a presence next to her.

A boy said, "What's the Orb?"

She blinked. Nicolas stood next to her, examining the book cover on Grace's table. The fog in her mind lifted. She was in Grace Yoholo's dining room.

Nicolas tugged on her shirt. "What's an orb?"

"Well," she said, the bizarre sensation of a moment ago fading. "An orb is something round, like a sphere."

"But what's *that* orb?" He placed a finger on the blueprint drawing.

What was that orb drawn on the inside of the book cover?

Michael observed her with concern from the other side of the table. "Are you okay?"

"Yeah." She forced a smile and closed the book. "How was stargazing?"

"Great," Nicolas said. "We saw Jupiter."

"Wow. Jupiter. That's very cool," she said.

"You know what else? Miss Grace says we can see rocket launches right from her back porch. There's one scheduled for tomorrow."

"Really?" she said. "Well, I'm not sure we'll be around for that but…

Her voice trailed off as Nicolas turned the book over, pulled off the cover, spread out the paper, and traced the drawings of the orb with his finger. Why did the image look familiar? Was it something her father had shown her as a girl? It had been drawn on the back of his book cover. He had written notes in the pages. Could the drawings have been his as well?

"What is it?" Nicolas said quietly to himself as he studied the picture.

Grace peered over Nicolas's shoulder and said, "It's a space station."

"You mean like in *Star Wars*?" the boy said, amazed.

"Sort of," Grace said. "I'm sure you've heard of Noah and the ark, right?" The boy nodded. "The Orb is like Noah's ark, but it's in space instead of on the ocean."

"Can we go there?"

"I'm afraid not," Grace said. "It was only an idea. It was never built."

Constance sensed that Grace knew more about the Orb than she was letting on. She glanced at Michael to gauge his reaction and discovered him watching her with such intensity that she blushed and looked away.

"Why didn't the people who designed it build it?" Nicolas said.

Grace put her arm around Nicolas. "For one thing, it's enormous," she said. "It would take a lot of people and a lot of money. And even if they got it up there, it would be dangerous. Only a special type of astronaut could operate it."

"I bet I could fly the Orb," Nicolas said. "Right, Mom?"

Constance smiled, but the moment he looked away, the smile disappeared. The thought of her son rocketing into space sent her pulse racing and sweat beading on her forehead. She shuddered, despite the heat.

"Remember," Grace said to the boy. "Noah only needed the ark because there was a flood."

Nicolas was silent a moment and then said, "You mean the Orb is only for an emergency?" Grace nodded. "What kind of emergency?"

Grace noticed Constance staring at the Orb schematics, reached across the table, and returned the cover to its proper position around the book. "That's a conversation for another time," Grace said.

Constance imagined the Orb floating through the book cover's swirling illustration of the universe. Grace said that the ship had never been built, but Constance sensed that it had. It was a gut feeling... No, more like a memory. But how was it possible to have a memory of something she had never seen before? Fuzzy imaginings of living quarters and corridors and animals flashed through her mind.

She glanced at Michael. He was like an old friend who understood her thoughts without her needing to say a word. But how could that be? They had only met hours ago. Like a static-filled radio message, she had flashes of Michael with her on the Orb—passionate images. Her pulse quickened. Her skin tingled. She broke eye contact, afraid that he could tell what she was thinking and feeling.

She observed Grace with Nicolas. Grace, too, seemed familiar. Comfort and warmth and profound sadness surrounded the woman.

"Are you okay, Mommy?" Nicolas said.

With Nicolas, there were no unsettling images or emotions. With her son, all was normal and real. She put a reassuring arm around his shoulder. "I'm fine."

"You think I can go to space school and be an astronaut on the Orb?" he said.

She wanted to hold him tight, keep him forever by her side, and forbid him from even thinking about going to space. But why? Children often dreamed of being astronauts ... including her. That didn't mean it would happen.

Michael mouthed, "Are you okay?"

She shook her head. No. She didn't think she was.

CHAPTER 12: ORB

Faraway voices trickled into the recesses of Constance's consciousness. "Is she okay?" "You think she's dying?" "Roy, can you hear me?" *Go away*, she silently told the voices. *Let me sleep.*

Her head was lifted and then lowered onto something cool and wet. "Constance, it's Michael," came a man's familiar voice.

How did she know him? *Oh, yeah.* "Michael?"

"She's coming to," someone said.

Her eyelids fluttered open. Michael, Lina, Zhang Yong, and Garcia stared down at her. She smiled dopily, feeling a little drunk. She raised her head, and the world swayed. She rubbed a knot at the back of her skull.

"What happened?" she muttered and then remembered... Maria had happened. She glanced up. The fan at the top of the chamber was still. She recalled stepping inside the compartment, the heat, the low oxygen, and Maria handling her like a rag doll. There was something else, too. Something Maria had said.

"You gave us a good scare," Michael said. "Belkin

changed the emergency shut-off code. We couldn't get in or override the system."

"Where is she?" Constance searched the compartment.

"She left," Lina said. "Like the coward she is."

"We would have stopped her," Zhang Yong said. "But we were worried about you."

"Besides," Garcia said. "Where can she go?"

Michael studied Constance's face. "How do you feel?"

"Like I've been run over by a Mack truck," she said, pulling herself to a seated position.

Maria's ferocious attack was disturbing. Constance took a deep breath and felt pain in her side. If the others had not been watching and she had not been able to fight back, Constance was sure Maria would have done worse, maybe even killed her. Her torso and legs throbbed. There were undoubtedly bruises. How much would they be like the bruises she had seen on Grace? Was it possible? Could Maria have killed Grace? Why would one inhabitant kill another? What could be gained?

"Did you learn anything about Grace?" Michael said.

"What about Grace?" Zhang Yong said. Like Constance, he had felt particularly close to Grace.

"I think Maria knows more about her death than we were told."

"Like what?" Garcia said.

"Are you suggesting Maria killed…" Lina trailed off.

The group fell quiet. The crew had always taken seriously their charge of creating a new and better society on a faraway planet. The thought that one of them was a murderer rocked the foundation of their utopian belief.

"I don't understand," Zhang Yong said. "What would she get out of harming Grace?"

Why would Maria want Grace dead when Grace was finding them a new home? Was it really about getting off the ship? It had been twelve months since Earth's destruction.

Only the solar system's uninhabitable outer planets remained. If Maria's goal was to escape from the Orb, where would she go? Constance considered the possibly that Maria had gone insane from the effects of the traumatic migration or as a result of her obsessive time in the crucible. They needed to speak with her before her mind was completely gone.

"We need to find Maria," she said. "I think she knows something about how to get off the ship."

"Not without a space suit," Michael said.

"Off the ship to where?" Zhang Yong said.

Garcia raised his hand to interrupt. "You're saying we have a murderer onboard?"

"I will kill her," Lina said.

"No," Constance said. "We need her to tell us what she knows."

Lina nodded. "Then I will kill her."

Lina was like a dog with a bone. Once she fixated on something, she didn't let go. Constance wouldn't want to be on Lina's bad side.

Constance pushed herself to a standing position and tested her legs. A little wonky but good enough to get moving. Michael helped her toward the exit.

"Get the others and find Maria," she said to the trio. "If she's in her cabin, keep her there until we get back. But remember, she's dangerous."

The crew followed Constance and Michael from the crucible. "What about you?" Garcia said.

"I'm going to talk to Kylos," she said.

"I'll stay with Roy," Michael said. "Now go. Who knows where Maria is right now?"

Constance waited for the others to exit and then said, "I think the Curators are abandoning the Orb."

"What?"

"Like when a queen bee deserts a hive," she said.

"Or rats on a sinking ship."

"I think they're taking Maria with them."

Michael shook his head. "Why would they take Maria, of all people?"

"I think it's payment for killing Grace."

"What did the Curators have against Grace? It doesn't make sense." He moved away, agitated.

"We need to go to the Curators' ring," she said.

He winced. The only time the inhabitants had been on A ring was during their initial migration. That was where their teleportation vessels had been housed and where they had been nurtured back to health before being transferred to their permanent residence ring. The Curators' ring also contained the Curators' living quarters and the control room for all functions of the massive ship. These were things the crew had pieced together from fuzzy recollections after their traumatic arrival. As far as any of them knew, the only way to gain access to the ring was with the aid of a Curator.

Of those who had survived the migration, Michael had suffered the most. She understood why he had no desire to revisit the ring. She touched his arm. "If there is a way to escape this ship, wouldn't you like to find out what it is before it's too late?"

He paced and then said, "Okay."

"Okay," she said.

Michael assisted her down the corridor and into the connecting strut. He kept a hand on her lower back, bracing her in case she lost her footing and fell backward—a distinct possibility given what Maria had put her through. They reached the top of the stairs, squeezed into the alignment chamber, and steadied themselves as the contraption took them from vertical to horizontal. Michael caught her as she stumbled onto the platform. They hopped into an open elevator compartment and rode in silence.

"Here's our stop," he said as the landing to the Curators' ring approached. "You sure about this?"

Constance jumped from the compartment and stepped into the alignment stall. He hopped in after her, barely squeezing into the cage. They stood nose to nose, waiting, hoping that the alignment stall would move. It didn't.

She peered around his shoulder. "Watch it," she said as the dumbwaiter moved past them.

He winced as the machinery scraped his back. "This thing isn't made for two people."

She shook the stall, frustrated. "Now what?"

"How about this?" he said, studying the stall and the connecting strut beyond it. "If we can squeeze through the mesh behind the alignment chamber, I think we can jump to the stairs."

She peered through the mesh. The stairwell landing was four meters below and operated under a competing gravitational field. If they were able to swing just right and adjust to the shift in gravitational pull while hanging from the mesh, his plan could work ... and, if not, they'd fall into the gap between the stairwell and the shaft and down nearly fifteen meters.

"What do you think?" he said.

She didn't relish the possibility of plummeting to her death in the connecting strut, but it was the best idea they had.

"I'll go first," she said. She would have an easier time squeezing through the small opening.

"I'll try to hold on to your waist for as long as I can, but once you're through you should try to get to the landing as quickly as possible."

She sucked in her gut, squeezed through the opening, and held tight to the mesh that cut into her fingers. Immediately, the A ring's centripetal force yanked at her legs and twisted them sideways. She winced as pain shot through her right hip.

Michael reached through the gap and grabbed the waist of her pants. "Got you."

She saw the twisting metal staircase below. Everything seemed to spin, making it hard to get her bearings. She eyed the landing and attempted to swing toward it, but every time she got momentum, the pull of the axle tugged her back from the platform and over the abyss.

"You can do this," he said.

She gave him a quick nod. She forced her body to swing harder toward the landing. He released her, and she felt the pull of the ring. Maybe she should use it rather than fight it. She stretched her arms to their full length and allowed the force to draw her entire body toward the abyss. Her wrists ached from being bent at an extreme angle. She swung again, this time going sideways, and felt her toe tap the landing.

"You got it," Michael said with such enthusiasm that she almost lost her grip.

She swung sideways again and again but each time only managed to touch a toe.

"You're gonna have to jump."

He was right. The only way she was going to make it to the landing was to let go of the mesh and take a leap of faith. She took a deep breath, got ready to swing, and let go. The competing forces arched her back and whipped her sideways. She slammed into the strut wall and onto the staircase landing with a thud. Despite the pain shooting down her right leg, she flashed him the victory sign.

"Now you," she said.

Michael moved to the gap between the alignment stall and wall. He pushed his arm through the narrow opening and tried to push through. He exhaled and tried again, this time using his foot on the opposite wall for leverage. No matter how he contorted his frame, he was unable to pass through the opening. He pulled his arm back through the gap and gazed down at Constance on the stairwell landing.

"I can't get through," he said. "You'll need to come back."

She looked down the stairwell and then back at Michael. "I can't," she said.

"I'll help you … like I did before but in reverse."

"I can't go back, Michael. I've come too far."

He shook the mesh. "What are you talking about, Roy?"

"I promise I'll be right back," she said, turning away.

"Roy, wait," he called after her. She gazed up. "What if the Curators find you?"

"Let's hope they don't," she said and hurried down the stairs.

CHAPTER 12: EARTH

Insects chirped as a gentle breeze blew across Grace's yard. After Grace's revelation about the Orb and her offer to give Nicolas a piece of her homemade blueberry pie, Constance had asked Michael to join her outside. Constance wrapped her arms tight to ward off the chilly spring air.

"You cold?" Michael said.

She shook her head. "It feels good."

They stood in silence, staring at the stars. How should she begin the conversation? She had never met Michael Whittaker before today, and yet she had an overwhelming sense that she knew him well—even intimately—as if she had another person's memories implanted in her brain. She needed to find out if he, too, was experiencing these visions.

"So you wanted to talk," he said.

"This is going to sound strange," she said. "But have you ever seen me before today?"

"No."

"I feel like I know you. That somehow we have a life together."

She stole a look at him and instantly wished she had kept

her mouth shut. He shifted his weight and rubbed his neck. She had made him uncomfortable. *Great,* she thought. *At best he thinks I have a crush on him, and at worst he thinks I'm a nut.*

"Never mind," she said. She moved away and sat on the porch swing. Schrodi crawled from under a bush and rubbed against her legs.

Michael joined her on the swing. She watched Nicolas inside with Grace. Seeing his contented face covered in blueberries comforted her.

"He's a good kid," Michael said.

She nodded.

"I know I have no right to ask, but…"

She rubbed her fingers. "Nicolas's father?"

He nodded.

The simple answer to Michael's question was that she had fallen in love. She had been terribly lonely at the time, and Nicolas's father had made her feel special. He was charming, intelligent, confident, and almost two decades older than her. He filled a void created when her father died. He told her from the start that he'd never leave his wife, but she didn't care that he was married and her professor. She was drunk on the high of being with him and got pregnant. She never told him, fearful that he might seek custody or, worse, tell her to terminate. She knew even then that she'd die before she'd let anyone take her son.

"I'm sorry," Michael said, breaking her trance. "It's none of my business."

"It's okay," Constance said. "Nick's father was a visiting professor when I was getting my doctorate. Age-old story of grad student falling for professor."

"Does Nicolas know?"

"His father was back at his regular university when I found out. I didn't see the point."

"Well," Michael said after a long pause, "however it happened, you have a pretty special kid in there."

She rose from the swing and studied the night sky. Schrodi followed and rubbed against her as she peered through the eyepiece.

"It's pointed at Jupiter," Michael said from the swing.

She gazed at the planet and heard her father's voice. He had recommended viewing the planet from a distance but also using it as a place to anchor before embarking on a long inter-stellar voyage. She wondered if that was what should be done to journey to a planet five hundred light years away, to the planet Grace had said was their Goldilocks planet. *How would we need to change to make the trip? Transposons?*

She removed her eye, studied the sky, and tried to recall where Grace had placed her finger on the map. There was no chance of spotting Grace's planet with the naked eye—it was doubtful she'd even be able to see the star that it was orbiting —but she'd bet the massive telescopes on Wallops could pick it up. She returned to the telescope and pointed it low in the sky, where she suspected the Goldilocks planet might be—some-where below Jupiter and east of Venus.

"What are you looking for? Jupiter is that way," Michael said, pointing to an area of the sky much higher than where she was focused.

"I'm looking for Grace's planet."

"Grace has a planet?"

"Apparently," she said and panned the horizon. She glanced at the sky where Jupiter was, trying to get her bearings.

Suddenly, Schrodi hissed, puffed, and ran inside through the cat door. Seconds later, Constance felt pressure in her ears.

"Did you feel that?" Michael said.

She nodded. "I think the cat did, too."

The sky flashed with lightning. Thunder rumbled in the distance. "Sounds like a storm," he said. "We should head in."

Constance squinted at the clear night sky and redirected the telescope to view the shoreline. She spotted boats tied to the docks rocking in the water, as if caught in a wake. Strange. No watermen were out at this hour. She scanned the channel and empty piers and caught sight of something fuzzy on a wooden jetty. She focused the eyepiece and gasped. Staring back at her was a now familiar figure: Kylos.

CHAPTER 13: ORB

Constance snuck from the connecting strut stairwell to the forbidden Curators' ring and paused at the entrance. She had never anticipated getting this far and, if she had, she would have expected to find Fifi or another Curator waiting for her. Instead, the ring was deserted and eerily quiet.

She poked her head around the entryway. The air smelled of electricity and sulfur and was cooler than the air in the inhabitant rings. The corridor was significantly darker than the rest of the Orb. She guessed that the difference in illumination was because the Curators' eyes required less light than that of the inhabitants, but it was only a guess. Although there had been much whispered speculation among the crew, no one had knowledge of the Curators' physiology or origins.

Kylos had maintained that the Curators' purpose was to serve as "the saviors of humanity when humanity could not save itself." For most inhabitants, that explanation had been enough. They were thankful to have survived when billions had perished and didn't question the motives behind the Curators' generosity. The few who had pushed Kylos for further explanation about the Curators' purpose or origins had been accused of lacking gratitude and shamed into silence.

She peered down the hallway and then stepped back into the stairwell. Michael watched from behind the mesh at the top of the stairs. She wanted to yell that she was okay and that she would be right back but was worried that the sound would give her away. She gave him a quick wave and exited.

She hesitated, uncertain as to which way to go, and then decided on a clockwise direction. The hall grew dark as the connecting strut entrance disappeared behind her. She crept forward to give her eyes a chance to adjust and used the soft green lights that lined the floor as a guide. She wondered what she'd find on A ring. The Curators alternated shifts patrolling the Orb. She had never seen more than three together at a time except on special occasions. She assumed they spent the rest of the time on their ring but had no idea what they did there.

She inched along, trying not to make any noise. The silence was absolute and made her want to scream. The corridor narrowed. Her pulse quickened as she drew closer to large metal objects lining the walls. They were approximately seven feet high, three feet wide, and two feet deep. She wondered if the containers were the Curators' sleeping compartments. The high-tech coffins seemed fitting for the likes of Kylos, Fifi, Dumbo, and the rest. She ran her hand along a vessel. Buttons lined one side.

She raised herself on tiptoe and felt the smooth, rounded top. Her cheek pressed against the cool metal, and the memory of the migration's pain hit her like a lightning bolt. These were the transportation tubes that had ripped them from their doomed planet to the Orb.

She stumbled back and bumped into another vessel. Her legs buckled, and she crumpled to the floor. The agony of the experience flooded back in vivid flashes—the screams, the terror, the feeling that her body had been torn apart limb by limb. Bile welled in her esophagus. *No*, she thought, and swallowed hard. She would not get sick; she would not be broken a second time. She willed herself to stand, took a deep breath, and exhaled. She repeated the breathing and with every blow out forced the memories from her head. Her legs strengthened, and she moved away down the corridor.

It wasn't the memories of the migration alone that bothered her. It was how weak they had all been afterward—how the Curators had used the shock of the transport to bend their will, make them more malleable and less likely to ask questions or rebel. Was it survivor's guilt that had made them compliant? Knowing that seven billion people and every living creature on Earth had died while they lived was a lot to handle. For some, it had proved too much.

Her pulse returned to normal. She stretched her shoulders and neck to relieve the tension caused by the flashback. She slipped down the hall and estimated she must be halfway around the ring. She was as far from the stairwell and Michael as she could be. If she continued, she would soon approach the stairwell from the other side and be back where she started. Thus far she had found nothing. No Curators. No Maria. No obvious way off the ship.

The light ahead brightened. A shaft of red and amber from Jupiter emanated from a room and washed over the floor. She hugged the wall and peered around the corner. She shifted her head out of the light so that her eyes could see the areas in shadow. The room was one of the largest on the Orb.

She entered and attempted to make out the room's contents. Anything not in the direct path of the light was dim. She listened to be sure nobody was coming and crept toward the room's center. She detected minor movement from the shadows, and something about the movement reminded her of laundry hanging out to dry.

She squeezed between two dark areas, careful not to touch anything. She heard a faint sound and froze. Was someone approaching? She heard the sound again. It was coming from above—quiet and soothing, like gentle waves rolling in on a beach. She scanned the ceiling, but it was too black to see.

The dark shadow to her right rocked slightly. Was it clothing hanging from the ceiling? Had she risked everything to discover tunics hanging in the Curators' closet? She gingerly reached out to touch the garment and felt cold flesh. She yanked her arm away and elbowed more cold flesh behind her. She stifled a scream and froze as the objects swayed and then became still. She guardedly circled one of the objects until she could see it in the Jovian light and suppressed a second scream. Dangling by her shoulders from two hooks was Fifi.

Constance gaped at the Curator's face. The eyes were closed. She gazed down Fifi's naked body and discovered what she and the others had long suspected: the Curators lacked obvious reproductive parts. She scanned Fifi's feet with their strange webbed toes and saw that the Curator was suspended inches above the floor. *That explains the swaying*, Constance thought.

She moved her eyes up Fifi's body. What was coming from her stomach? She leaned closer and saw what was making the soft whooshing noise. A translucent tube ran from where a belly button would be up to the ceiling. Dark fluid rolled back and forth within the tube. She followed the tube and stretched on her tiptoes to see where it led but couldn't make anything out.

Constance lowered her gaze and came face to face with Fifi again … only this time Fifi's eyes were wide open.

CHAPTER 13: EARTH

Constance stared through the telescope eyepiece at Kylos on the pier. Kylos's mouth turned up in a V-shaped grin. His bony hand came into view. He curled his index finger and beckoned her. She jerked away and shivered.

"What is it?" Michael said beside her.

She heard Grace's warning in her head. *You can't let that creature discover Nicolas. It would be dangerous for everyone.* She peered through the window at Grace and Nicolas finishing the last bites of blueberry pie. She had to keep Kylos away. But how? If she tried to leave now with Nicolas, Kylos would see him. If she stayed put, Kylos might approach the house. If she told Michael, he would confront Kylos. There was only one option. She would meet Kylos on the dock.

"I need you to do something for me," she said to Michael. "Stay here with Grace and Nicolas."

"Where are you going?"

"Please, just stay here," she said and strode toward Kylos and the water a couple hundred feet away.

The screen door opened and closed behind her. She couldn't see Kylos but felt his eyes boring into her as she made her way toward the shore. She arrived at the landing, stopped near several small boats docked at land's end, and searched for him. Clouds blocked the moonlight.

She crept down the wharf and squinted into the gloom, but it was as if Kylos had disappeared into the brackish air. Water lapped at the pylons. A board sank under her weight. The cool night air gave her goose bumps. She heard a splash and peered over the edge. No sign of the man. Her heart raced. Had he lured her to the pier so he could do harm to Nicolas? Could Kylos be at the house right now?

"It's good to see you again, Ms. Roy," Kylos said from behind her.

She whirled around. The gaunt man she had come to hate —the one Grace had called a creature—stood under a hazy light perched above him on a post. The light hadn't been on when she stepped onto the walkway. Insects buzzed around him and reminded her of an incident when she was a girl— how a childhood friend had whacked a hive, sending a swarm of bees into the air, how she had frozen in fear, and how not one bee had stung her, beginning her fascination with bees. Kylos didn't seem to care or notice the bugs or the curious fact that they never flew closer than five inches from him.

"Why are you here?" she said.

"Father wishes to continue his discussion. I have been tasked with retrieving you. I had dispatched Mr. Whittaker to bring you back, but when he failed to return I grew ... concerned. I believe Father would find your detour to Dr. Yoholo's residence curious. I know I do."

"Dr. Malic isn't your father," she said, tired of his lies.

"I see Dr. Yoholo has shared one of her fanciful stories," he said, circling her. "What else did she tell you?"

She eyed him as he orbited. "Nothing," she said, regretting she had said anything.

"Come now," he said. "The Dr. Yoholo I know isn't shy about her theories. She must have said something ... something about the work your parents did with the FSI, perhaps?"

"What do you know about that?"

He stopped circling and stood before her. "The better question is … what don't I know?"

When she had met with him at the FSI, the man had been nothing but cryptic. She found it hard to believe he would be forthright now.

"Try me," he said. "Ask me anything."

"Grace mentioned a ship," she said, testing him.

"Ah," he said and pointed to the sky. "She discussed the Orb, did she?" Her eyes widened in surprise. "What did dear Dr. Yoholo tell you?"

"That it doesn't exist."

He nodded. "That is true."

She squinted at him, doubtful.

"You think the Orb does exist," he said.

"Yes."

He nodded again. "That is also true."

"That's not possible," she said. "We can't both be right."

"You contemplate the universe and think big. But," he said, snatching an insect from the air by its delicate leg and holding it before her, "sometimes it's better to think small." He studied the bug, struggling to break free of his grasp, and then released it. "You feel strongly that you are correct. Why is that?"

She wasn't about to tell him about the visions she'd had of strangers and Michael and what she guessed were areas of a spacecraft.

"Don't worry," he said in a hush. "Your secret's safe with me."

The comment unnerved her. It was as if he could read her thoughts. "I don't know what you're talking about," she said.

He smirked. She'd had enough of his games. Time to get Nicolas and run as far from this man and Wallops as possible. She darted past him and marched off the dock.

"Don't you want to know what happened to your mother?" he said.

She stumbled to a stop. Her throat went dry. *Keep going and don't listen*, a voice in her head commanded. But the heartsick kid in her wouldn't let her move. What if he had answers to her questions? How could she walk away?

She stormed back. "Tell me what you know."

"I'll do better than that," he said. "I'll show you."

"Show me?" she said, stunned.

"Of course. But you need to return to the FSI. Dr. Malic says you have more to learn … and do." He slinked toward her, the bugs buzzing like a cape behind him. "You don't think you were asked to come all this way to pick up an automaton, do you?"

She heard the click of a gun hammer behind her. "She's not going anywhere with you," Grace said.

Grace stood several yards away, a shotgun aimed at Kylos's chest. Michael stood beside her.

"I thought our paths would never cross again, Dr. Yoholo," Kylos said. "You look well."

"Wicked creature," Grace said and spat on the ground.

"Be careful," Kylos warned.

Despite the grin plastered on his face, Constance could tell Kylos was no more pleased by Grace's presence than she was his.

"Mr. Whittaker," Kylos said. "When I requested you return Ms. Roy to the FSI, I don't recall telling you to bypass her past Dr. Yoholo's humble abode. I didn't know you two were acquainted."

"We're—" Michael began.

"Don't say anything," Grace said, cutting him off.

"Very well," Kylos said with a sigh. "Shall we, Ms. Roy?" He moved toward her.

"Don't take another step," Grace said. "Connie, it's time you got on your way home."

Constance hesitated.

"You're free to go," Kylos said with a motion of his arm. "But if you do, you'll never hear your mother's voice again."

"Don't listen," Grace said. "He speaks nothing but lies, especially when he feigns being supportive."

Constance's head told her that everything Grace said was true, that Kylos wasn't to be trusted, that he was lying to manipulate her back to the FSI. But her heart held out hope that Kylos or Malic possessed information that could solve her life's greatest mystery. Oh, to hear the voice that had sung her to sleep at night, that had admonished her for returning from playing in the woods with mud caked on her feet, that had patiently tutored her on math homework.

"Mom?" came a voice from a distance away.

Nicolas stood in the doorway of Grace's house. Adrenalin surged into Constance's bloodstream. "Nicolas, go back inside," she yelled.

Kylos's eyes twinkled. "Nicolas," he said, tilting his head and gazing at the boy with interest. "Who is Nicolas?"

CHAPTER 14: ORB

Constance stared into Fifi's glassy corneas and saw her own reflection. She stood inches from the Curator's face —terrified how Fifi might react to her presence in their inner sanctum—held her breath, and willed herself not to blink. She studied Fifi's nostrils and mouth. As far as Constance could tell, she wasn't breathing. Was Fifi in a state of hibernation? If so, why did her eyes open? Had it been an involuntary behavior triggered by Constance's presence?

Fifi's eyes snapped closed. Constance squeezed her own lids, relieving her burning eyes, but remained motionless lest she alert Fifi a second time. She waited several seconds and then backed away. Her retreat was slow, every step carefully placed so as not to make a sound. The entrance to the room became visible in her peripheral vision. She took several more steps and was in the corridor.

Time to return to the connecting strut and Michael. She took off and was pulled up by a charley horse in her calf. She spotted a dark entranceway and hobbled inside. She hugged the wall, listened to see if she had been followed, and worked out the cramped muscles in her calf, arms, and neck. She didn't know whether it was the beating from Maria, the tense face-to-face encounter with Fifi, the unusually cool air of the Curators' ring, or a combination of these factors that had caused her muscles to spasm, but her body ached in a way she hadn't felt since recovering from the migration.

She massaged her shoulders and thought of Fifi hanging by hooks inserted into her humerus bones. Two other Curators had been hanging in the same slumber-like state. She wondered where the remaining Curators were. If they were patrolling the Orb in their usual grouping, that would only account for an additional three or four. Had the rest abandoned the ship?

Better keep moving and ponder these questions later. As she turned to leave, she heard a thump. She squinted to see if she had found another sleeping chamber. Again, the thump. She spotted the dark outline of what looked like a console. She inched forward, careful to keep her arms by her side so she didn't bump into anything, and made her way to the far wall and a large portal that looked out into space. She had stumbled into the control room.

A sizeable console ran the length of the window. Had she really found the ship's cockpit? She ran her fingers over what she suspected was a controller. It was unlike any she had seen before. Instead of buttons, switches, levers, or wheels, the top was covered with flat screens and panels. She placed her right palm on a panel. A spark of static discharge shocked her. She yanked her hand away, studied the panel, and then pressed her palm to the surface again. Nothing.

She placed her left palm on another panel next to the first. She hoped the controller would spring to life under her touch, that somehow she would be able to gain access to the Orb, but the console remained dark and quiet. Kylos had told the inhabitants that only the Curators could control the Orb. It seemed he had told them the truth. *Damn Kylos*, she thought and slapped the controller. The slap echoed in the room and beyond. She whipped her head around. What if she had awakened the Curators from their suspended sleep? Time to go.

She moved along the edge of the console and heard another thump. This time it sounded as if it was coming from the other side of the wall. She spotted a smaller window. She peered inside the chamber. Small red lights along the walls pulsed like warning lights atop a tower.

Suddenly, Maria's face popped up and her hands slammed into the glass. Constance jumped. Maria's eyes widened upon seeing Constance. She thumped on the glass and yelled something Constance couldn't hear. Constance searched the wall for a control panel and pressed it. Nothing. Maria pounded harder, pointed to the hall, and shouted.

Constance crept to the doorway. The corridor was deserted. She was about to return to the room when she noticed a hatch. That was what Maria had been trying to tell her—to unlock the door to the chamber she was in. The hatch looked thicker than the usual doors. The only other door that looked like this one was the one that sealed off the disposition chamber. Constance's heart skipped a beat. The Curators were preparing to jettison Maria into space.

She tugged on the latch. It didn't budge. She heard Maria banging on the other side. She glanced down the hall. If that didn't wake the Curators, she didn't know what would. She'd have to hurry. She rushed back to the observation window in the control room. The panel near the window was now lit and running down a clock. The lights inside Maria's chamber pulsed faster.

Maria pounded the glass with a look of terror. Constance pressed the panel in various places. The countdown continued. "Hold on, Maria," she said. She ran to the main console and pressed panel after panel. Nothing. Less than a minute was left on the clock. She ran into the hall, no longer caring if the Curators saw her. She placed a foot against the wall, wrapped her fingers around the latch, and pulled with all her strength and weight … but it was no use. The chamber was sealed.

She darted back to the window. Maria peered at her, tears in her eyes. There were only seconds left. There was nothing she could do. The woman had been horrible, perhaps had even killed Grace, but she was still one of the last survivors of Earth, a member of their crew.

"I'm sorry," Constance said.

The chamber doors opened, and Maria was sucked away. Constance ran to the large observation window. Maria's body twitched and then was still. She watched as Jupiter's gravity embraced Maria's frozen remains and carried her to her resting place.

The sound of feet softly padding down the hall sent Constance's heart racing. She dashed into the corridor, glanced toward the Curators' sleeping sanctuary, and saw Fifi's waxy, naked form ambling toward her. Fifi stopped. The two stared at one another. Constance glanced at the door to the expulsion chamber and then back at Fifi. The Curator gave Constance a sly smile.

Constance took off running. Despite the dark interior, she sprinted at full speed, using the green lights along the floor as a guide. She didn't see the migration vessels lining the walls, hit her shoulder against one, and fell back. She winced and took off again. She saw light spilling into the corridor from the connecting strut and pumped her arms.

She grabbed the entranceway wall and swung herself into the strut and up the first few steps. "Michael," she yelled between breaths.

Her lungs burned, and her muscles felt like Jell-O. *Keep going*, she told herself. *You're almost there.*

"Where the hell have you been?" he said when she reached the top.

"I'll explain later." She eyed the distance to the gap where Michael stood ready to pull her through.

"Just jump," Michael said. "I'll catch you."

"I can't," she said.

"Then you'll have to climb along the mesh. It's the only other way."

Constance heard footsteps below, grabbed the mesh, and started climbing. Her arms trembled with exhaustion. She squeezed her fingers harder as the gravitational force of the axle tugged her sideways. Michael grabbed her legs and pulled them through the gap. She clung to the mesh as the centripetal force of the Curators' ring tried to tug her back.

Michael clutched her waist and shirt. "Tuck your head," he said.

She did as instructed. He yanked her through the opening and clipped her ear on the jagged mesh before rolling her onto the platform. She wiped the cut with her shirt.

"Sorry," he said. "You okay?"

She held out her arm for him to help her up. "Get me outta here," she said.

CHAPTER 14: EARTH

Insects buzzed in a deafening symphony. Constance wanted to run, grab Nicolas, and blast into space, far away from Kylos and the FSI and transposons, but every muscle in her body had locked up when Kylos spotted Nicolas.

"Ms. Roy, is that your son?" Kylos said, gazing at Nicolas in a way that made her shudder.

"That boy's none of your business," Grace said.

"You and I know, Dr. Yoholo, that if Ms. Roy has a child, it is a great deal my business."

"If the FSI wants its money back, it can have it," Constance said. She was sick of the organization and its unreasonable contracts.

Kylos tsked and wagged a finger at Grace. "You haven't told her," he said.

Constance turned to Grace. "Told me what?"

"You and Michael get out of here," Grace said, not taking her eyes from Kylos. "I'll deal with this one."

"I'm not leaving until I get answers," Constance said. She turned to Michael. "Do you know what's going on?"

Michael gave a quick shake of his head.

"Mom, is everything okay?" Nicolas said, stepping from the porch.

"Everything's fine," she said, trying to sound calm. "Go back inside."

"But Schrodi's acting funny," the boy said.

"'Cause he smells a rat," Grace said, eyeing Kylos.

"Nicolas, please, do as I say," Constance said. "I'll be there in a minute."

Nicolas hesitated and then entered Grace's home and closed the door.

Constance studied Grace and Kylos. "You two know something about my son. I demand to know what it is."

"I'm afraid I no longer have time for our chat," Kylos said. "But I'll be at the FSI if you'd like the answers you seek." He walked away toward the dark end of the pier.

"Wait," Constance called after him. "What about my mother?"

"You know where to find me," Kylos said and disappeared.

"Where'd he go?" Michael said.

"Into the primordial ooze where he belongs," Grace said.

"His departure was so sudden," Constance said.

"That's what concerns me," Grace said, lowering her gun. "Kylos wouldn't leave unless he's planning something."

Constance studied the end of the dock, straining to detect if Kylos was still out there watching them.

"We don't have much time," Grace said. She hurried toward the house.

Constance took a final look at the pier to be sure Kylos was gone and then dashed after Grace. Michael followed. She grabbed the woman as they reached the porch. "I'm not going anywhere until you tell me what is going on," she said. "He says he knows what happened to my mother."

"He only thinks he knows," Grace said.

"And you?"

Grace motioned for Constance and Michael to move away from the door toward the swing. "None of this was supposed to happen," she said. "No one was supposed to get hurt."

"I don't understand," Constance said.

"Remember how I asked you what it would take to cross the galaxy?"

Constance nodded.

"Cross the galaxy?" Michael said with raised brows.

Grace held up her hand to silence him. "Edward found a way at Wallops. It was miraculous," she said. "We could move matter on the atomic level."

"What does that have to do with my mother?" Constance said.

"The program was daring. It required enormous energy. Tests indicated the migration process would be fatal to the hosts."

"It would kill people?" Michael said.

Grace nodded.

"So the program was abandoned," Michael said.

"No," Grace said. "They modified the host."

Constance's eyes widened in understanding. "With transposons," she said.

Michael looked at the women. "I'm not following."

"They genetically altered the host in order to survive the migration process," Constance said.

Michael shook his head. "That's insane."

"That's what I thought," Grace said. She turned to Constance. "But your mother didn't. She, your father, and Edward all believed that the end was near and that the only way to save humanity was to change it."

"My mother was involved? How?"

"She volunteered for a genetic experiment. She was injected with self-replicating transposons."

Michael paced, agitated. "How could they do that?"

"I tried to stop them," Grace said. "But they had help."

Constance glanced at the water. "Kylos," she said.

"Your mother died testing their theory and the capability of the transposons. I wasn't there when it happened. I warned your parents and Edward against it. Just because we can test something doesn't mean we should. When they refused to listen, I cut off ties. I didn't want to be a part of... That was the last time I saw them. And the last time anyone saw your mother."

Constance turned away, stunned. How could her father have allowed such a thing? "My father and Malic ... they were a part of my mother's—"

"No," Grace said. "Your father didn't want your mother to go. He tried to take her place, but the genes replicated better in a female line. Your mother insisted she be the one. They never meant for any harm to come to her."

"What the hell did they think was going to happen?" Michael said.

"Your father was a broken man when she died," Grace said, ignoring him. "It may sound clichéd, but a part of him died with her."

Constance remained with her back to Grace and Michael. Tears welled in her eyes picturing the suffering her mother had endured ... all in the name of science.

"You said the transposons replicated better in women," Michael said. "So these things are passed on?"

"They get stronger with every generation," Grace said.

Constance swung around. "I have them?" she said. "And Nicolas?"

"When I saw your son..." Grace stopped herself. "I believe so, but only Edward can tell for sure."

"What else has the FSI done to people?" Michael said.

"I don't understand what you mean," Grace said.

The muscles in his jaw tightened, and his fists clenched. "I think you do," he said.

Constance was surprised by his anger. Why was he

concerned about what the FSI had done to her mother and Nicolas? Then it hit her. "Did the FSI alter Michael's genes when he was ill as a boy?" she said. "Is that how he got well?"

Grace sighed. "It's possible."

He ran his fingers through his hair. "So I'm what … a science experiment?"

"I don't know," Grace said. "Only Edward has the answers."

"Like he'll tell us anything," he said.

"We need Edward's help in order to keep Nicolas safe."

"Safe from what?" Constance said. "You still haven't told us why he's in danger."

"If Nicolas has the ability I think he has, Kylos will want to exploit it. There's nowhere anyone could take him that he'd be protected."

"Aren't Malic and Kylos working together?" Michael said.

"The Edward I knew would never let anything happen to a child," Grace said.

"Forgive me if I don't believe you," Michael said.

"Even if it's true that Dr. Malic wouldn't hurt Nicolas," Constance said, "you knew him twenty years ago. People change."

"I refuse to believe that," Grace said.

Nicolas peeked around the door. "Mom, can I come out?"

Grace took Constance's hands and looked her in the eye. "Do you trust me to save your son?"

Constance felt the force of the woman's sincerity. Nicolas watched from the doorway. As his mother, it was her duty to protect him, no matter what.

"Yes," she said. "I trust you."

CHAPTER 15: ORB

Constance leaned against a table on the far side of the dining room. The commissary was packed with inhabitants asking questions and talking noisily about what little Michael had told them about what had happened on the Curators' ring. She hadn't shared everything she had witnessed with him. She was still processing it herself. She had told him enough to buy her time to think.

She tried to shake Maria's pleading eyes and frantic banging from her mind. She had no doubt who had been the architect of Maria's merciless end. Fifi's grin had told her everything. Maria must have killed Grace with the promise of leaving the ship, but in making a deal with the Curators, Maria had brought about her own demise. The truth could no longer be ignored. The Curators intended to let them die.

"Where's Belkin?" someone said.

"We couldn't find her," Lina said.

"Bet she doesn't have the guts to show after what she did to Roy," Garcia said.

Zhang Yong eyed the crew's angry faces. "If she knows what's good for her, she'll stay in hiding," he said to Muhammad, who nodded agreement.

"Maria is dead," Constance said, unable to take the crew's speculation any more. Talking ceased. "She was ejected from the ship."

"How?" Muhammad said.

"From another disposition chamber on A ring. I saw her…" She took a breath. "Fifi did it."

The inhabitants fell silent, worried and confused looks on their faces. She wouldn't share the details of Maria's final moments. Better that she alone be haunted by them.

"Why would Fifi discharge Belkin from the ship?" Hashim said.

"I think it was punishment for talking."

"To you?" Zhang Yong said. "Did Maria tell you something when you were in the crucible?"

"She said she was getting off the ship," Constance said.

"That's impossible," Dru said. "She must have been messing with you."

"I can assure you," Constance said, "she was quite serious. Ask Whittaker, Lina, Zhang Yong, and Garcia if you don't believe me."

"We didn't actually hear what she said to you," Garcia said. He turned to the others. "Isn't that right?"

Lina and Zhang Yong nodded.

"This is ridiculous," Dru said. "A Curator wouldn't kill an inhabitant. We should to talk to Kylos."

Others muttered agreement.

It would have been hard for Constance to believe, too, if she hadn't seen it herself. She hesitated telling them more, but if they were going to figure out a way to save themselves, the others needed to know what they were up against.

"There were only three Curators on the ring," she said. "I think Kylos is gone. I imagine the others will soon follow, if they haven't already."

"That doesn't mean anything," Lina said. "They could be on patrol."

"Really?" Constance said, her patience gone. "Have you seen them? Have any of you?"

"Maybe they're coming back," Muhammad said.

She gazed at Muhammad, ever the optimist, and shook her head.

"But why?" he said. "Why would they save and then abandon us?"

Michael made his way through the crowd and joined Constance. "When Roy and I asked Kylos about how we're going to find our new planet without Grace, he said something about all of this being an experiment … and that it is over."

"The experiment is over?" Hashim said. "What does that mean?"

"That they're going to let us die," Dru said.

"And you two didn't think to share this with us?" Garcia said.

"What would you have done if you knew?" Michael said. "Fly this thing to another planet?"

"Maybe," Garcia said.

Tension filled the air. If Constance didn't do something, the cafeteria would turn into Thunderdome.

"I found the controls," she said.

"What?" said several people.

"When I was on the Curators' ring," she said. "I found a room, like a cockpit. I think that's where the controls for the ship are located."

"Did they work?" Lina said.

"No."

"Only the Curators can move the ship," Michael said.

Constance caught Hashim's eye. Before his life on the Orb, Hashim had been a leading researcher on artificial intelligence and air travel at Carnegie Mellon University. If anyone had a chance of deciphering how the ship worked, it was him. "Perhaps Hashim could get the console to work," she said.

"I'll give it a shot," Hashim said. "It's certainly better than waiting to die." He turned to Dru. "You're the computer whiz. Wanna give me a hand?"

"Absolutely," Dru said.

"I hate to sound negative," Zhang Yong said, "but even if Hashim and Dru gain control of the ship, where will we go? We don't have back-up resources. We probably only have one shot at getting to the right destination."

His words hit hard. They had less than forty-eight hours until they plunged into Jupiter's atmosphere.

"I know where to go," Constance lied. "Grace told me."

Michael's eyes widened in surprise. "When was this?"

She looked away to avoid his scrutiny.

"Why didn't you say so in the first place, Roy? You trying to give me a heart attack?" Muhammad said.

"Yes," Michael said, all seriousness. "Why didn't you say so?"

She had never been a good liar, and it was clear Michael was wondering why she had told this one. Her legs trembled. Was her body betraying her? *No*, she thought, feeling the shudder through her entire body. *It's more than that.*

A metal cup rattled to the floor. Silverware and plates vibrated across tables. Everyone grew quiet as a low vibration ran through the room. The ship shuddered. A low metal wail followed as if the Orb itself was in pain. Constance watched the ceiling quiver. Suddenly, the shaking stopped. They waited, but neither the tremor nor sound returned.

"What was that?" Dru said, voicing the question on everyone's mind.

All eyes fell on Constance. It wasn't because she had the answer. They all had the answer. The crew turned to her because she was the only one brave enough to say it.

"That," Constance said, "was the beginning of the Event."

CHAPTER 15: EARTH

Constance rushed Nicolas down the steps of Grace's house. She had no idea what the specific threat Kylos posed to Nicolas was, but Grace was adamant about the danger and the need to protect him. She pressed her hand against Nicolas's back to keep him from stopping to examine a bug or play with Grace's cat, which raced alongside them on the path.

"Where are we going, Mom?" he said, clutching *A Map to the Galaxy*.

"Remember the bookstore you liked so much?" Constance said.

Michael waited at Grace's car with the back door open and scanned the area. Schrodi jumped inside and meowed.

"Schrodi wants to come with us," Nicolas said with delight and slid onto the backseat.

"Schrodi needs to stay and guard the house," Grace said. She lifted the cat from Nicolas's lap and draped it over her shoulder. "But how would you like to take this?" Grace produced a glass ball that had been hanging from her porch.

Nicolas gazed at the bright yellow feather inside and nodded.

"Buckle up, and Dr. Yoholo will hand it to you," Constance said.

Nicolas did as instructed and then took the glass ball from Grace.

Michael slammed the door closed. "I still don't know how I'm going to get into the FSI," he said, keeping his voice low. "Won't Kylos have alerted security?"

"Perhaps," Grace said.

"So you expect me to walk through the front door?"

"Unless you have a secret passageway." Grace removed a necklace hidden underneath her clothing. "You're going to need this," she said and handed it to him.

The disc pendant on the chain was unusual, with tiny notches and holes. Constance wondered if Grace had made it or if the marks had meaning to the Algonquian or Cherokee.

"What is it?" Michael said, examining the jewelry in the light.

"Take it to Edward and tell him to meet me at our special place. He'll know it's from me and where to go."

"And if I encounter Kylos?"

Grace patted him on the arm. "You're a strong fella. I'm sure you'll think of something." Schrodi squirmed in her arms. "I better put him inside," she said and retreated.

Michael studied the pendant. "What do you think it is?"

"Maybe something Malic gave her?" Constance said. "They were close at some point."

He placed the necklace in his pocket. "Guess I should get going."

"I'll understand if you back out," she said. "You don't have to do this."

"Yes, I do," he said. "But if I sense for one second Malic isn't being honest with me, I'm coming back alone and escorting you and Nicolas home to Blacksburg."

The two locked eyes. She felt like she was saying goodbye

to a paramour, not a virtual stranger, and had a sudden impulse to kiss him.

"Don't worry, Alice," he said, trying to lighten the mood. "I'll be as invisible as the Cheshire cat. Kylos won't even know I'm there."

"Why are you still *here?*" Grace said as she joined them. She looked back and forth between Constance and Michael and said, "Ah."

Michael cleared his throat and said, "I'm on my way."

"Good luck," Constance said.

He got into his car, started the engine, waved, and then disappeared down the road.

"It's time for us to leave, too," Grace said.

"Where's Mr. Whittaker going?" Nicolas said as Constance and Grace slipped into the front seat of Grace's car.

"On an errand," Constance said. "But he'll be back."

"Good," Nicolas said with relief.

Grace started the engine and pulled onto the road.

"You like Mr. Whittaker?" Constance said, surprised by her son's reaction to Michael's departure.

"Yes," Nicolas said, gazing out the window. "And he has my automaton."

Constance grinned. The automaton was on the back seat of Michael's car. Her son was still an innocent boy. But for how long?

"He'll be back," Grace said, noticing Constance's look of concern.

"Who?" Constance said.

"Michael."

"Oh, yes," she said, letting the misunderstanding go.

They rode the rest of the way to Sundial Books in silence. The roads were deserted at this hour, and it made for a short trip. They pulled into a space next to the back entrance.

"It looks closed," Constance said.

Grace cut the engine, exited, and crossed to the bookstore. Constance helped Nicolas. In one hand he held her father's book and in the other the glass ball with the feather. Grace stepped onto the back porch. The door opened, and the couple that had helped her and Nicolas appeared in the entrance.

"It's good to see you again, Grace," the man said.

"May we come in?" Grace said.

"We've been expecting you," said the woman.

Constance pushed Nicolas ahead of her into the store. The man nodded to the woman, who locked the door and pulled the window shade. The man turned on a lamp on the counter. It cast a soft, warm glow over the room. Truffaut, the tabby, blinked at the guests and then returned to napping on a wicker chair.

"It's been too long," Grace said to the woman. The two embraced. Grace turned to the man. "I'm glad to see you looking well, Jon."

"Good to see you, too," Jon said.

"Constance, Nick, these are my dear friends Jane and Jon Richstein. I believe you met them earlier."

"We certainly did," Nicolas said and smiled at the couple.

Grace, Jane, and Jon exchanged a look.

"I'm sure they won't mind if you look at their books," Constance said to her son.

"Not at all," Jane said. "You know where they are."

"Yep," Nicolas said with enthusiasm. "Here, Mom, you take this." He handed Constance *A Map to the Galaxy*.

The group watched him bounce to the children's section, the glass ball swinging from its string.

"Didn't I tell you it was her?" Jon said in a hushed tone to Grace once Nicolas was preoccupied with looking at books.

"We knew the moment she came in," Jane said.

"Knew what?" Constance said.

"That you are your mother's daughter," Grace said.

The three stared at her as if she was a fascinating museum artifact. She shifted *A Map to the Galaxy* in her hand, and it occurred to her that the discovery of her father's book had been no accident.

"You planted my father's book," she said to Jane.

"Let's just say it was only for sale to the right buyer," Jon said.

"Jane and Jon have been the book's custodians for many years," Grace said.

"And the picture?" Constance said. "Where's the Devil's Back Porch?"

Jane and Jon chuckled. "It's not a place," Jon said. "More like a group."

"That had shared interests," Grace said.

Constance motioned to the three. "And you're members of the group the Devil's Back Porch?" she said.

Jane smiled. "I'm sure Grace has much to discuss with you," she said. "We'd be happy to look after Nicolas."

"She's right," Grace said. "There are things you need to know before…"

"Before what?" Constance said.

"Let's talk outside."

Constance glanced at Nicolas contentedly scanning the shelves and playing with the glass ball. She wasn't crazy about leaving him alone a second time in the store.

"Believe me," Grace said. "This is the safest place for your son right now."

"Nick," she said. "Jane and Jon are going to keep you company while I talk with Grace."

The boy nodded and resumed his book search. Grace and Constance exited to the back. Constance positioned herself so she could keep an eye on Nicolas through the screen door. Grace leaned against the pole and gazed at the dock.

"That pier is all that's left of the original swing bridge," Grace said. "Before the new bridge, the road used to come over from Wallops and let out right here. I miss that old bridge."

She sighed. "I suppose there comes a time to tear down the old and build the new."

"Are we talking about bridges or you and Dr. Malic?"

Grace smiled. "Maybe both."

"You loved him."

"Very much."

"And you haven't seen him since…" Her voice trailed off. *Since my mother's death,* Constance thought.

"Your father told me later that Edward had regrets about what they had done—what had happened to us—but by then it was too late. Edward was already entangled with Kylos."

Constance wondered how Michael was getting on. Would he succeed in gaining access to the building and Dr. Malic? The things Malic had said at their meeting had made her question his sanity. Would he remember Grace? Was Grace placing her hopes on a man who didn't exist anymore? And if he was the man she remembered, would he be strong enough to travel?

"I know you believe Dr. Malic will be able to explain things to us, to help Nicolas," Constance said. "But you should know that when I saw him at the FSI, he was quite weak."

"The radiation from the experiment," Grace said. "Edward and your father paid a terrible price."

Her father's lung and stomach cancer had never made sense to her. Her father had been neither a smoker nor a drinker, and cancer didn't run in his family. When she had pressed him as to how he could come down with both illnesses, he had brushed her off and told her he must be unlucky. After all these years, she finally understood the cause.

The wind chimes tinkled in the breeze. She scanned the bridge that swept low around the island for headlights. It seemed an eternity since they had said goodbye to Michael in front of Grace's house.

"What do we do now?" Constance said anxiously.

Grace sat on the bench and looked out over the water. "Wait."

CHAPTER 16: ORB

The Orb's tremor had only lasted seconds, but the crew's realization that the ship was beginning its journey into the Jovian atmosphere had proven a great motivator. They needed to break into the Curators' ring, gain control of the ship, and fly themselves to their new planet … now. The temperature on the ship had risen several degrees as the climate controls fought against Jupiter's force, and the water supply was at a critical level. Those who had been in denial could no longer refute the impending Event and the likelihood that they would all perish.

The commissary had been transformed into a bustling command center. Michael helped organize the inhabitants into several groups, each assigned to work on a particular aspect of their survival. Everyone looked to Constance to lead because she was the only one who had visited the Curators' ring and because of the lie she had told about Grace revealing the location of their new home. Her lie weighed heavy on her mind. She had given them hope. What would happen when they found out the truth?

Lina and Garcia were in charge of the group assigned to

maintain and repair essential functions of the ship and were preoccupied with negotiating duties with their crew. Several members would need to take on double and triple shifts to allow others time to work on the exodus. Lina had to recruit two members to replace Grace and Maria in tending to the animals and performing other menagerie duties. Despite his lack of experience with animals, Zhang Yong volunteered to care for Grace's creatures and help tend the gardens.

Muhammad's group would oversee accessing and securing the Curators' ring. After cutting open the alignment stall mesh, they would fortify the area so the competing forces of the axle and ring didn't rip the stairwell apart or injure the crew as they traveled between them. Securing the ring also meant defending against any potential Curator attack and, if they did encounter Curators, subduing them so that they could navigate the Orb to their new home.

Once Muhammad's group made the ring accessible, Hashim and Dru's team would work on deciphering the controller. This team had the most daunting task because they had little knowledge of the ship's technology. The only hints they had as to the cockpit's functions were Constance's experiences with the console's static discharge and the panel's countdown clock. Constance hoped Dru and Hashim's research expertise would enable them to crack the Orb's code.

Constance studied Michael from the opposite side of the commissary. He had fallen into the role of coordinator, ensuring team leaders had what they needed and troubleshooting disputes. The crew had assumed that Michael would assist Constance with whatever planning or calculations she needed to perform in preparation for setting off on the journey to their new planet. Nobody seemed to notice that the two hadn't spoken since she told her lie. She couldn't avoid him forever.

She grabbed a cup of weak coffee, zigzagged her way through the crew, and joined Michael in surveying the activity.

"You know," Michael said, keeping his voice low, "you're a terrible liar. The only reason these people believe you is because they need to."

"I didn't lie," she said, avoiding eye contact.

"Really? Grace told you where the planet is?"

"She could have."

Michael shook his head in disgust.

"You were the one that said that if Grace told anyone where the planet was, it would be me," she said.

"So?" he said.

"Maybe she did leave a message. Maybe I just haven't figured it out."

"You don't really believe that, do you?"

Constance watched the teams working with purpose and determination. The Curators had abandoned them like a queen bee deserting a hive. Without a queen, a colony was doomed unless a new queen was introduced or the workers helped raise one. In order to survive, they needed a leader.

"Let's say you're right," Michael said after a long silence. "Let's say Grace left instructions for finding the planet, and you discover what they are—you really think we can figure out how to move this thing?"

"It's worth a try, isn't it?" she said and walked away.

"Where are you going?" he said.

"Grace's cabin," she said and exited.

Michael was right. There was a sliver of a chance of finding another planet, but it was in that sliver where hope— and their salvation—resided. She refused to have their final hours end in despair. Better to go down fighting. Maybe she'd find something in Grace's cabin that could give her a clue about where to go. She worked her way along the empty corridor, up the stairwell, into the central axle elevator to the inhabitants' residence ring. She hesitated when she reached Grace's cabin. It had only been a day since her death.

She slid the door open and stepped inside. The wall panels

glowed with light, a cup of cold tea sat on the bedside table, and everywhere was Grace's art. Grace had had one of the few single-occupancy cabins and she had transformed the cool interior into an inviting one. The room was so alive with Grace's spirit that Constance half expected her friend to appear.

Constance approached a primitive painting fashioned from a homemade canvas that hung on the far wall. Flowers and animals dotted the landscape. She squinted at a figure cresting a hill. It bore a striking resemblance to Constance.

She crossed to the neatly made bed and looked through stacks of readouts that had been laid on the blanket. In the upper right-hand corner of each paper there was a simple computer rendering of a planet with a corresponding number: 452, 440, 269. Under the planet and number was a twenty-four-digit location code and below that a table indexing the planet's similarity to Earth. Measurements of gravity, temperature, atmospheric composition, gases, etc., were listed vertically. Beside those numbers was a column marked *Survival Scale*, in which Grace had written numbers for each condition, followed by a circled final survivability assessment. Perhaps the answer to where they should go was in these pages.

Constance sat in a nearby chair and scanned the survivability percentages … 20.31%, 30.25%, 42.55% and so on. Not a single planet had been assigned a survivability factor of more than fifty percent. She sighed. Would she be willing to bet their lives on a fifty-percent chance?

She returned the papers and gazed across the room at a canvas mural that covered the entire wall. Unlike the other works, the mural was an odd impressionistic rendition of the galaxy. The light from Jupiter streaming in through the cabin window brought the mural's celestial bodies to life. Constance had an overwhelming feeling of futility. Their survival depended on her proving her lie the truth. How was she supposed to do that? She hung her head in defeat.

"I've always found humanity's capacity for mourning puzzling," said a familiar voice from the doorway.

Her heart skipped a beat. Even before she looked up, she knew who was there ... Kylos.

CHAPTER 16: EARTH

Constance checked her watch for the umpteenth time. Forty-five minutes had passed. Several cars had crossed the bridge, but Michael and Malic had failed to appear. Had Michael been forbidden from entering the facility? Had he been forced to find another way in? If so, why hadn't he called to let them know? Maybe Kylos had caught him. She glanced at Grace waiting on the bench. The woman didn't appear to be the least bit anxious about Michael's mission or the possibly of seeing the man she loved after decades apart.

Maybe she should take a walk to the pier to see if she could see anything from there. But then she wouldn't be able to keep her eye on Nicolas, who had fallen asleep in a chair on the porch after the bookstore owners had left for the evening.

"You think something has happened to them?" Constance said. She looked at Grace to determine if the question had disturbed her. She hadn't intended to voice her fear aloud.

"They'll be here," Grace said with Zen-like calm.

"How can you be so certain?"

"I believe in Michael and Edward. You should, too."

The comment irritated her, and she didn't want to be irritated at Grace. "I'm going for a walk on the—" she said but stopped when something in the distance caught her eye. A tiny light was approaching from the channel. "Do you see that?"

Grace rose and scanned the horizon. "It's them."

As the light drew closer, Constance heard an outboard motor. Two figures sat in a boat. The engine stopped. The boat drifted to the dock, and then she saw Michael and Malic. Michael steadied the frail Malic as he stepped from the boat.

Grace watched the men intently, but if she was apprehensive about seeing Malic again, it didn't show. Constance glanced at Nicolas. She'd wake him only if or when Malic needed to speak with him.

Michael held Malic's arm and helped him to the porch. Grace and Malic stared at one another. Michael nodded to Constance to meet at the end of the porch, handed Malic his cane, and left Malic and Grace to have a moment alone.

"What took so long?" Constance said. "Did you run into trouble?"

Michael shook his head. "I got in, called Malic on the monitor, and that was it. We moved as fast as we could."

"How did you convince him to go with you?" she said.

"I showed him the necklace on the surveillance monitor. He came through the decontamination chamber within minutes. No questions asked. The boat was his idea. Said it would be quicker."

They watched Grace and Malic on the bench. She wondered if, after all these years, it was possible for the couple to pick up where they had left off. She recalled recently meeting a childhood friend after having lost touch for nearly ten years and how it was as if no time had passed. But meeting an old friend was one thing; forgiving a former lover was another.

"You look beautiful," Malic said and touched Grace's hand.

"My hair's white now," she said.

"So's mine," he said with a chuckle.

Grace looked at him with concern. "How are you, Edward?"

"What do people say? Every day above ground is a good one."

"That's not an answer," she said, gently scolding.

He gave Grace a dismissive wave and pulled her necklace from his pocket. "You found our Goldilocks," he said.

She nodded. "But that's not why I called you here." She waved Constance and Michael over.

"Good to see you again, Ms. Roy," Malic said.

Constance wasn't sure if it was good or not. It would all depend on what he told her about Nicolas.

"And who do we have here?" Malic said, nodding toward the sleeping boy.

"My son," Constance said and protectively stepped near him.

Malic nodded. "Let's meet him, shall we?"

Grace gave Constance a reassuring nod.

"Nick," Constance said, touching her son's shoulder.

Nicolas shifted in the chair and rubbed his eyes. "Is it time to go?"

"Not yet. First I'd like you to meet someone."

"Who?" he said, sitting up.

"Dr. Malic," she said and gestured to the head of the FSI. "He's the man who gave you the automaton."

"It's really neat," Nicolas said.

"I'm glad you think so, young man." Malic retrieved an object from his pocket. "What do you think of this?" he said and held up a tiny silver astronaut figurine.

"It's cool," Nicolas said.

Malic smiled. "Would you like to see a magic trick?"

Nicolas nodded, slid from the chair, and moved to Malic's side. Constance sensed that whatever the man was about to show Nicolas was more than a simple trick. Was it a test to see if Nicolas had the abilities Grace had alluded to earlier?

Malic held the figurine. "Now watch carefully."

He pointed with his right hand to the figurine in his left, wrapped his right hand around the figurine, and removed it. Nicolas watched Malic tap his right hand, open it and ... the figurine was gone.

Nicolas examined Malic's empty hands. "Where is it?"

"Well ... let's see," Malic said and pulled the figurine from behind Nicolas's ear.

Nicolas clapped with delight. "Did you see that, Mom?"

Constance forced a smile. She had seen magicians perform the trick with coins, rings, and other small objects, but something about seeing the little astronaut disappearing and reappearing disturbed her.

"You can keep it," Malic said and handed the figurine to the boy.

"What do you say?" Constance said.

"Thank you." Nicolas moved the astronaut through the air like it was flying and made soft whooshing sounds. "You know I can do magic, too," he said.

Constance wondered why Nicolas was telling Malic he could do magic. Did her son feel like he needed to impress the elderly man?

"I'd love to see it," Malic said.

Nicolas landed the astronaut on the arm of the bench and removed the glass ball with the yellow feather from his sweat-shirt pocket. He carefully held the ball in both hands. Seconds later, the feather rose and vibrated in midair inside the ball. Then the feather floated back to the bottom and was still.

Malic and Grace exchanged a look. "That's very good," Malic said.

"Nick, honey," Constance said. "How did you do that?"

"Magic," he said with a smile. "Isn't that right, Dr. Malic?"

"Magic, indeed," he said. "Ms. Roy, you have a talented boy."

"What do you know about my son?" she said.

"Nick," Michael said. "Why don't you and I take a walk on the pier?"

"No," Grace said. She turned to Constance. "The boy needs to know."

Constance hesitated and then nodded.

Malic met Constance's eye. "Your parents were my dear friends. I cared deeply about them and, by extension, you. When your father passed, I kept an eye on you … and your life."

Constance swallowed. Had Malic known about Nicolas all along? If so, why had he waited until now to tell her? Was there a reason he had kept information about Nicolas from her?

Malic turned his attention to Nicolas and leaned forward on his cane. "You have the power to move air, young man. You can move like them."

Constance shivered. She dreaded who Malic meant by *them*.

Nicolas cocked his head. "What does that mean?" he said.

"It means," Malic said. "I brought your mother all this way to meet her when the person I needed to meet was you."

CHAPTER 17: ORB

Constance gaped at Kylos looming in the doorway of Grace's cabin. An instant later, she was on her feet, ready to fight.

"What are you doing here?" she said, scanning the room for anything that could be used as a weapon.

"Checking on your progress."

He surveyed Grace's cabin and crossed to the mural. Constance backed away and watched with apprehension as he examined the art.

He leaned close, scrutinizing a particular brush stroke. "It's remarkably detailed," he said, his eyes inches from the work. "Dr. Yoholo was a fine artist."

"And you killed her," Constance said, anger replacing fear.

"Ms. Belkin killed Dr. Yoholo." He studied her. "Ah, but you already knew that."

"Maria killed Grace because you ordered it."

"Not true," he said with a wag of a bony finger.

"Maria told me about your deal," she said. "You were going to take her with you."

"I promised no such thing."

"I saw Fifi eject Maria from the ship."

"I'm sorry you witnessed that. It was most unfortunate and, I would imagine, traumatic." He crossed to the window and gazed at Jupiter. "My colleague and I have different opinions about your kind. She was quite displeased with your insubordination. I'm afraid she exhibited a rather primitive human response … revenge. Ironic, really."

"Humans may be primitive," she said. "But we're smart enough to see that the other Curators don't do anything without your permission. You let Fifi kill Grace. Her death is on you."

He turned to face her. "I was needed elsewhere. I was not entirely aware of the events that had transpired until now."

"So what are you going to do about it?"

"Nothing," he said. "Humans die. My colleague merely accelerated the process."

She stared at him, dumbfounded. She had always known Kylos was cold but hadn't thought him to be cruel.

"My response disturbs you. I don't know why. The inevitable fate of the vegetables you grow is that they will die, but nothing stops you from killing them before the natural course of things."

"Are you serious?" Constance said. "That's a plant. We eat vegetables for food. What Fifi did was murder."

"I must admit I find her disobedience troubling. It appears you've made an enemy of my colleague and that she's gone rogue. We, too, have a delicate balance, Ms. Roy. One that must be restored. I had instructed her to leave the Orb."

"So it's true. You're going to let us burn up in Jupiter's atmosphere. You're not even going to try to help." She sat on the edge of the bed, overcome.

"You and the others are an experiment that has failed. It's time for us to make a new start."

"Failed? How?"

"It's complicated."

"Try me."

"Your view is so … limited. This world you inhabit is a dream." He made a sweeping gesture with his arm. "All you see here is only one of an endless sea of possibilities."

"What do mean possibilities?"

"In every scenario, humanity has been the cause of its own extinction. We had hoped to save you. Sadly, we have failed. It is no longer a prudent use of our resources to assist you. It's time for us to move on."

Kylos exited into the corridor.

Constance dashed after him. "Why have we failed? Just tell me that."

He stopped. "It seems we miscalculated the effects of the migration. The process has made your group lacking in a critical variable for survival."

"What?"

"None of you are able to reproduce."

Constance watched him retreat. She felt like she'd been kicked in the gut. Even if they were able to get the Orb running, find their Goldilocks planet, and make it there, the human race was doomed to extinction.

She sprinted down the corridor. "Kylos!" He turned. "Why did you come back?" she said. "Why not just let us die?"

He paused. It was the first time Constance had known him to be at a loss for words. "I suppose I wanted to say goodbye."

She raised a brow. "That sounds rather human of you," she said. "Almost like you care."

He grinned, his tiny teeth showing. "Contrary to your impression, Ms. Roy, I have always cared. You have the power to save yourselves, if not your race. The solution is right in front of you, if you look." He disappeared into the connecting strut.

What was he talking about? Constance raced into the stairwell to get more answers, but he was already gone.

CHAPTER 17: EARTH

"What do you want with my son?" Constance said and wrapped an arm around Nick's shoulders.

"Your son may have the ability to save us," Malic said.

"How's a boy going to save humankind?" Michael said.

Malic pointed at Nicolas. "You, Nicolas, may be the first of your kind."

"Really?" the boy said with gusto and stepped toward Malic.

Constance pulled him back.

"I've spent my life building bridges to cover vast distances, bridges from one world to another." Malic leaned toward Nicolas. "Your grandmother was the first to travel across one of my bridges."

Nicolas gazed at Malic, wide-eyed. "She was?"

Constance clenched a fist. There was no way she'd let Malic take the kind of risk with her son that he had with her mother.

"Your son doesn't need a bridge to travel," Malic said to Constance. "He can do it on his own."

"You hear that, Mom?"

"Yes," Constance said through gritted teeth. "Dr. Malic has interesting theories."

"You must listen to him," Grace said.

"Not only can your son travel over distances," Malic said. "He can travel through possibilities."

"What does that mean?" Michael said.

Nicolas tilted his head. "Maybe I can travel to the Orb," he said.

Malic turned to Grace, stunned. "He knows about the Orb?"

"He saw the drawing on the back of the book cover," Grace said.

"That's right," Nicolas said. "*A Map to the Galaxy*."

"You think Nick is some type of savior because a feather moved?" Constance said.

"You require further proof," Malic said.

"I know I do," Michael said.

"Very well." Malic motioned to the empty bench. "Please," he said to Nicolas. "Have a seat."

Constance clutched the boy.

"I promise," Grace said. "Edward won't hurt him."

Constance reluctantly released Nicolas. The boy slid onto the bench.

"Are you comfortable?" Malic said. Nicolas nodded. "Good. I'd like you to close your eyes."

Nicolas closed his eyes and swung his legs back and forth, back and forth, and then stopped. He cocked his head to the side.

"Now," Malic said. "Tell me what you see."

CHAPTER 18: ORB

Constance clutched Grace's bed and waited for the tremor to subside. They were becoming more frequent. Time was running out. She rifled through the papers on Grace's bed. Kylos had said that the answer to how they might save themselves from the Event was right in front of her. She had been looking for the better part of an hour and was no closer to a discovery. What was Grace trying to tell her in this mountain of data? She gazed at the sheets for the two planets that had fifty percent survivability. Could one of these planets work? *No*, she thought. Grace and Kylos seemed to believe there was a single solution ... which meant a single planet.

She tossed the documents onto the bed and flopped into the chair. Her neck hurt from bending over the papers, and the back of her legs cramped. She leaned back and stretched her entire body. What she wouldn't give for a hot shower, a good meal, and a nap. *You'll have plenty of time to sleep when you're dead*, she chided. She cracked her fingers. Maybe examining something new would give her a fresh perspective.

She stood and faced the beautiful mural with its twinkling stars and celestial bodies. Grace had collected nutshells and other items from the dining hall to craft dyes for the homemade canvas. She noted bits of these items on the paper, carefully added to create shadows, highlights, and texture. Kylos was right. Grace was a fine artist. Constance hadn't known the Curators to be art lovers, yet Kylos had examined the mural down to a brushstroke. She had found his close examination of the work odd. Perhaps his Curator eyes allowed him to see something she couldn't. *The solution is right in front of you, if you look.*

Constance scrutinized the work for recognizable constellations, clues that might help her get her bearings. Nothing looked familiar. She shouldn't be surprised. As her father had predicted years ago in his book, the Goldilocks planet—if it existed—would be located beyond the known solar system. Perhaps this was Grace's imagined map rather than a representation of an actual vista.

While Kylos had admired the entire piece, he had been most interested in one particular area. *Open your eyes and see what Kylos saw.* She crept closer, trying to recall exactly where he had stood when he was inches from the canvas. Had Grace drawn or marked the work with an *X* like on a treasure map? She squinted at the brushstrokes and bits of organic matter. A small grouping of stars or moons caught her eye. Where had she seen this pattern?

She leaned closer, and Grace's necklace bumped against the wall. She stopped it from swinging and felt tiny notches in its surface. She examined the pendant. Jupiter's light streamed in through the window and hit the disc, creating a pattern of tiny lights on the mural. Could it be? Was the necklace, not the mural, her treasure map? She removed the jewelry and adjusted its position so that the light pattern shining through the pendant became crisper against the mural. She rotated the pendant. The pattern turned. *The solution is right in front of you.*

The mural vibrated. Seconds later, the entire room rumbled. She felt the whoosh of a cool breeze at her back, and then all was quiet. How much more could the Orb take?

She raised the necklace into the light. Slowly, she moved the light pattern across the area of the mural that had attracted Kylos's attention. The pinpoints danced across the mural's sky. Her eyes widened in disbelief. The pattern perfectly matched an area on the painting.

The room lights flickered. Then came a second gust of cold air and the smell of electrical discharge. *That's new*, Constance thought. The necklace shook in her hands as she held the disc steady and caught the light. Had she found their Goldilocks planet? "Are you seeing what you think you see?" she said quietly.

"I see you, Mommy," came a voice from behind her.

She froze, took a breath, and peered over her shoulder. Standing in the doorway with his head cocked to the side was the boy she had seen in the corridor.

CHAPTER 19

Nicolas opened his eyes and stared as if in a trance at the bridge that connected Chincoteague Island to the mainland and Wallops. It frightened Constance to see her typically active son inert and expressionless.

"What do you mean you see me?" she said, worried that whatever Malic had done was causing her son to hallucinate. "I'm right here, Nick."

"Yes, Mommy, but you're also there," he said and pointed into the distance.

Malic raised a hand to silence Constance. Grace nodded in agreement. Michael appeared as concerned as she about what was transpiring.

"What does your mommy look like?" Malic said.

"Like Mommy … but different."

"Different how?" Grace said.

"She has white hair."

Constance raised her brows. "You mean I'm old?"

The boy paused and then said, "No, your hair is just white."

"Look around," Malic said. "Can you see anything else?"

Constance observed the boy from near Grace's mural. He

appeared almost translucent in Jupiter's light. Was he real or an hallucination? Why had he called her his mother and mentioned her white hair? He gazed about the cabin at the art, the papers on the bed, and the necklace in her hand.

"Grace's necklace," he said.

How did the boy know about Grace's necklace?

"Where are you, Nicolas?" Malic said.

The boy looked at her. "Is this the Orb?"

She forced herself to speak. "Yes," she said in a whisper. "Who are you?"

The boy's brows furrowed in confusion. "I'm Nicolas, your son."

Constance felt a tug at her heart and sensed that what the boy said was true ... and not. She wished Michael were here. A child on the Orb. What would Kylos think given the inhabitants' apparent reproductive deficiencies? Maybe neither would see the boy. Maybe this vision was for her alone.

"Why are you sad?" the boy said.

"Because I don't know if I'll be able to save the crew and animals on this ship," she said, not caring that she might be speaking to a figment of her imagination.

"You can do it," he said. "I'll help."

His encouragement made her smile. The ship trembled, and the smile was gone.

"What's happening to him?" Constance asked Malic as Nicolas trembled on the bench. She put her hands on Nicolas's shoulders. "Nick? Nick, are you okay? Nicolas, please, wake up."

Nicolas stopped shaking and blinked.

Constance hugged him tight. "Don't do that, you hear?" she said. "You scared me to death."

"I'm fine," he said.

"Where were you?" Grace said to Nicolas after Constance released him.

"I was with Mom on the Orb."

"The Orb doesn't exist," Constance said. "Remember, Grace told you that."

"But it does exist. I saw it. And you were there."

Constance squeezed Nicolas's hand and forced a smile.

"They've done it," Malic said. "They've built the Orb."

"I'm sorry," Michael said. "Does someone mind explaining what's going on here?"

"Our world exists next to many other worlds, Mr. Whittaker," Malic said. He held his palms a centimeter apart. "Only a thin membrane like the air between my hands separates them. The difference between the two worlds is the difference between what could have happened and what did happen. Young Nicolas has the ability to see between those two worlds."

"Are you saying that the world he saw was real?" Michael said.

"As real as the one you're in right now."

"That's enough," Constance said. "He's not doing that ever again."

"But I have to," Nicolas said. "They need me."

"Need you?" Constance said. "Need you how?"

"You told me you didn't know how to save the people and animals on the Orb."

Constance tried to control the feeling of panic welling within. She felt Nicolas slipping away. She grabbed his hand. "We're going home," she said.

"You can't," Grace said.

"I will not lose my son to whatever is going on here. Say goodbye, Nicolas."

"But Mommy," Nicolas said.

"What if your mother explained it to you?" Malic said. "Then would you be convinced?"

Constance glared at Malic. How dare he use her mother. "My mother is dead," she said.

"Barbara predicted how you would react," he said, unde-terred. "She made a recording for you if this day ever came."

"I don't believe you."

"Edward is telling the truth," Grace said.

After all these years … to hear her mother's voice again. "Where is this recording?" Constance said.

"At Wallops," Malic said.

"You expect her to go back to the FSI?" Michael said.

"The tape is hidden," Malic said. "Nobody knows where to find it but me."

Everyone fell silent and waited for her decision. How could she walk away from what Malic was offering? She sighed, closed her eyes, and nodded. Yes, they would return to Wallops.

CHAPTER 20

Constance placed a hand on the wall to steady herself and felt the intensity of the ship's vibration against her palm. The Orb groaned. She lightened as Jupiter's pull interfered with the ring's spin and the centripetal force that gave the ring its gravity. Papers on the bed fluttered into the air like feathers.

The entrance to the cabin where the boy had been was empty. He had disappeared when the tremor started. Constance wanted to push him from her mind—chalk the vision up to exhaustion—but she couldn't dismiss how his presence made her feel. She had never been particularly interested in children, and yet she had felt a strong mother-child bond. Was it simply because he had called her his mother? Or was her mind playing tricks on her after Kylos had told her everyone on the ship was unable to create offspring?

The ship jerked. The trembling ceased. And the papers fell back to the bed. The ferocity and length of the quakes were increasing. She needed to find their new planet before the Orb was ripped apart by the goliath Jupiter. She pushed from the wall and again aligned the light pattern streaming through Grace's pendant with the painting's celestial bodies.

"How's it going?" Michael said from behind her.

"You're a sight for sore eyes," she said.

"Aw, Roy, are you sweet on me?"

She shook her head and returned to the pendant and mural. "Did you feel the tremor?" she said, scanning the painting.

"The worst yet," he said. "Thankfully, I wasn't in the central axle." He observed her squinting at the art, her nose inches from the canvas. "What are you doing?"

"Finding our new home." She rotated the pendant and watched the light configuration. "Find me something that writes," she said.

Michael searched the cabin and returned with a home-made brush. Constance checked to be sure that it was wet with dye and then carefully drew a circle on the painting where the largest light was shining through the pendant. She filled in the circle.

"What is it?" he said.

She lowered the pendant. "Our new home."

"You found Grace's planet?" Michael said, stunned. "How?"

She held up the jewelry. "You see the light coming through the notches on the disc?"

He nodded.

"Watch." She moved the disc over the panorama until the pattern lights aligned with painted stars.

"The lights match images on the mural," he said, excited. "Except there isn't a match for—"

"The sphere I drew," she said.

"If Grace's pendant is some type of key, why didn't she draw the sphere on the mural too? Why draw everything and leave the most important element out?"

"Maybe she didn't want the Curators to know where it was. Don't you see? The small lights were to help us find the location on the mural so that when we lined them up we'd see where to find our planet." She admired the painting. "That sphere is our new home, and this mural is the map that tells us how to get there. Grace left us a message, after all."

"This is great," he said. "But we still don't know which way we're looking."

"Not yet," she said, studying the map. "But as soon as I identify some constellations, I'll be able to get our bearings."

She lowered her head to place the necklace around her neck and stumbled.

"Whoa," Michael said, catching her. "Maybe you should sit down."

She attempted to shake off the vertigo and nearly fell again. *Not now*, she thought. *I need to find the constellations.* But past experience had taught her there was no willing the vertigo away.

"I'm okay," she said, easing onto the bed.

"You need rest. You won't be any good to us if you pass out or lose your mind."

She gave him a sideways glance. "Before you showed up, before the tremor, I saw something."

"On the mural?"

She shook her head. The room spun. She inhaled deeply and said, "I saw a boy."

"A boy? Here? See, this is what I'm talking about, Roy."

"Wait, you have to listen—"

"No, *you* have to listen," he said. "You need sleep."

"But the constellations."

"The constellations can wait." He moved papers aside and pulled back the blanket. "We probably won't be done breaking through the alignment stall to the Curators' ring for another fifty minutes. That's fifty minutes you're going to use to recharge your gray matter."

He was right. If she continued as she had been, she might not be of any help and risked putting the crew in jeopardy. She propped a pillow against the padded wall.

Michael pulled the blanket over her legs. "I want you to sleep," he said. "No getting up to work on that mural. Promise?"

She nodded.

He kissed her on the forehead and then crossed to the entrance. "I'll get you as soon as we're through."

Her eyelids grew heavy. Seconds later, she drifted off. She had the sensation of rocking, like on water. Michael, Grace, the boy, and an older man came into focus. They were on a small boat skimming through a marsh toward a rocky shore in the distance.

CHAPTER 21

The outboard motorboat bobbed across the choppy channel toward the Wallops launch pad and the FSI. Constance and Michael watched the shoreline. Constance wrapped an arm around Nicolas to keep him secure. Grace held Malic's hand and steadied him whenever the boat rocked too violently. Behind them, daylight broke over Chincoteague and gave the island a hazy amber glow. If they didn't reach land soon, they'd be visible in the morning light.

Malic had insisted the group approach by boat rather than by car. Neither Grace nor Nicolas had clearance to visit the facility, something NASA required in advance, and by now Constance's clearance had expired. Michael had also pointed out that even if Malic was able to convince the guard at the gate to let them on-site without proper authorization, Kylos might be alerted to their presence. The water was the safest route. Constance still wasn't sure how Malic was going to get them into the facility once they made it on the property. One step at a time, he had said when she had asked, which had done nothing to reassure her.

"I feel like a pirate," Nicolas said.

To Nicolas this was an adventure, but she couldn't help

feeling as if they were caught in a whirlpool pulling them toward the eye of a terrible storm. By pursuing answers to questions about her mother's death, was she placing her son in danger?

The motor squealed as Michael pushed on the steering handle and navigated the marsh. He tapped Nicolas on the shoulder. "How'd you like to try?"

"Really?" the boy said. He turned to Constance. "May I?"

She looked at Michael with concern. "Is it safe?"

"I think he can handle it. Besides, I'll be right here."

"Okay," she said. "Be careful."

Nicolas picked his way to the back and sat next to Michael, who placed the boy's hand on the steering handle.

"When I tell you to go right, pull toward you, and when I say left, push," Michael said while demonstrating. "Got that?"

Nicolas nodded.

"You see those reeds? Let's go a little left," Michael said, holding the handle until he was sure Nicolas had it and then released control. "There you go," he said.

Nicolas grinned at Constance and then turned his attention to steering the vessel. Michael joined her. A white gull soared above them, caught an air current, and banked away from the boat.

"He can handle it," Michael said to Constance and gave her a reassuring pat on her arm.

"Thank you," she said.

"For what?"

"For taking me to see Grace … for coming with me to the FSI. This could cost you your job."

"Nonsense. I'm with the boss," he said, indicating Malic sitting in front of them.

"Why are you helping me?"

He shrugged. "Maybe I want to see how this all turns out."

"Up ahead," Malic said and pointed. "Left at the marker."

"Yes, sir," Nicolas said and saluted.

The rocky shore drew nearer. "What are we going to do when we get there?" Constance said.

"You'll see," Malic said with a sly smile.

Michael moved back to join Nicolas. "Nice work, Captain," he said. "Mind if I take over?"

"That was fun," Nicolas said.

Michael cut the engine. The boat rocked as the water lapped at the rocky shore and rippled back at them. He steered the drifting boat until it bumped against granite stones. He hopped out, secured the boat, and held the vessel steady as everyone exited.

"This way," Malic said, climbing the granite berm with his cane.

Grace helped Malic navigate the rocky terrain as Constance and Michael helped Nicolas. They reached the top of the rocks and flat land. They followed Malic along the water. He took a right inland, headed to a wooded area near the wildlife refuge, and stopped. Constance could just make out the rocket and FSI building farther down the property. She was grateful they were partially hidden by trees but wished to get out of sight as soon as possible.

"Now what?" Constance said.

Malic stomped his cane. To Constance's surprise, the ground beneath him echoed. It was a metal plate that had been painted brown and green to resemble earth.

"Now," Malic said. "We go down."

He motioned for Michael to lift the plate. A ladder led into a deep, dark hole. Constance grabbed Nicolas from the edge.

"I'll go first," Michael said. He stepped onto the ladder and disappeared.

Malic stepped forward. Seconds later, he disappeared too. She hoped Michael was prepared to catch him if he fell.

"It's okay," Grace said, noticing her look of concern, and then descended.

"You ready?" Constance said to Nicolas.

"I climb ladders all the time at the gym," he said.

"I'll be right below you," she said. "Just take your time."

She grabbed the side of the ladder and found her footing. Seconds later, Nicolas joined her. She moved slowly so Nicolas would have to do the same. The sunny opening grew small. She peered below and saw Michael, Malic, and Grace waiting in a dimly lit area at the bottom.

"You're almost there," Michael said.

Her feet hit solid ground. She helped Nicolas from the ladder.

"I'll be right back," Michael said. He scurried up the ladder, pulled the metal plate over the opening, and then rejoined them at the bottom.

The tunnel had curved concrete walls. Conduits ran along the walls and ceiling. Flickering fluorescent tubes lined the walkway. A metal pipe about five feet in diameter ran through the corridor's center. The passageway curved in both directions, giving her the impression they were at one point on an enormous underground circle.

"This way," Malic said.

Their echoing footsteps sounded like an irregular, fluttering heartbeat, and she had the sensation they were in the bloodstream of a concrete giant.

"Is this it?" Grace said to Malic.

"Yes," Malic said.

"Is this what?" Constance said.

Malic stopped, halting the group. "This is what we built, Ms. Roy," he said, tapping his cane on the floor for emphasis. "This is our bridge."

CHAPTER 22

A rapping sound stirred Constance from sleep. She groggily scanned her surroundings … star charts on the bed … the landscape painting … the space mural. She was in Grace's cabin.

"We're almost through," Michael said, crossing from the doorway and sitting on the bed.

As the Orb's environment seeped back into her consciousness, she pushed herself up and mentally grasped at the fading dream images: a boat, a tunnel, Michael, Grace, and the boy.

"You okay?" Michael said.

She rubbed her eyes and focused on Grace's landscape picture. Animals roamed a big-sky mountain terrain. A woman watched from a distant hillside. A white bird soared in the bright orange sky. Was this Grace's vision of their new home?

"Constance?" Michael said, touching her arm.

"What?" she said, startled from her daze.

"I asked if you're okay." He studied her face. "Were you seeing the boy again?"

The boy steering the small boat came vividly into focus.

"No," she said. Michael was already worried about her. There was no point in telling him about her dream.

"We're close to entering the Curators' ring. Everyone's waiting for you."

She retrieved Grace's pendant from the nightstand.

"What's that?" He pointed to the image of a bird on the pendant's back.

"A dove, I think."

"Why a dove?"

Constance shrugged. "Doves are symbols of love, peace, even messengers. Some believe the bird offers protection."

"I'm not sure it's done a good job of that," he said. "Besides, it's a strange-looking dove." He studied her. "You sure you're ready to return to the Curators' ring after—"

"I'm fine," she said. "Tell everyone I'm on my way. I'll just be a minute."

"See you soon," he said and exited.

The dove on the necklace was strange and unlike Grace's accurate depictions of other animals. The bird's neck was longer than expected, and the feathers on the wings weren't as fanned out as was normally the case. And there was something odd about the way it was flying. Why was the dove more abstract than the other artwork? Perhaps the metal on the pendant had been harder to work with. Whatever the reason, she didn't have time to figure it out. The crew was waiting.

She placed the jewelry around her neck, threw off the blanket, and stretched. Her body felt terrible, but her mind was clearer. It was good that Michael had forced her to sleep. It was unlikely she'd have another opportunity until they were safe or… She shook the thought from her head. She had to remain positive.

She moved to the mural to commit the area that charted the path to their new planet to memory. She burned the sphere and its surrounding stars into her brain. Grace must have had a motive for not painting the planet. Thank goodness she had discovered the pendant's secret. She glanced at the disc hanging upside-down around her neck—like Grace must have viewed it when she wore it. The dove, now inverted, was no longer taking flight but appeared to be preparing to land, its long neck stretched forward and its wings out. Why hadn't she seen it before? She had been able to identify the shape since she was a young girl. The bird wasn't a dove but rather a swan. It was the constellation Cygnus, the constellation that would give them their orientation. Now all she needed to do was find a way to pilot the Orb.

CHAPTER 23

Constance stared at the enormous pipe running down the tunnel's center and seized Nicolas's hand lest his curiosity and fearlessness tempt him to touch it. If she understood Malic correctly, they were feet from the Wallops Flight Facility's top-secret supercharged ion collider, the collider conspiracy theorists and bloggers had speculated would bring about the end of the world.

"It sure is a funny-looking bridge," Nicolas said, studying the cylinder. "How does it work?"

"All will be revealed," Malic said. He checked his watch. "Come. It's not much farther, and we don't have much time."

"What's the hurry?" Michael said.

"In ten minutes Dr. Yablonski will be down here on his rounds."

Malic hastened away with Grace's assistance. Constance and Michael followed. Nicolas skipped between them. If they were in the bloodstream of some concrete giant, Constance imagined they'd soon enter the heart or maybe the brain. Some thirty or forty feet above them, the Wallops Flight Facility was springing to life as people began their morning duties. Her pulse quickened, thinking of Dr. Yablonski's impending arrival. She glanced at Nicolas to be sure he wasn't fatigued. He contentedly bounced along, holding her hand and rocking his head from side to side.

Malic's breathing grew heavy, and he leaned against Grace for stability. Constance tapped Michael and nodded toward Malic.

Michael caught up to the older man. "Take my arm," he said.

"Humph," Malic said and swatted Michael away.

Grace suppressed a smile as Michael shrugged and dropped back to walk with Constance. Moments later, Malic stopped and said, "Ah-ha!" He pointed to a large metal door on the left. A keypad was set into the concrete next to the door.

"Are we here?" Nicolas said.

"Yes, young man. We are here," Malic said. He pressed a thin finger over numbers on the keypad: 1-6-7-1-2.

Weren't those the numbers for the hours missing from the clock on the Sundial Books sign? Constance ran the numbers several times in her head to be certain they were committed to memory. The sound of mechanisms turning and clicking behind the door echoed in the corridor and reminded her of the automaton. There was a final click, and then the door swung inward with a hiss. Air from the tunnel rushed around her body and into the opening. Malic motioned to Michael, who pushed the door completely open.

"Oh, Edward," Grace said, peering inside and shaking her head.

"Geez, that's worse than my room," Nicolas said, underscoring Grace's sentiment.

Constance covered Nicolas's mouth with her hand. They stared into Malic's book- and antique-filled lair. The vantage point was different from the last time she had entered his sanctuary, but the chaos was the same.

Malic hobbled inside. Grace and Michael followed. Nicolas broke free and rushed in after Michael.

"Come, come," Malic said, waving her inside.

She hesitated, remembering the bizarre decontamination chamber. She wondered why Malic no longer seemed concerned with infection, first traveling outside his sanctuary and now inviting them into his inner sanctum without any safety measures. Footsteps approached from the corridor. She quickly stepped across the threshold. The door closed and locked.

She followed the group toward the interior. She glanced over her shoulder at the sound of movement behind her and saw a mountain of junk slide in front of the door. No wonder she hadn't noticed the entrance when she had been in the room before. She joined the rest of the group winding its way along a narrow path. She studied Michael's, Grace's, and Nicolas's stunned faces as they took in the room. Not too long ago, she had been equally astonished.

Malic stopped before a bookshelf cluttered with DVDs, CDs, eight-track and VHS tapes, and records. He leaned on his cane and reached for the top shelf. He took a deep breath and tried again.

"Up here?" Constance said, stepping forward.

"Yes," Malic said. "It's a tape."

She glided her hand along the objects on the shelf, felt a VHS tape, and pulled it down. Written on the tape's spine in thick black marker was *AUG 21 FSI BOARD MTG.* "Is this it?" she said.

"That's the one," Malic said, taking it from her.

"You sure that's the message from my mother?"

"Oh, yes," he said and tapped his finger on the spine. "I marked it that way as a ruse. Nobody wants to watch a board meeting." He chuckled, amused by his cleverness.

Nicolas pointed at the tape. "What is that?"

"It's called a VHS," Michael said.

"VHS?" the boy said.

"It's a video," Grace said. "Before we had DVDs or online TV."

"Oh," Nicolas said. "I've never seen a VHS."

"I imagine there are a lot of things in here you've never seen," Grace said, eyeing the mess around her.

"Is one of them a VHS player?" Michael said.

"Right this way," Malic said. He motioned for them to follow him along a tight path.

Constance didn't remember traveling this way on her previous visit. When they came to the end, Malic checked to be certain everyone was with him, pressed his cane into a circular opening in the floor, and turned it like a key. The floor in front of them and the belongings on it shifted to reveal a large oval door that reminded Constance of a submarine hatch. Malic crossed to the wall and placed his hand on a screen. Seconds later, the latch turned.

"Mr. Whittaker, would you mind?" Malic said. "I'm afraid the door is too heavy for me."

Michael and the rest of the group remained where they were, staring at the yellow and black radioactive trefoil symbol on the door.

"This is where it happened," Grace said.

Malic nodded. "It's been sealed ever since."

"This is where what happened?" Michael said.

"Where my mother left me," Constance said. She stared at the radiation symbol. "My father's cancer was caused by whatever is behind this door."

"Yes," Malic said. "During the transport. But there's no lasting danger." He coughed. "Well, not for you or your son."

She eyed Malic. "You're sure it's safe?"

"I wouldn't allow any of you to enter if it wasn't."

Malic motioned to Michael, who stepped forward and grabbed the latch.

"You're certain you want to do this?" Michael said to Constance.

She nodded.

Michael yanked hard on the latch. The door swung open with a sorrowful moan and revealed a room so devoid of light, it was like staring into an abyss.

CHAPTER 24

Constance rode the dumbwaiter toward the Curators' ring, eager to tell the others that she had found their new planet, and it was located within the constellation Cygnus. She smiled, allowing herself a private moment of victory, but then recalled that she had already told the crew that she had found their planet. To announce her discovery would reveal her a liar—even if the lie had become truth—and undermine the crew's confidence in anything she might tell them in the future. It was best to keep her recent findings between Michael and herself.

Her heart raced as the opening to the Curators' ring became visible. The last time she had been there was a harrowing experience. She jumped to the platform and was yanked by the ring's gravity toward a gaping hole in the alignment stall. Michael grabbed her arm to keep her from falling head first through the hole to the bottom of the stairwell.

She clutched him and moved away from the opening. "Thanks," she said.

Muhammad's team had cut a cavity in the stall mesh and secured the flap with materials pilfered from other parts of the ship. The hole would enable her to drop directly over the top step. She peered down the stairwell tube. The crew stared up at her. The hopeful look in her fellow inhabitants' eyes troubled her. She knew only a little more than the others about the Orb and the Curators' ring. Once they made it to the control room, she didn't have a clue how to navigate the ship.

She studied the gap between the alignment stall and the first step with apprehension.

"It should be easier than the first time," Michael said as if reading her mind. "But it's still tricky so be careful. You ready?"

"Ready as I'll ever be," she said.

She dropped to her hands and knees, inched toward the opening, and felt the tremendous pull of the centripetal force of the Curators' ring. She locked her fingers into the mesh to keep her legs from being sucked through. Michael grabbed under her arms to keep her within the stall until she was ready to drop.

"If you don't hit it right, you could fall to the bottom," he said.

"Let's hope I hit it right then."

She edged her feet over the hole. The ring's gravity jerked her legs through the cavity. The opening's edge cut into her gut, causing her to lose her grip and twist in the vortex of the competing gravitational forces. Those on the stairs scrambled to catch her. She tumbled as if caught in an ocean undertow, and she lost sight of which way was up. Her head banged hard against the wall.

"I got you," Garcia said, snatching her by the arm. "Someone mind giving me a hand?"

She felt more hands on her waist and legs as she teetered over the gap. The group pulled her to the top step, and she collapsed against the wall. She looked up at Michael. "That was easy?" she said.

"I said *easier*."

She stepped aside to allow Michael to drop through the

hole. With the crew's assistance, he quickly joined her on the stairwell.

"Nobody's been on the ring?" she said to Michael, Muhammad, and Garcia, who stood nearby.

"You're the only one who knows what's down there," Muhammad said.

"So we don't know if they're waiting for us," she said. She recalled her final conversation with Kylos. *It is no longer a prudent use of our resources to assist you. It's time for us to move on.* In all likelihood, they were on their own, but the image of Fifi ejecting Maria from the Orb gave her pause.

"We made these," Garcia said, clutching a makeshift weapon.

The crew displayed hammer- and knife-like weapons.

Muhammad handed her a light that had been removed from a wall and rigged with power. "This should help," he said. He flipped a switch, and a narrow beam illuminated the stairwell. "Almost everyone has one."

Constance shifted her grip on the light. Etched into the metal was a serial number and ORB-2.

"Everything okay?" Michael said.

Constance nodded.

As she passed crew on the stairs, they squeezed against the wall and clicked on their lights. She held her light before her and briefly made eye contact with Hashim and Dru. The group followed her like miners down a shaft. She reached the bottom and gazed into the corridor's dark interior, thankful that this time she had more than the floor illumination to guide her. The inhabitants joined her in the passageway.

"Which way?" Zhang Yong said.

"Here," she said and pointed right.

She retraced her steps. The crew whispered comments about the smell of electricity and sulfur, the coolness of the air, and the strange green lights. Then the group grew quiet, so quiet Constance could hear their clothes swishing as they walked. She held the light high. Despite its brightness, the corridor's curvature made it impossible to see far ahead. She passed the migration vessels lining the walls and glanced at the others. They stopped and stared at the containers, dumbstruck, no doubt with a flood of emotions overwhelming them.

Michael ran his hand along one of the vessels. Constance watched him a moment. He was clearly lost in the horror of his transport. She touched his shoulder.

"We need to keep going," she said, aware of how difficult this moment was but also concerned about how little time they had. "The control room is up ahead."

"We're almost there, everyone," Michael said.

One by one, people turned away from the vessels and followed Constance down the hall. She spotted light streaming in from the windows of the Curators' sleeping quarters, approached the entrance, and motioned for everyone to stop. She peered around the corner and panned the light into the room's dark interior. The room was empty.

"They're gone," she said.

Michael and the others entered, casting their lights over the hooks, tubing, and tunics.

"What are these?" Michael said, pointing to the tubes.

"Some type of feeding tubes," Constance said from the doorway.

"Are we sure they're gone?" Lina said.

"Only one way to find out," Constance said. The team followed her to the next room. "I believe this is the control room."

Hashim and Dru crossed to the controller under the enormous window and began discussing possible mechanisms for hacking into the ship's system. Constance drifted to the smaller observation window that looked into the chamber where Fifi had locked Maria. Constance touched the glass where fingerprints streaked to a sudden stop on the other side.

Michael joined her. "Is this where Maria…"

She nodded and turned away from the glass. "You think that's the control console?" she said to Hashim and Dru.

"Certainly appears to be," Dru said.

"You said it did something when you touched it," Hashim said.

Constance sat on the console stool and placed her hand on a blank panel. A spark arched from the panel and shocked her.

"Whoa," Dru said and glanced at Hashim, who looked equally surprised.

"Could be a type of biometric ID system," Hashim said. "Could you try again?"

Constance returned her hand to the panel, but, as on her previous visit, the spark did not repeat. "That's what happened before," she said. "The initial shock and then nothing."

"Mind if I give it a try?" Hashim said.

Hashim placed a hand on a panel. Nothing. Dru tried next with the same result. One by one, crew members attempted to get a response from the machine. One by one, they failed.

Constance motioned to Michael. "You're the only one who hasn't tried," she said.

"I think we know the outcome," he said but attempted to activate the console anyway. "See?"

Constance watched Dru and Hashim hunched over the controller, speculating on its operating system. "What are we missing?" she said.

"A Curator?" Michael said. "Sorry, bad joke."

"No. You may be on to something," she said.

He raised his brows in surprise. "Really?"

"The Curators obviously have something in their makeup that allows them to communicate with the ship through touch … something we lack."

"Okay," Michael said. "But what?"

She shrugged. "Hashim and Dru, what do you make of it?"

"We'd like to open it up—see what's inside," Hashim said.

"But we need tools," Dru said.

"I'm on it," Muhammad said, heading toward the hall.

"Wait," Constance said. "Take some folks with you."

"I'll go," Garcia said.

"Me too," Lina said and exited with Muhammad and Garcia.

Constance watched them disappear down the corridor.

CHAPTER 25

Constance huddled in the dark with Nicolas, Michael, and Grace as Malic searched for a wall switch with a tiny key chain flashlight.

"The switch is here somewhere," Malic said.

"It smells funny," Nicolas said.

Constance pressed her son's head against her side. The air smelled of ozone, as if there was an electrostatic charge nearby. She squinted in an attempt to ascertain what type of room they were in and whether or not it was safe.

"Ah," Malic said.

Fluorescent tubes buzzed and flickered to life.

"Wow," Nicolas said in awe, pulling away from his mother.

"Exactly what I was thinking," Michael said, gazing about the space.

Constance turned in a circle, taking everything in. They appeared to be inside a control room or command center. Computers lined the walls. On one side was a large console with a window above it with a view of a concrete wall. A smaller window was on the adjacent wall. It, too, looked out on concrete.

"What is this place?" Michael said.

Malic limped to the control console and removed a remote from a slot in its side. "This is where dreams were forged," he said and clicked a button on the remote.

The monitors and panels sprang to life and displayed three-dimensional schematics of a spaceship.

"The Orb," Nicolas said.

Malic grinned. "Isn't it spectacular?"

Constance wandered to a monitor. "It's like something from a dream."

"Your mother's dream," Grace said.

"My grandma did this?" Nicolas said, pride in his voice.

Constance turned to Malic. "Is that true?"

"Some of it," Malic said. He hobbled to a stool near the console, sat, and leaned on his cane. "The FSI employed a lot of people. This is the result of their hard work. But the initial kernel that sparked all of this was your mother's."

"I had no idea," Constance said, appreciating for the first time her mother as a fellow scientist.

"She was a visionary designer," Grace said. "We could see that even in the early sketches."

"The ones on the back of the book jacket," Constance said.

"*A Map to the Galaxy*," Nicolas chimed in.

"That's right," Grace said. "Your mother developed the initial design of the ship. Your father and I worked on locating our new planet."

"What was your role in everything?" Michael said to Malic.

"I worked on the bridge to get us there." Malic looked away and added, "With help."

Constance studied the man's face. "From Kylos," she said.

"Him and his kind," Grace said.

Malic gestured to the console. "We couldn't have made this without him."

"What does it do?" Michael said, reaching to touch a panel.

Malic raised his cane and intercepted Michael's hand before it made contact. "This is a wondrous system, but it must be treated with the utmost care. What is contained within is … delicate and alive."

Constance raised a brow. "You mean biological?"

"Partly. It's highly sensitive. You'd no more take a hammer or screwdriver to it than you would any living thing."

"I'm finding this all a little hard to believe," Michael said.

"You will come to understand in time," Malic said.

"So what was this room for?" Constance said.

"This is where we ran simulations, experimented with the Orb's functionality, tested the possibility of it becoming a reality, and transported…" Malic's voice trailed off. He cleared his throat. "In the end, it wasn't meant to be."

"Because my mother died," Constance said.

"Barbara believed in what we were doing," Malic said.

"She was certain we could save humankind," Grace said.

The adult Constance understood why her mother had done what she had. If there were a possibility that she could somehow save the human race, wouldn't she do the same? But the child Constance was hurt and confused by her mother's abandonment.

"I want to see the tape," she said.

Malic shuffled to a monitor tucked on a desk in the corner and inserted the tape into the machine beneath it. Constance glanced at Nicolas. Perhaps it was better if she watched it alone. She made eye contact with Michael.

"Hey, buddy," Michael said and placed a hand on Nicolas's shoulder. "Care to join me in exploring the stuff in Dr. Malic's big room?"

"Don't I get to hear from Grandma?" Nicolas said.

"Why don't we let your mother hear first," Michael said.

"Mom, do I have to?" the boy said.

"I think it best," she said. "Maybe Dr. Malic has another automaton."

"Do you?" Nicolas said, brightening.

"My room contains many wonders," Malic said with a wink. "If you find one you like, it's yours."

"Let's go," Nicolas said and tugged on Michael's arm.

Michael exited with Nicolas. She sat in the chair before the monitor.

"Just press play," Malic said. "We'll be right over here."

Grace and Malic moved to the far corner of the room. Constance stared at the black screen. What would her mother tell her that would convince her that the Orb world that Nicolas had "visited" and that had caused him to convulse in that terrifying way existed? What could her mother say to persuade her to allow her son to be involved in Malic's experiment—the experiment that had given her father and Malic cancer and had ripped her mother from her life? Since Nicolas was born, she had done everything in her power to keep him close. Now, according to Malic and Grace, her mother had information that would induce her to do the opposite. She hit PLAY.

The machine whined as gears turned the tape. The screen filled with static. She heard rustling and whispers, and then a blurry image appeared as the camera operator focused. Her parents came into view. They were bunched together, obviously worried that they might be out of frame. The background was the control room she was in now.

"Hi, Connie," her mother said. "I hope this message finds you well. If you're watching, it means Edward has told you of the experiment and why I must go away. Leaving you and your father is the most difficult decision of my life."

Her mother's voice broke. Her father squeezed her mother's hand and whispered something in her ear.

"While I'm away, your dad will take care of you and make sure you're not too much of a wild child."

Constance smiled. Her mother had always scolded her for her rambunctiousness, affectionately calling her a wild child. It had been years since anyone thought of her as wild.

"I want you to listen carefully to what I'm about to say and understand that I am of sound mind," her mother continued. "Friends have entrusted me with a very special gift. This gift has been passed on to you and comes with a great responsibility—one you didn't ask for but one you must honor and accept. This gift allows us to travel to faraway places that humans have never seen. In a little while, I am going to test the gift. If all goes well, we will have found a way to save the human race. I hope you see why I don't have a choice … that it would be selfish of me to put my desire to stay with you and your father above the needs of billions of people. I'll miss you, Connie. Never doubt how much I love you. If all goes as we predict, I will see you again. If it doesn't, you must carry on my work. It's the only way. Be strong and take care of your father. You know how he is with laundry."

Her mother smiled through tears, blew a kiss, and then the screen went to static. Constance's heart broke all over again. Upon learning of her mother's death as a child, she had run into the woods and yelled at the stars and trees and moon to the point of exhaustion. Constance had believed that her childhood stubbornness and tiffs with her mother had been the cause of her mother leaving. Her father's refusal to tell her what happened had only added to the impression that she was somehow to blame. There were still so many unanswered questions, but one thing was clear: her mother had not left because of Constance, but rather because she believed she had been given a gift that enabled her to save humanity.

Grace touched her shoulder. "Are you okay?"

Constance nodded and turned off the monitor.

Nicolas ran into the room. "Mommy, Mommy," he said, out of breath.

Michael rushed in after him.

"Everyone, look," Nicolas said. He held the glass ball with the feather high in the air. The feather floated and vibrated inside.

Constance forced a smile. "That's very good," she said, her mind still on her mother's recording.

"But it's not me," Nicolas said. "The feather's doing it all by itself."

The adults exchanged knowing looks. If Nicolas wasn't moving the feather, it could only mean one thing: Kylos was coming.

CHAPTER 26

The Curators' ring bustled with activity. Crew not needed elsewhere on the Orb had made their way to the ring and broken into squads, preoccupied with keeping the ship intact long enough for Dru and Hashim's team to figure out the navigational system. Life support had been cut to the storage, crucible, disposition, and garbage shoot rings; the animals had been sedated; and inspections for breaches had been completed. The command center glowed with Muhammad's makeshift lights. Everyone was focused on the one thing that controlled the ship and their fate: the console.

Constance and Michael watched from the entry as Dru and Hashim's group studied the panels and debated the best method for accessing the console's inner workings. Constance wiped sweat from her brow. The ring's previously cool temperature had been increasing as Jupiter pulled the ship nearer. The presence of so many people in a small space escalated the rise. Constance guessed the temperature to be close to thirty-six degrees Celsius. If they weren't able to move the Orb soon, they'd be cooked—if the radiation didn't kill them first.

Since entering the ring, Constance hadn't had an opportunity to discuss her discovery about the Cygnus constellation with Michael. She tapped him on the arm and motioned for him to join her in the corridor so they could speak in private.

"The planet is in the Cygnus constellation," she said in a low voice.

"What?" Michael said.

Constance removed Grace's necklace from under her shirt and pointed to the swan. "See that? It's not a dove." She flipped the pendant. "It's a swan. The swan constellation Cygnus."

He squinted at the design. "Are you sure?"

She nodded. "What Grace gave us is amazing, really … on so many levels."

"I'm not following."

"Some Native Americans believe the swan has the ability to enter dreamtime and bring back knowledge to the tribe, that it teaches humans to be one with all planes of consciousness." Constance suddenly thought of the boy and wondered if he had also visited Grace.

"And?" Michael said.

"The swan can also mean grace … like her name."

"So maybe she was just labeling her work."

"Don't you see? The swan is the Cygnus constellation. It all makes sense now … why she was so confident she would find our planet."

"Because she already had," Michael said. "But if Grace had known all along where our planet was, why didn't she tell us?"

During the conversation with Grace in the menagerie, Grace had indicated that her job would be over once their planet was found. Had Grace felt that if she told the others she had already found the planet, she would no longer be relevant or useful? Would she gamble with their lives like that? It didn't sound like the Grace she had known, but nothing made sense to her anymore.

"I'm ready," Hashim said to Muhammad.

Muhammad passed Hashim a screwdriver. Hashim pried open a section of the console's outer shell below one of the touch panels. The room grew quiet. Constance's pulse quickened. Hashim carefully handed the metal piece to Dru, who handed it to Muhammad. Dru held a light as she and Hashim peered inside the cavity. They whispered to one another and leaned back, dumbstruck.

"Is something wrong??" Constance said.

"Look for yourself," Dru said and moved aside to allow Constance to examine the console's interior.

Constance squinted into the opening. While it wasn't her area of expertise, she had worked with a fair amount of sensitive scientific equipment and had become familiar with that on the Orb as well. The system inside the console was unlike anything she had seen before. Lead lines ran from the panel to translucent optical circuit boards and glass spheres. But what surprised and puzzled her were the small, fleshy sacks floating in clear liquid.

Constance motioned for Michael to take a look.

"What is that?" he said.

"Our best guess," Hashim said. "A quantum computer."

"How about for those of us who don't speak geek," Michael said.

Hashim raised a brow.

"Sorry," Michael said, wiping the back of his neck. "I think this heat is getting to me."

"Let me see if I can explain," Dru said. "This computer uses the principles of quantum physics to increase its processing speed."

"Astronomically," Hashim said. "It's really quite cool."

"So how does it move the ship?" Michael said.

"We don't know," Dru said. "The technology is advanced beyond anything Hashim and I have worked on."

"What are the sacks?" Constance said.

"A type of biometric sensor, I believe," Hashim said. "Dru

thinks they must be there to detect a biological marker in the operator. It's a pretty good theory."

"Thank you," Dru said.

Michael shook his head. "So you're saying those sack things identify the operator and grant access by looking at … what did you call them?"

"Markers," Hashim said. "Think of it like this: in order for the console to work, the operator must contain the right code or combination, like on a lock."

"Something sequential but complex at the same time," Dru said.

"Like a DNA sequence," Constance said.

"Exactly," Dru and Hashim said with enthusiasm.

"So how do we fake these DNA markers to get the ship moving?" Michael said.

Hashim's smile disappeared. "You can't," he said. "You either have the markers or you don't."

"Could we bypass the sensors?" Constance said.

"You mean like hotwire it?" Michael said.

Dru raised a brow at Hashim. "I suppose," Dru said.

"How long would it take?" Constance said.

"It's hard to say," Hashim said.

"Best guess," Constance said, trying not to lose patience.

"Two hours. But are you sure you want us to try?"

"Why wouldn't we?" Michael said.

Dru pointed at the sacks. "Those sensors … we think they're living."

"If we monkey with them," Hashim said. "There's a good chance we'll destroy them."

Michael ran his hands through his hair. "So let me get this straight," he said. "If we leave it alone, we can't get this thing to work, and if we take it apart, we might never get it to work?"

Dru and Hashim nodded and looked at Constance. She'd put the decision to circumvent the console sensors to a vote.

She glanced around the room. Everyone had stopped working. She studied their faces. A vote wasn't what they wanted. They wanted a decision from her. She crossed to the observation window. Jupiter's eye filled the entire vista. The slimmest of fissures were appearing in the glass.

She turned to Dru and Hashim and said, "Do it."

CHAPTER 27

"I thought we were safe here," Constance said to Malic while keeping an eye on Nicolas watching the feather in the glass ball.

"Kylos won't hurt Nicolas," Malic said.

Grace shook her head. "This is what comes of that deal, Edward."

"What deal?" Michael said.

"My mother was part of a deal?"

"No, of course not," Malic said defensively. "She insisted."

Constance folded her arms. "Where's the tape of the experiment?"

"There isn't one," Malic said.

"What was on the VHS?" Michael asked Constance.

"You're a scientist, Dr. Malic," she said, ignoring Michael's question. "I find it hard to believe the experiment that killed my mother wasn't recorded."

"It was," Malic said, clutching his side. "But it was destroyed with the radiation. What you watched is all I have."

Malic gasped, dropped his cane, and stumbled.

"You okay?" Michael said, catching and steadying him.

"I think I need to sit."

Michael and Grace helped Malic sit in the chair by the VHS player.

"I'm telling the truth," Malic said. "You believe me, right, Gracie?"

"Hush now, Edward," Grace said, stroking his cheek. "You've worked yourself up."

Constance was reminded of Malic's frailty when she had first met him and how he had had to wheel an IV around as he gave his tour. Had he endangered his own health to help her?

She checked to see if Nicolas had been upset by the heated exchange and froze. The console's monitors and panels flashed with activity as Nicolas ran his hands over the panels like a pianist. The glass ball sat on the controller, the feather flipping, swirling, and fluttering as if in response to sudden changes in gravity and air pressure within the sphere. She crept around her son's side. His eyes were glazed, as if he was in a faraway place—like when he had quivered and told her he had seen an older version of herself on the Orb.

"Nick," she whispered, fearful that it might be dangerous to wake him from the trance.

He cocked his head in her direction and extended his hand. She reached toward him, touched the tip of her index finger to his, and felt a jolt of heat, fear, and desperation. She yanked her hand away. What was happening to her son?

CHAPTER 28

The crew watched, stock-still, as Hashim began the delicate operation on the Orb's quantum computer. The strategy he and Dru had outlined was simple. Hashim would use a pair of tin snips to remove the organic biometric sacks from the panels, reattach the leads directly to the panel, and bypass the security protection. While the plan was straightforward, Constance sensed the procedure would be anything but. She prayed that her decision hadn't doomed them to dying in Jupiter's fiery belly.

Dru held a light steady as Hashim stretched into the cavity and placed the cutting tool's sharp edge around the leads. Once the leads were cut, there was no going back. Everyone held their breath as Hashim squeezed the clips, the blades millimeters from slicing through the clear tubing.

Without warning, the ship trembled. Hashim lost his grip on the tin snips. Instead of falling onto the sacks, however, the tool floated and spun within the console. The Orb shook and violently knocked the crew into one another and the walls. Constance attempted to grab hold of something and was pulled into the air. Bodies bounced off the walls, ceiling, and one another. The ring had stopped spinning.

Michael grabbed the console chair bolted to the floor and righted himself. Constance spun by and seized his arm to keep from flying into the corridor. She ducked as Hashim sailed across the room and hit the far wall hard.

"What's happening?" Dru said, twisting uncontrollably in the air.

"We've lost gravity," Michael said. "We must have hit debris in the atmosphere."

Constance dug her fingers into Michael's clothing to anchor herself and peered out the large observation window. Bright lights streaked by the ship like angry shooting stars. But it wasn't what was outside the window that caused her the most alarm. The tiny fissures in the glass were rapidly elongating into an ever-widening web of cracks.

"The hull's going to breach!" she yelled.

Michael waved toward the corridor. "Evacuate!"

The crew scrambled toward the hall, pushing against objects, walls, and one another to propel them toward the exit. Michael repositioned his feet against the chair and crouched in preparation for kicking out and sending him and Constance through the doorway.

"Ready?" he said to Constance.

She tightened her grip. As Michael pushed off, flashing lights in her peripheral vision captured her attention. She stole a look over her shoulder and discovered that, in the midst of the chaos, the control console had sprung to life. She released her hold on Michael, hooked her feet into the seat back to keep from floating away, and pulled her body back to the controller.

"Roy!" Michael said, snatching the doorjamb as the last of the crew exited. "Get out of there!"

She floated above the controller, her back pressed to the ceiling, and watched in fascinated awe as images of star charts, maps, schematics, and Grace's planet flashed across the monitors. Controlling it all from the stool like a maestro at his podium was the boy who had appeared to her in Grace's cabin … the boy who had called her his mother.

"Constance!" Michael said from the corridor.

She made eye contact with Michael and pointed at the boy. Michael's jaw dropped. Despite the dire situation, she smiled with relief. Michael saw the boy, too. She wasn't crazy after all. The exit doors moved to close. Michael thrust his arm into the opening to keep the door from sealing Constance inside and cried out in pain.

"I got it," Muhammad said and threw a wrench into the opening to keep the doors open.

Beeps and clicks from the console below drew Constance's attention back to the boy working on the panels. She stretched to touch his shoulder to alert him to her presence when suddenly—as if she was having an out-of-body experience—she saw a younger looking, still redheaded version of herself appear behind the boy. As her other self watched the boy's activity, Fifi materialized across the room behind them. Constance watched in horror as her other self inexplicably moved away from the boy toward… Her heart skipped a beat. Was that Grace and Michael? Constance stared at the two, temporarily stunned, and then noticed Fifi crossing to the boy. Constance opened her mouth to warn the boy and the other Constance of Fifi's presence, but no sound came out. Fifi tapped the boy on the arm and beckoned him to follow. Constance attempted to push off of the ceiling and tackle the Curator, but she was unable to move. It was as if she was caught in a terrible nightmare. She watched in anguish as the boy turned away from the controller, followed Fifi, and vanished. She silently screamed at…

Constance crossed the FSI control room to Michael, Grace, and a pale and shivering Malic.

"How is he?" Constance said.

"Burning up," Grace said.

"I'm fine," Malic said. "I just need a little rest."

"That's the first smart thing you've said since we sat you down," Grace said.

"I need your help," Constance said into Michael's ear.

"What's up?"

"It's Nicolas," she said, turning in the direction of the console. "He's…" Her voice trailed off. The panels and monitors were black; the feather was still; and Nicolas was gone. "Nick?" Constance said, searching the room. "Nick?" she said again.

"Maybe he went back to Malic's room," Michael said.

Constance dashed from the control room and into Malic's den. "Nicolas?" Her voice echoed against the high ceiling. "Nick, are you in here?"

Michael joined her. "I'm sure he's here. I bet if we—"

Constance pressed her hand against Michael's mouth to stop him from speaking. Had she heard her son's voice? She tilted her head and listened.

"Is everything okay?" Grace said as she and Malic entered.

Constance held up a finger to silence them. She listened again. She heard air blowing through the vents … Malic's labored breathing … and her son.

"Who are you?" Nicolas said from somewhere deep within Malic's labyrinth.

"Someone who has been eager to meet you," came a woman's voice.

Constance's knees buckled. She didn't understand how or why—perhaps it was mother's instinct—but she knew her son was in imminent danger. Adrenalin flooded her system. She dashed into the maze, bumping into junk and knocking objects over as she went. She wanted to call out to tell her son to run away from the strange woman but was afraid that she'd lose her trace on the direction of his voice.

"I understand you like machines," Constance heard the woman say.

"Yes," Nicolas said. "Do you?"

"Yes," the woman said.

"I have an automaton."

No no no no no, Constance silently shouted as she hit a dead end and had to turn back. She met up with Michael and signaled they go left.

"Is your automaton a horse?" the woman said.

"How did you know?"

"Because I have it."

"Nicolas!" Constance called out, panicked.

"Mommy?"

"Don't you want your automaton?" the woman said from the direction of the decontamination chamber entrance.

"I guess," he said with hesitation.

"Nicolas, don't go with her," Constance said, turning in a circle trying to find a way to her son.

"Your horse is this way," the woman said, this time with more insistence.

"I don't think I should—"

Nicolas was cut off. Constance bolted toward the entrance, plowing through walls of objects and tossing aside anything that blocked her way. Michael helped clear a path. She reached the decontamination entry. The door to Malic's room and the one to the hall were open.

She raced through the decontamination chamber. Michael sprinted after her. They ran around the corner and caught sight of the stranger pulling her son around another corner. They dashed down the hall and saw the elevator doors close.

Constance pressed the elevator wall panel to stop it, but it was too late. Nicolas and the woman were gone. She thought of the numbers Malic had used earlier and pressed them into the pad. Nothing.

"Let me try," Michael said. He swiped an ID card, but the panel failed to come to life. "That's strange," he said and tried again.

Constance banged on the elevator doors in frustration.

"I'm coming, I'm coming," Malic said, turning the corner with Grace.

He hobbled to the wall panel and pressed his palm against the screen. The panel displayed a shrinking bar graphic indicating that the elevator was returning. "I'm still good for something," Malic said.

The bar shortened and disappeared. A second later, the doors opened. The elevator was empty. Constance held the doors while Grace and Michael helped Malic inside. She stared at their worried reflections in the mirrored wall as they ascended. The elevator slowed and stopped. She held her breath. Who or what would she find on the other side?

CHAPTER 29

The FSI elevator doors slid open with a quiet whoosh. The conference room had been empty on Constance's previous visit; now twelve figures whispered around the large table, as if in the midst of a board meeting. Kylos perched at the head of the table, his usual suit replaced by a gray tunic. The individuals seated around him wore similar garments and, like Kylos, had pale, waxy skin, willowy limbs, pointy features, and silver hair parted in the center. The strangers varied slightly in size, and some appeared more masculine or feminine, but they all looked as if they were descended from the same genetic line.

To Constance's horror, Nicolas sat in the middle of the conference table—a human centerpiece—with the horse automaton in his lap.

"Mom," Nicolas said as she rushed into the room.

A female figure near Nicolas grabbed his wrist and yanked him back. "Silence," she said.

"Take your hands off my son," Constance said, charging forward.

Michael seized Constance by the arms. "Careful," he

whispered. "We don't know what we're dealing with … and they have Nicolas."

The woman smirked.

"What a surprise. We weren't expecting you," Kylos said. He turned to Malic. "I see you granted them access."

Malic opened his mouth to reply but coughed instead. Grace scowled at Kylos.

Constance's cheeks flushed. What type of people kidnapped children and upset ailing old men? "Why have you taken my child?" Constance said, pulling away from Michael and stepping toward Kylos.

Several of the strangers moved to intercept her. Kylos raised a hand and stopped them.

"We are all your children, Dr. Roy," Kylos said, motioning about the room. "In fact, that is a topic of this council meeting."

"What are you talking about?" Constance said.

"Nonsense," Michael said.

"We've come for Dr. Roy's son," Malic said, finding the strength to speak.

"The son that never should have been," the female said, glancing at Nicolas with disdain.

Nicolas wilted under her stare.

"Leave the boy alone," Grace said. "Can't you see you're frightening him?"

Kylos walked around the table, placed his hand on Nicolas's head, and turned the boy to face him. "You're not scared, are you?" He flashed Nicolas a toothy grin.

Nicolas paused and then said, "No, sir."

"Please," Constance said to Kylos. "He's nothing to you."

"Oh," Kylos said. "That's where you're wrong. Your son has a rare ability … perhaps the rarest."

Constance's mouth went dry. This was about more than moving a feather in a glass ball. "Ability?"

Kylos glanced at Malic with a raised brow. "You haven't told her," he said and wagged a bony finger at Malic.

"Told her what?" Michael said.

Kylos motioned to the female who had kidnapped Nicolas. "My colleague witnessed your son operating the control console." He turned to Nicolas. "Isn't that true?"

"I saw him," the woman said.

Kylos held up a hand to silence her. "I'm asking the boy."

"Nick, don't answer," Constance said, fearful of the consequences if her son revealed what she, too, had witnessed.

"Yes, it's true," Nicolas said with confidence. "Why? Do you need me to fly the Orb?"

"All in good time," Kylos said, taking the automaton from Nicolas and examining it at eye level.

"The boy's not part of this," Malic said.

"But he is," Kylos said. "You've allowed him to inherit a gift that was only meant for Dr. Roy's mother, Dr. Roy, Mr. Whittaker, and the other candidates."

"Me?" Michael said.

Kylos noticed Constance and Michael's confused expressions. "You've been kept in the dark. Allow me to enlighten you. You two were selected to participate in an experiment to save your species. Sadly, an experiment that has repeatedly failed."

"What do you mean failed?" Malic said.

"What experiment?" Constance said, looking from Kylos to Malic and back.

"Your ancestors had much promise generations ago," Kylos said. "They created amazing objects." He turned the key to wind the automaton, set it on the table, flipped the switch, and watched the horse gallop. "Two thousand years ago your race gave birth to an astonishing revolution ... a revolution of ideas and steam and mechanisms. Over time, these machines became more complex and, eventually, sentient."

The strangers at the table turned in their seats and gazed intently at Constance and Michael, as if awaiting their responses. But it was Nicolas who spoke.

"You're an automaton," the boy said with awe.

"From another timeline and more biological than mechanical," Kylos said. "But yes. Your kind created our kind to protect you from yourselves. Your ancestors had the forethought to understand that eventually humans could destroy themselves."

"So you're our overseers?" Michael said, gazing at the strangers.

"We prefer the term Curators," Kylos said. "We weren't programmed to rule or interfere, only to guide you in the proper direction."

"And still they destroy themselves," the woman Curator said. She turned to the others. "How long must we help them when all they're capable of is bringing about their own extinction?"

The strangers whispered among themselves and nodded agreement.

"It's true," Kylos said, addressing his fellow Curators. "We've watched them destroy their land, their sky, their planet—"

"What are you saying?" Constance interrupted.

Kylos gazed at her, Michael, Malic, and Grace. "We've watched you all die."

"This can't be true," Malic said.

The woman Curator looked pointedly at Grace and smirked. "It is."

"Funny, I feel pretty alive right now," Grace said, clenching her fist.

"You haven't perished in this world, Dr. Yoholo, but in another," Kylos said. "Imagine my gratification when I saw you again."

"I don't think I can," Grace said.

"Perhaps not," Kylos said. "But it is true."

"Where do Michael and I fit into all of this?" Constance said. "And how does this concern my son?"

"Mr. Whittaker's miraculous recovery from boyhood illness and subsequent physical prowess are no accidents. We assisted with that, Mr. Whittaker, but I believe Dr. Malic has told you as much. As for you, Dr. Roy, you inherited the ability we gave your mother."

"What exactly is this ability?" Michael said.

"You have the capacity to withstand a long and difficult journey."

"Like your mother," Malic said, struggling for breath. "You can survive the transport … to find a new home."

"Your experiments have failed," Kylos said to Malic. "We've watched you transport candidates time and time again and, in the process, the by-product has been the creation of strangelets and the destruction of the world."

Malic crumpled as if hit in the chest. "No," he said.

"I'm afraid so," Kylos said.

"Why didn't you stop me?"

"We are not programmed to do so."

Malic collapsed to his knees and clutched his heart.

"Edward," Grace said, wrapping an arm around his back to help him up.

"I'm sorry," Kylos said, sounding sincere. "But every time you've attempted to save the world by migrating candidates, you've annihilated this planet with your machine. At this very instant, candidates are trapped in a universe without a new home and, I regret to say, on a course toward ruin."

"The people on the Orb," Nicolas said with dismay.

"Yes," Kylos said.

Malic hung his head. "What have I done?"

"You said candidates … like Michael and me?" Constance said.

"Not *like* Michael and you," Kylos said. "*Actually* Michael and you and Dr. Yoholo … in another universe. Your son has told you as much."

Constance recalled Nicolas in the trance on the bookstore back porch and his vision of her on the Orb. "Yes," she said, as unbelievable as it seemed.

"This is absurd," Michael said. "How could you possibly know this?"

"Because I've been there," Kylos said. He glanced at the other Curators. "We all have."

"So if they—we—are doomed, what's all this about?" Michael said, gesturing to the Curators around the table.

Kylos gazed at Nicolas. "This is about hope."

"No," the female Curator said. "This is about ending our association with humans."

"I'm afraid my colleague no longer believes in our mission," Kylos said. He turned to the female Curator. "But it's not up to you or me. It's up to the council to decide."

"Decide what?" Grace said from the floor where she held Malic.

"Whether or not we continue," Kylos said. "Whether or not Nicolas will be allowed to use his unique gift."

"You still haven't said what that gift is, exactly," Michael said.

"Haven't you figured it out?" Kylos gestured to the other Curators. "He's like us. He can do what we can."

"I'm an automaton?" Nicolas said.

"No," Kylos said. "You're very human. Which is why being able to do what we can is so special."

"What exactly is it you think my son can do?" Constance said.

"Move through time and space," Malic said in a rasping voice before Kylos could answer.

Nicolas stared at the Curators with wonder.

Constance took a step toward Kylos, her heart filled with dread. "You said it was up to the council to decide if Nicolas will be allowed to use his ability. What happens to my son and those on the Orb if the council votes no?"

The female Curator grinned. "They perish."

CHAPTER 30

Constance clutched a groove in the ceiling as she hovered in the control room, kept an eye on the console below, and waited for the boy to reappear and work his magic on the controller. The fate of the Orb's inhabitants hung in the balance.

Suddenly, Michael grabbed her ankle and yanked her free of the ceiling toward the exit. Somewhere in her consciousness she heard him yell "Come on!" but her attention remained on the console chair, even as she sailed across the room and into the corridor. She pried his fingers away and pushed off the hallway wall to propel back into the control room. But it was too late. The crew released the doors, and the exit vacuum sealed closed. Constance peered through the door window and willed the boy to return. But he was gone, and Fifi with him.

"I need to get back in there," she said to Michael.

Michael turned to the others floating in the passageway. "Can anyone get a status report on the rest of the ship? We need to know if we've lost structural integrity on the other rings."

"I can go," Garcia said. He pushed off the wall and floated away toward the stairwell.

Constance made her way to Michael. "You saw them, didn't you?" she said, floating in front of him. "You saw Fifi and the boy."

"Fifi?" Dru said, traveling toward them with Hashim. Dru braced herself against the wall. "You saw Fifi? Here?"

"We're not sure what we saw," Michael said.

It was time the others knew. "We saw Fifi … and we saw a boy operating the controls."

"A boy?" Hashim said. "On the ship?"

The crew looked at her with concern. Whatever respect she had earned as their leader could evaporate if they no longer had confidence in her sanity.

"Whittaker saw them, too," she said. "Tell them, Michael."

Michael hesitated and then said, "Yes. I saw them."

Murmurs of disbelief rippled up and down the corridor as others joined them. They floated in a semicircle around Constance and Michael.

"A boy on the Orb?" someone said. "Impossible."

"We saw what we saw," Michael snapped.

Constance touched his arm. She sensed he was having a hard time accepting what he had observed.

"The important thing right now is that we need to get into the control room and secure it before the window ruptures," she said. "Anybody have an idea about how to do that?"

The Curators had been responsible for the ship's integrity. The inhabitants had been left to fend for themselves with little knowledge of the vessel's inner workings. Maybe Muhammad and his team could figure something out. They had done a good job with accessing the alignment stall. She spotted Muhammad. Blood drops drifted from a gash in his forehead.

"Muhammad, you're injured," she said.

He pressed his hand against the cut. "I'll be fine."

"You sure?" she said, worried he might have a concussion. Muhammad nodded. "What do you need?"

"Any ideas how we might secure the control room?" she said.

Muhammad pushed through the group to the control room door and examined the area through the glass. "The window hasn't breached yet. I'm surprised the protective shutters weren't triggered when the fissures began."

"Maybe the sensor didn't pick up any loss of pressure," Dru said.

"Or maybe it no longer works," Hashim said.

"Could the shutters be jammed?" Michael said. "There was a lot of debris out there."

Muhammad turned from the door. "It's possible. We could try closing them manually."

"That can be done?" Constance said.

"If it's like the other portals on the ship, we should be able to remove the wall panel and access the mechanism."

"You mean someone would need to go in there," Constance said.

"Yes. And there's no guarantee I'm right."

"So if it breaches, what's the worst-case scenario?" Michael said.

Hashim reluctantly held up his hand. "Remember the organic sensors in the computer? The cold and loss of pressure will kill them."

"So? We were going to bypass them anyway," Michael said.

"We're not bypassing anything," Constance said. "Not anymore."

"We can't just wait and see what happens," Michael said.

"No," she agreed. "We can't risk losing the sensors. Someone is going to have to go in and manually close the shutters."

"I'll do it," Muhammad said. "It was my suggestion."

Constance shook her head. "It should be me."

"Now's no time to play hero, Roy," Michael said. "Muhammad knows the mechanism."

"Yes," she said. "But if something goes wrong, if the room loses oxygen or pressure or temperature…" She pushed the possible crises from her mind. "After Maria, I hold the endurance records in the crucible. It's not about playing hero. It's about being able to withstand the deteriorating conditions long enough to get the job done."

Hashim stole a look at Michael. "She has a point."

"Fine," Michael said. "But at the first sign of trouble, I'm pulling you out."

"Let's hope it doesn't come to that," Constance said. "Muhammad, I'll need you to walk me through it when I'm inside."

"Absolutely."

"Hashim, is there any way to restore the gravity?" she said.

"Not until we gain access to the control console."

She turned to Muhammad. "How long until you think your team will be ready?"

"Five minutes tops."

"Let me know when you are. Then we'll evacuate this section so we don't depressurize the entire ring. Agreed?"

"Agreed," the crew said and began preparations.

"Can I talk to you in private?" Michael said.

She knew that look. He was unhappy about the plan. They floated away from the others. No need for them to hear their disagreement.

"I don't like this," he said when they were out of earshot.

"You know I'm the best person to go in," she said.

"I understand trying to prevent a breach, but what you were saying about not disconnecting the sacks on the computers … that I don't get."

She took a breath. "What I'm about to say may sound crazy, but hear me out. The boy you saw in the control room—"

"Maybe I just thought I saw him," Michael said. "Maybe he was a—"

"Whittaker," she interrupted, trying not to lose her patience. "I need you to listen. The boy spoke to me back in Grace's cabin. He said he was my…"

"Your what?"

She locked eyes with him. "He said he was my son."

"What?" he said after a moment. "But you don't have a son."

She understood Michael's disbelief, and yet she knew with every fiber of her being that what she had said was true. "I don't have a son here," she said. "But somewhere I do."

He ran his fingers through his hair and looked away.

"Michael," she said, gently taking his face in her hands and forcing him to look at her. "This boy … I saw him steer the Orb."

When she was sure Michael understood that she was serious, she released him.

"So what are you saying?" he said. "That you want to wait for the boy to show up again to pilot this ship to our new planet?"

"Yes."

"This is crazy."

"Please, Michael."

"Okay. Let's say any of this is true. Why would this boy come and help us?"

"Because he knows we're in trouble."

Muhammad cleared his throat. Constance and Michael broke apart. "Sorry to interrupt," Muhammad said. "But I thought you'd like to know that Garcia's back. The other rings with life support are fine except for a slight diminishment in gravity. Seems this ring sustained the most damage from the debris."

"Thank you," Constance said. "Anything else?"

Muhammad pointed to the control room. "We're ready when you are."

CHAPTER 31

Constance analyzed the council debating Nicolas's fate. The moment the female Curator had announced that the group would vote on whether Nicolas lived or died, Constance had wanted to grab her son and make a run for it. Unfortunately, her group was significantly outnumbered, and in the time it took her to reach Nicolas, the female Curator could snap his neck. It was impossible for them to take on all twelve members and also ensure Nicolas's safety.

Constance, Michael, Grace, and Malic had been ushered to seats along the wall near the elevator. Despite repeated requests to let Nicolas sit with them, the boy remained on display in the center of the enormous conference table. Constance studied the interaction between the strangers. There was a clear divide within the group, with Kylos at one end of the table and the female Curator who had kidnapped Nicolas at the other. If the meeting became heated, they might have an opportunity for escape.

Constance leaned forward in her chair and studied a door at the far corner of the room. There didn't appear to be a security code panel or lock. At best, the door led to a fire exit stairwell, at worst to a closet or storage area. She considered the elevator again. Even if they managed to get to the elevator, the Curators would disable it. Breaking the window wasn't an option either. The glass was thick and the office too high. Their best chance was the unlocked door. She sat back and turned her attention to the Curators. When the time came, she'd take Nicolas and run.

The female Curator pointed at Constance and the group. "This," she said with venom. "This species is what we've wasted centuries protecting, helping, and nurturing. For what? They have demonstrated time and time again that their quest for knowledge is greater than their need to survive. They've had enough time to prove themselves. We have arrived at the moment when we must end our association with the humans and move on."

Curators around the table nodded and muttered agreement. Nicolas squirmed and pulled his arms around his legs.

"My fellow Curators," Kylos said, rising from his seat. "What our colleague has said is true. The humans have been —how shall we say—reckless with their inventions. Their atomic bomb, sarin gas, even their desire to cool themselves rather than be concerned about the health of their planet or their descendants is of grave concern. I don't deny that when given a choice to pursue invention, no matter the cost, or walk away, they find it impossible to do the latter."

"So why have you called for a vote if we're all in agreement?" one of the Curators said.

"Because I believe they have a chance to save themselves."

"Save themselves?" one Curator said. "How? With this child?"

"Precisely," Kylos said.

"We've watched humans take a yellow dye and turn it into an explosive and develop chemicals to kill plants and use it to kill their own species," the female Curator said. "This boy is a thousand times worse."

"He's only a boy," another Curator said.

The female Curator pointed at Nicolas. "But one day he'll be a man, a man who will create more like him. If we don't destroy him, there could be an entire race of humans traveling across membranes to multiple universes and spreading their destruction like a virus. No," she said, pounding the table. "They cannot be trusted with such technology."

"My son is not technology," Constance said.

"You have no voice here," the female Curator said.

Kylos turned to Constance. "Like it or not, Dr. Roy, from our perspective your son is no different from the innovations my colleague mentioned. You have created a powerful weapon, one that would never have existed had you not violated the terms given you by the FSI … terms put in place to protect your kind … and all that is."

"That young man wouldn't hurt a soul," Malic said.

"Perhaps not," Kylos said. "It's never the invention's fault it is created. Nor is it the invention itself that brings about destruction. It is what your kind does with something such as Nicolas that troubles the council. You, too, have found it hard to resist the seduction. You brought about death and illness, not to mention the strange matter that has repeatedly wiped your planet from existence in other universes. Isn't your inability to resist scientific pursuit the reason why Dr. Yoholo broke off ties with you?"

"Don't listen to that creature, Edward," Grace said.

"How dare you," Constance said, jumping from her seat. "My son is a human being, not some *invention*, and Dr. Malic shut everything down once he realized the outcome of his experiment."

"You see," the female Curator said with a smug smile. "That is exactly my point. Dr. Malic could have chosen not to proceed with the experiment in the first place once he realized the risks. And once you discovered you were pregnant, you could have—"

"Enough," Kylos said. "Curators are designed to protect the humans, not propose—"

"Stop it!" Grace said. "Have you no decency, no compassion? There's a child in this room. A human being with a mind and soul. I will not stay another moment and listen to this." Grace helped Malic from his chair. "Come, Edward. We're leaving."

"You're not going anywhere," the female Curator said, moving around the table to intercept Grace and Malic.

"You'll have to get through me," Michael said, stepping forward to block the Curator.

The strangers looked at one another, uncertain as to how to respond. Now was the opportunity Constance had been waiting for. She made eye contact with Nicolas and mouthed "Ready?" He nodded and shifted his weight to a crouching position. Never had their countdown ritual been more important. She held up one finger for "tick," two fingers for "tack," waited until the female Curator had reached Michael, and yelled, "Go!"

Nicolas sprang to his feet and ran down the table.

"Get him," said the female Curator.

Curators reached for Nicolas's legs as he scurried by them and leaped from the table. Constance grabbed his hand, raced to the unlocked door, and threw it open. Behind it was a stairwell. She turned back for Grace and Malic.

"Come on!" she called to the others.

Michael held the female Curator back as Grace and Malic hurried toward the exit. The Curator scratched Michael in the eye. He lost his grip. Another Curator slipped past him and rushed at Grace and Malic. Constance let go of Nicolas's hand and said, "Run." She watched Nicolas race down the stairs, then turned back in time to fend off a Curator. Despite their frail appearance, they were remarkably strong.

"Go," she said to Grace and Malic, kicking the Curator in the thigh.

Grace rushed into the stairwell, but Malic broke free, turned back, and, with all the strength he had left, charged the female Curator, sending them both to the ground.

"Edward," Grace said.

"Help Nicolas," Constance said. "Michael will get Edward."

Grace dashed down the stairs. A Curator swung an arm into Constance's gut and knocked the wind from her. She stumbled back, and everything went blurry. She blinked. Kylos grabbed the Curator and tossed him aside. Was Kylos helping her? She searched for Michael and Malic.

Michael pulled the female Curator from Malic's limp body. Blood oozed from his ear. Michael threw Malic's body over his shoulders as Curators closed in on him.

Constance rushed toward Michael and felt a steely grip on her shoulder. She whipped around and discovered that Kylos had a hold of her.

"You must leave," he said urgently.

Constance tried to yank away, but he held her strong.

"It's the only way to save Nicolas," he said.

The sincerity in his voice took her back. She stole a look at Michael carrying Malic. If she stayed to help, she might end up the strangers' prisoner or dead, and Nicolas would be in danger. If she left, she could protect her son, but Michael and Malic might suffer a terrible fate.

"I can help," Kylos said. "But you must go now."

Forgive me, she thought, turned away from Michael and Malic, and fled into the stairwell. The door closed with a thud behind her.

CHAPTER 32

The control room doors closed tightly behind Constance. She floated toward the console and the cracked observation window. By choosing to wait for the boy, she was gambling with the lives of everyone on the Orb. What if Fifi harmed the boy and he was unable to return? She pushed the thought from her mind. It was too late for other options. She needed to focus on closing the jammed shutters. If she didn't, there wouldn't be a ship for the boy to come back to.

She felt Michael and Muhammad's eyes on her through the door glass. The rest of the crew had retreated behind a central bulkhead as a safety precaution in case the window shattered while the control room door was open.

She heard a quiet hiss and floated toward it across the room. The hiss grew louder. She took several deep breaths and then forced the air from her lungs. It was a technique Maria had boasted of using in the crucible. She had claimed it was best to expel air from your system when in an atmosphere experiencing decompression—that if you filled your lungs and held your breath, the pressure inside the lungs would push out and rip you apart. Constance had no idea if Maria was correct, but she wasn't taking any chances.

She reached the window. The hissing became a piercing squeal. If the window shattered, she'd only survive a few seconds before her life and those of the other refugees ended in an explosive roar. She examined the fracture in the glass. The crack started in the lower right corner, a thin line no thicker than a human hair. Centimeters from the start, the nearly invisible fissure split into two distinct cracks, and each of those split into two more. The pattern repeated across the glass, creating a web of fractures. The damaged window bowed outward, warping under the strain.

She glanced over her shoulder at Michael and Muhammad watching from the corridor. Michael pointed to the observation window's left side. She gave him a thumbs-up. Just as Muhammad had explained, there was a small panel near the window. She had noticed these panels on the ship's portals before but had never thought much about them.

Constance removed a screwdriver from her waistband and pried the panel loose. ORB-2 was engraved on the back. She released the panel and focused on the opening. There were two switches and a crank with a small circle cut into it. As Muhammad had instructed, she pressed the switch on the right and then the one on the left. Mechanisms clicked into place. She inserted her finger into the crank and turned counterclockwise.

Metal shutters slowly lowered over the exterior and interior of the window. The glass bowed more. She turned the crank faster, but the shields moved at a snail's pace. Her finger ached from where the sharp metal of the hole cut into her skin. She switched hands. The amount of visible window shrank to twenty, eighteen, sixteen centimeters … and then the tremor hit.

The knob vibrated, causing the metal to cut into her finger like an electric knife. She lost her hold on the crank. Blood drops floated into the air. She pushed against the exterior wall, felt the tremendous force of the vibration, and was reminded of when freight trains rumbled through her West Virginia town as a kid.

She hooked a finger into the hole in the crank and turned. The squeal from the window jumped in decibels, and a tiny diamond-shaped piece popped from the glass and flew into space. Constance braced against the wall, dug her finger into the knob, and cranked faster. Blood flew out through the small hole in the glass.

Air rushed around her toward the hole as more and more pieces broke away. She tightened her muscles as her body was pulled toward the opening and pushed any remaining air in her lungs out. The glass burst into space like confetti.

The squealing ceased, the temperature dropped sharply, and Constance felt tremendous pressure on her eyes. She squeezed her lids closed and blindly turned the knob. She had not taken a breath in what seemed an eternity. She desperately wanted to inhale, but with the breach there was no air left.

She strained to keep her body from being squeezed through the window like toothpaste. She didn't know how much longer she could hold on and move the shutter. Maybe she should give up. It would be so easy. She fought to maintain consciousness. She wanted to open her eyes to see if the shutters were down but kept them closed and tucked her head. Visions of the boy flashed through her mind. He was her son. She was certain of that now. Somehow she knew that his name was Nicolas, that she had named him after her father, and that he was more important and precious to her than anyone or anything in her life … and Fifi had him. She shuddered. She had seen what the Curator did to Maria.

She felt helpless to save her son. Helpless to save her crew. Helpless to save herself. Her mind grew cloudy. *This is what it feels like to die*, she thought, and let go.

CHAPTER 33

The FSI stairwell door burst open. Constance stumbled out, sucked in air, and scanned her surroundings. The exit had spat her onto a parking lot behind the building. She shielded her eyes from the sun, turned in a circle to get her bearings, and searched for Nicolas and Grace. The Wallops grounds and launch area were deserted. Where would Grace have gone? The rocket rose above the landscape—the one landmark visible from anywhere on the complex and shore. *Of course*, she thought. Grace would head to the boat.

Constance dodged between parked cars to stay out of sight of the FSI windows. Once clear of the building, she had an unobstructed view of the launch site. Off in the distance and dwarfed by the enormous rocket, two figures ran toward the water. Seeing Nicolas and Grace so close to the boosters gave her pause. An ignition would incinerate them in seconds. She resisted the urge to call out to let them know she was coming. The sooner they were clear of the rocket, the safer they'd be.

She sprinted after them. The rocket's size had given her a false sense of the distance to the shore. Despite her speed, she felt like she was making little progress. Sunlight reflecting off the concrete flight pad blinded her. The temperature soared. She ran into the rocket's shadow and caught sight of Nicolas and Grace at the end of the launch pad. Soon they would reach the rocky erosion barrier and boat and be safe. She reluctantly slowed to catch her breath. Her quads trembled and burned from exhaustion.

Nicolas spotted Constance over his shoulder and stopped.

Constance waved and said, "Keep going!"

Grace took the boy's arm and guided him down the rocks.

Constance pumped her arms and made a final push toward the water. She ran off the hard pavement onto marshy soil. The mud swallowed her foot. It was as if she was running in quicksand. She grunted in frustration. She was less than fifty feet from the boat.

Grace helped Nicolas into the boat.

"Mom!" he said, seeing Constance lose her balance.

"Stay there," she said. She pushed herself onto her hands and knees.

"Mom," Nicolas called out again and struggled against Grace's grasp to exit the boat.

"Don't wait for me," Constance said. "Just go."

"Go where?" someone said behind her.

The voice was unmistakable. Kylos. The Curator gazed intently at the boy.

"Get out of here!" Constance said to Grace.

Grace gripped the pull on the motor and gave it a tug.

Nicolas wobbled to the end of the boat and stretched his leg over the side. "Mommy!"

"Nicolas, no!" Constance said.

Grace released the pull and lunged at Nicolas. The two fell back hard against a seat.

"Where do you think your son can go that we won't find him?" Kylos said. "Look how easily I located him. My colleagues will do the same."

"What would you have me do? Let them take Nicolas? Kill

him?" She shook mud from her hands. "If you didn't think we should run, why'd you help us escape?"

"Did I?" Kylos said.

Her eyes narrowed to slits. Was he toying with her?

He gazed across the channel at Chincoteague and gestured to the water and sky. "No matter how hard we have tried, your species always destroys this magnificent habitat. My colleagues have lost faith." He extended a hand toward Constance. "But I have not."

She had no idea if he was sincere or if this was part of his game. But what choice did she have? If what Kylos said was true, there wasn't anywhere that Nicolas would be safe ... not without his help. She grabbed his cool, bony hand and allowed him to help her to her feet.

"I can take your son someplace safe," he said.

"Why should I trust you?"

"Because I was encoded three hundred years ago to help ensure humankind's survival. Nicolas is the first real hope for your kind in centuries."

"Where would you take him?" she said.

"Out of this world and into another."

"On the Orb," she said. "But aren't they doomed?"

"If Nicolas can assist them in finding their new home, my colleagues might change their minds about humankind and your potential to help yourselves."

"And if Nicolas can't help them?"

Kylos locked eyes with her. "Then you are all lost."

If she turned down the offer, one of the other Curators would kidnap Nicolas ... or worse. If she took the offer, she might never see him again.

"You want me to give up my son ... to you," she said.

"Not to me," he said. "To you and Michael and the others on the Orb."

What if she refused Kylos and the one chance her son had at being safe and then the others found him? What if they carried out their threats? To keep him with her would be dangerous. She could never live with herself if something happened to him because of her own desires.

"Nick," she said. "I need you to come here."

The boy hopped from the boat and climbed the rocks. Grace followed.

"Nick," Constance said, kneeling and taking his hands in hers. "I need you to do something, something that is going to be hard but is quite important."

"You need me to go to the Orb?" he said, a hint of excitement in his voice.

Constance nodded.

Grace yanked Nicolas back. "What are you doing?"

"Protecting my son."

"By handing Nicolas over to *him*?" Grace gestured at Kylos with contempt. "His kind—they're unnatural. You heard what they want to do."

Kylos cocked his head as if hearing something in the distance. "Dr. Roy," he said. "We don't have much time. My colleagues will be here shortly."

As if to confirm his warning, lights on the flight pad flashed and alarms sounded.

"They'll track him until they find him," Constance said over the alarms. She took Nicolas's hand. "He'd be in hiding forever. What kind of life is that?"

"If you let that thing take Nicolas, you'll never see him again," Grace said. "Trust me."

"Is that true?" Constance said to Kylos.

"The trip he'll make is not an easy one. Surely you realized that. But if returning to you is within his power, he will come back."

Nicolas tugged on her sleeve. "Don't worry, Mommy. I'll come back. I promise."

What if this was the last time she would see Nicolas? What

if she never again heard his silly laugh or touched his platinum locks? "Could I go with him?" she said.

Kylos shook his head. "Your dedication to your son is admirable. But the universe is not that pliable. You would not survive."

"And you're sure Nicolas will?" she said.

"Yes."

"You always said to help people," Nicolas said. "The people on the Orb need me."

She rubbed his head. "How'd you get so smart?" she said, fighting back tears.

"Please, Dr. Roy," Kylos said. "We need to depart."

Constance kneeled before her son and put on a brave face. "I'll miss you," she said.

"I'll miss you, too." He reached into his pocket, took his mother's hand, and placed the tiny astronaut figurine in her palm. "You keep this for me, Mommy, until I come back."

Constance clutched the figurine and wrapped her arms tight around Nicolas. He did the same.

"I love you," Constance said. "Don't ever forget that."

"I love you more," Nicolas said.

The intensity of the flashing lights and alarms increased.

"It's time," Kylos said.

Constance looked intently at her son, attempting to burn every detail of his face into her memory.

"Make sure Mr. Whittaker takes good care of my automaton," the boy said. Constance nodded. "Give Schrodi a hug for me, Miss Grace."

"I'll do that," Grace said, her voice shaking.

Nicolas kissed his mother on the cheek. "Goodbye, Mommy," he said. He crossed to Kylos and took the Curator's hand.

Kylos stared at Nicolas's hand, stunned for a moment by the boy's touch. Three figures raced toward them. The lights flashed. Alarms sounded. A deep rumbling shook the Earth.

Constance's eyes widened in horror. The lights and alarms weren't for security—they were for a rocket launch—and Kylos and Nicolas were heading straight toward it.

"No!" Constance screamed.

Grace grabbed Constance to keep her from running toward the launch. Boosters blew smoke and fire. The rumbling deafened. They fell to the ground and wrapped their arms around one another. Then came the blast.

CHAPTER 34

Constance felt her spirit leave her body, but she didn't float into the void of space or toward a bright white light. She didn't float at all. Instead she ran, fast and hard, twisting around corners and occasionally tripping when she misjudged a step. Down, down she ran. Was it from the impending doom of the ship? The Curators? Fifi? No. Her goal didn't seem to have anything to do with the Orb or its inhabitants. Her goal was saving her son.

She slammed open a door, stumbled, and fell. She thrust her hands in front of her to brace for impact but wasn't quick enough and hit the ground hard on her stomach. Wind rushed from and around her. She drew in air and felt its warmth.

"You did it," a voice said. It was Michael. But which Michael? From what world?

She squeezed her eyelids tight, unprepared for the answers.

Arms wrapped around her waist and shoulders and turned her face up. She was gently propped against someone's chest.

"Open your eyes," Michael said and lightly brushed hair from her face.

Was this real, or was this a hallucination caused by neurons firing in her brain for the last time?

"It's okay," he said. "You're okay."

She blinked. Everything came into focus. She was cradled in Michael's lap in the control room.

"What happened?" she said.

"You did it," he said. "You closed the shutters."

"But I didn't," she said.

"Not all the way," Muhammad said over Michael's shoulder. "But once the window blew, the shutters did their job and sealed the rest of the way."

She pushed up to check the window. The shutters were down and the view of Jupiter gone. "I don't remember," she said. She noted they weren't floating. "You've restored gravity."

Michael shook his head. "I'm afraid not."

She pointed about the control room. "But how are we…"

Michael stole a look at Muhammad.

"What is it?" she said.

"We've gone into an uncontrolled spin," Michael said. "It's the end."

No, she thought. *Not yet.* "Help me up," she said.

Michael and Muhammad helped her to her feet. Blood rushed hot and fast to her brain and upper body. She felt a force push down on her and then a pull to the left side of the room, followed by a pull a few seconds later to the right. The crew leaned in unison in one direction and then another as if adapting to ocean waves. The entire Orb, not just the ring, was spinning.

"What's the status of the rest of the ship?" she said, noticing the others' grim expressions.

"The central axle is down," Garcia said. "Lina's trapped there but says she's okay."

"What about the other rings?" she said.

The room fell silent. Some looked away.

"We've lost F ring," Michael said. "When the tremor struck, Zhang Yong was stopping a water leak in the protective layer. The outer layer cracked. He's…"

She sighed. Grace and now Zhang Yong. "What about D and G rings?" she said, dreading more bad news.

"As far as we can tell, the menagerie and garden rings are intact and still spinning," Michael said. "But since the central axle is down, we can't confirm."

The ship was like a comet streaking across space, spinning and casting off pieces as Jupiter pulled her into its atmosphere. How long did they have? Would it be the heat or radiation that killed them? Or would the ship's outer layers crack under the stress and send them into space to die of suffocation, decompression, and exposure?

"Should we try bypassing the computer?" Hashim said.

It was too late for that. She had gambled their lives on the belief that a son she had seen in a vision would magically appear and pilot the spacecraft to their new planet. All they could do was wait. The Orb let out an ear-piercing wail. Jupiter's force was ripping apart another section of the ship. The wail was followed by an increased gravitational force. Like an out-of-control carnival ride, the force suddenly shifted and sent them flying.

It was as if the entire room had been flipped on its side. The wall was now the floor, and the floor with the console and chair was now the wall. The force pressed everyone against the wall. Constance tried to push away but found it difficult to move even her head. Like test pilots on supersonic missions, soon the blood would be diverted from the brain, and she and the others would lose consciousness. Her cheek flattened under the pressure. She and Michael locked eyes, and Constance realized in that instant that she loved him. She gave him a slow blink, and he returned one of his own.

Suddenly, a burst of light filled the room. She attempted to turn her head to see the light's source, but the gravity was too much. A shadow entered from the corridor, unaffected by the ship's strange orientation. The figure made its way to where the console and chair sat sideways. They were tossed again, and the room righted itself.

Constance sat up and froze. One by one the rest of the crew did the same. Standing before them at the control console was Kylos.

"Looks like I've arrived just in time," he said.

"I'm going to kill him," Garcia said, moving to get up.

Kylos held up a hand. Garcia stopped as if expecting to be hit by an invisible beam. The crew rose and stood along the wall, wary of what the Curator might do next.

"What are you doing here?" Constance said.

"I've brought help." Kylos stepped aside and spun the console chair to face them. Sitting in the chair was the boy. "Nicolas, I'd like you to meet the crew of the Orb. Everyone, this is Nicolas."

"Hello," Nicolas said.

Constance was overwhelmed with feelings of relief, joy, and love. The boy spotted her, hopped from the chair, and ran into her arms.

"It's good to see you," Nicolas said with a smile.

She tentatively wrapped her arms around the boy. "It's good to see you, too," she said.

Michael and the others studied the boy. Constance knew the question that was on their minds. It was the same one on hers. Could this boy really save them?

CHAPTER 35

Constance's nostrils burned, her ears hummed, and her skin felt as if it had been singed. The rocket's thunderous takeoff had knocked her onto the rocky shore. Her wrist bled and throbbed where it had hit a chunk of granite, and a bruise was forming on her forearm. Her hand smarted too. She uncurled her fingers and discovered the shiny astronaut figurine. She had been clutching it so tightly that it had created an impression in her palm. She tucked the figurine in her pocket, cradled her forearm in her other hand, and searched for Grace.

Several feet down the hill at the water's edge, Grace stirred. She spotted Constance and gave a weak, reassuring wave. Constance gingerly descended and helped Grace to her feet.

Grace said something.

Constance pointed to her ears and said, "I can't hear."

Grace nodded.

They picked their way up the rocky hill. A mist of steam and smoke, a by-product of the burn, rolled over the empty launch pad. The final image of Nicolas flashed before her. In the seconds before the launch, she had looked back and, despite the exhaust and intensity of the light during blastoff, seen Nicolas and Kylos on the pad. They had turned to face one another and then, like a magician's illusion, were gone. As fantastic as it seemed, Kylos had used the launch as a cover for their departure. Nicolas was safe.

Her thoughts turned to Michael and Edward. Had they escaped or been overtaken by the Curators?

Three figures jogged toward them. She shielded her eyes from the sun. She expected to see the female Curator with the others but instead saw three military police officers, two men and a woman, with weapons drawn. She wrapped her arm around Grace's waist to support and protect her. One of the male officers yelled what she thought was, "Don't move."

"You don't need those guns," Constance said. "We don't want trouble."

The officers holstered their weapons. A man and the woman helped Grace climb the rocks to solid ground while the other man helped Constance.

"You shouldn't have been out here, Dr. Roy," the soldier said. "It wasn't safe."

"You know who I am?" Constance said, her hearing improved. It took her a moment, but she placed his face. He had been the guard at the entrance when she first arrived at Wallops. "You work at the gate," she said.

"That's correct, ma'am," the guard said.

"Are you going to arrest us?"

"No, ma'am," the woman soldier said. "We have orders to take you to Dr. Malic."

"Edward's alive?" Grace said and braced herself against the soldier.

"Yes, ma'am," the woman said. "He just arrived in the infirmary with Mr. Whittaker."

Was it possible Michael had fended off the Curators' attack? "How is Mr. Whittaker?" Constance said.

"Fine, I think. He brought Dr. Malic in," the woman

soldier said. "The doc wants Dr. Malic to go to the hospital, but he's refused transport until he speaks with you."

"You two look like you should be examined, too," the soldier helping Grace said.

Constance couldn't agree more. Grace looked shaken up, and she needed the gash on her wrist checked out. She was also eager to see Michael and Malic to be sure they were okay. "Show us the way," she said.

One of the soldiers left to retrieve a Jeep and returned a few minutes later. They helped Grace into the front seat. Constance sat in the back with the soldiers. She gazed out the window at the last of the rocket's contrail as they traveled from the flight pad to the facility's main campus. They entered another gate and drove past military barracks and bungalows to a nondescript building deep on the grounds.

Constance leaped from the vehicle, entered the building, and spotted Michael seated with his head in his hands in a small waiting room. The officers escorted Grace to a wheelchair and rolled her to an examination room.

"Dr. Malic is this way," one of the officers said to Constance.

"Give me a second," she said. She crossed to Michael and placed a hand on his shoulder. "Hey," she said.

He looked up with tired eyes. "Hey."

She eased into a seat next to him. "I'm glad to see you. I thought you were... What happened?"

"I held them off for a while, but there were too many. They had us. Then the female one raised her hand, and they all just stopped, walked to the elevator, and left."

Hopefully not to find Nicolas, she thought.

"Malic's not well," Michael said. "I brought him here as fast as I could."

"The MPs told us."

He noticed Grace in the nearby exam room. "Is Grace okay?"

"I think so."

He spotted Constance's wrist. "Are you okay? Where's Nicolas?"

If she told Michael how she had let Nicolas leave with Kylos, she'd shatter into a million pieces, so she said the only thing she could … what she needed to believe above all else… "He's safe."

A woman in a white coat approached. "Dr. Roy?"

"Yes?"

"I'm Dr. Belkin. I'm treating Dr. Malic. Would you come with me?" Constance and Michael rose. "Dr. Malic has only asked for Dr. Roy, sir. You'll have to wait here."

"Mr. Whittaker brought him in," Constance said. "I'm sure Dr. Malic wouldn't mind if—"

"*I* am not sure," Dr. Belkin said, cutting her off.

Constance's eyes narrowed. She looked at the doctor's nametag. Maria Belkin, M.D. was in serious need of lessons in bedside manners.

"Are you coming?" the doctor said.

"Go ahead," Michael said. "I'll check on Grace."

The doctor turned and walked away.

Constance hobbled after her. "How is he?" she said, keeping her voice low.

Belkin stopped in front of a door at the end of the hall. "Dr. Malic is quite ill. I've been overseeing his care. For some reason, today he's taken a turn for the worse." She stared pointedly at Constance. "He needs treatment at a facility better equipped than Wallops. He refuses to go until he talks to you."

Constance reached for the door. Belkin grabbed her arm. Constance raised a brow, and the doctor released her.

"Dr. Malic seems to think your opinion matters, Dr. Roy. You must convince him to leave for proper care."

Constance studied the woman. Despite her brusque

manner, the doctor was genuinely concerned about her patient. "I'll try," she said.

Belkin gave her a curt nod. "After you speak with Dr. Malic, I'll look at that wrist," she said and opened the exam room door.

Constance entered. Malic appeared small in the bed. IV tubes ran into the back of his hand and the crook of his arm. A heart monitor silently displayed the organ's activity.

His eyes fluttered open. "Constance," he said in a dry voice and motioned with a finger for her to come closer.

She crept forward and took his outstretched hand.

"You've met my doctor," he said. She nodded. "She's tough, doesn't give an inch. Whatever you do, don't cross her."

"I'll keep that in mind," she said. "She tells me you won't leave for treatment until you speak with me. I told her I'd try to convince you."

"It's too late for treatment," he said, his breathing labored. "But it's not too late for me to make amends."

At the end of his life, her father too had had regrets, and it had pained her to see him so troubled. "You have nothing to apologize for," she said and rubbed Malic's hand to reassure him.

"I'm sorry for what I've caused, how I've affected your life. I thought we could fix humanity, save it … what hubris."

"My parents believed, too. It wasn't all you."

"How many people have died because of my bridge? It must never be used again. Promise me you won't let that happen. Tell me you'll stop them from doing any more damage."

How could she deny him a wish that might be his last, no matter how impossible it seemed? "I'll try," she said.

He leaned back into the pillow. His hand slipped from her grasp.

"I'll tell the doctor they can take you to the hospital," she said.

"No," he said. "That isn't why I asked for you. It is young Nicolas I want to know about. Tell me. Is he safe ... from them?"

"Yes," she said and swallowed hard.

"Good," he said and closed his eyes. "I thought you'd be the one to lead us to the stars ... a new generation to a new home. But it was your son. He's the one that will travel through this universe and the next. He's the one that will rescue us."

It saddened her to think of Nicolas traveling alone through time and space.

"You're quiet," Malic said. "Is something on your mind?"

"Just you getting well," she said, not wishing to upset him with her concerns.

He opened his eyes, forced himself up, and studied her face. "You've seen and heard things you don't understand."

"I don't know what you mean," she said.

"You've seen another you, another Michael perhaps?" Her eyes widened. He nodded at her silent confirmation. "You have been entangled with them since you walked through the door to my chamber."

She thought about the visions of her on the Orb, the strangely passionate connection to Michael, and the other moments over the previous days that had made her question her sanity. She rolled back the hours, moment by moment. When had the visions started? Of course. They had begun after she had walked through the decontamination chamber leading to Malic's lair.

"You did this to me?" she said. "But how? Why?"

"The how is technology not our own. The why is the critical question."

Malic coughed and motioned toward a pitcher and paper

cup on the bed's tray. Constance poured water and handed him the cup. He swallowed and handed it back.

"You needed to be convinced," he said. "You needed faith. How could you believe in something that was impossible otherwise?"

Her mind reeled. Had he really used her as a guinea pig so that she would have faith in his grand experiment? Her cheeks flushed with anger, but the anger was only the surface emotion. Underneath were feelings of betrayal and sadness. This had been the man who was friends with her parents, who had paid for her education, who had seemed so concerned about Nicolas. How could he have done this to her? Then a realization hit her that instantly washed away the anger. Because of the entanglement, she had the ability to sense, even see, into the Orb universe where Nicolas was. Malic had unwittingly given her a gift. No matter what, she'd always be connected to her son.

There was a knock at the door. Grace and Michael peeked in.

"You have visitors," Constance said.

Grace crossed to Edward and smoothed his hair.

"How'd you get by Dr. Belkin?" Malic said.

"I had one of the soldiers distract her," Michael said.

"Then we gave her the slip," Grace said.

"That's my Gracie," Malic said with affection. He coughed and sank into the pillow.

"Hush now," Grace said and poured him water.

"I'm glad you're here," Malic said to Grace. "Remember the box? The one I gave you after…" He wheezed and struggled for breath.

"I remember," Grace said.

"Do you still have it?" Grace nodded. "I want you to give it to Constance."

"What box is this?" Constance said.

Malic closed his eyes. "Something you need to see. Something you've needed to see for a long time." His voice faded, his muscles relaxed, and then he was still.

The blips on the heart monitor stopped. They watched the flat line cross the screen in stunned silence.

Dr. Belkin charged into the room. "Code blue, room four!"

Medical personnel rushed in and pushed Constance, Michael, and Grace aside.

"Get them out of here," Belkin said.

One of the soldiers who had helped Constance and Grace held out his arms. "Please," he said. "Let's let the doctor do her job."

As they reluctantly retreated to the hall, Constance watched the code team work on Malic. Grace clutched Michael. The door closed, and he was gone.

CHAPTER 36

The inhabitants gaped at the boy embracing Constance. She took in the boy's warmth and affection and felt time and space disappear in a dreamy haze. Maternal love unexpectedly washed over her, and it was as if a missing piece of her heart had been restored.

"The Orb's stability is only temporary," Kylos said, bringing her back to the crisis.

Kylos moved his hands over the console panels. The crew gazed at him with suspicion, but Constance only felt gratitude toward the Curator—something she never imagined possible a few days ago. Kylos had stabilized the ship and brought Nicolas to help them.

"What are you doing to the controller?" Hashim said.

"Sabotaging it, no doubt," Michael said.

"You were on a crash course to Jupiter," Kylos said. "Now you're not. I'd hardly characterize that as sabotage."

"The only reason we were spinning in the first place is because you abandoned us without any knowledge of how to pilot this ship," Muhammad said.

"My colleagues have lost faith. My intervention gives you a chance."

"You can get us out of here," Michael said.

"I'm afraid not. I broke protocol in halting your descent—something I will not do again. The spin will resume shortly." Kylos removed his hand from the console.

"You have the ability to get us to our new planet, and yet you'll do nothing?" Dru said.

"I mean no ill will," Kylos said. "But there are matters more important than helping you."

"Like what?" Dru said.

Kylos approached Dru. "Like you helping yourselves."

"How are we supposed to do that?" Garcia said. "You're leaving us with nothing."

"On the contrary," Kylos said. "I have provided you with the only tool you need."

Nicolas released Constance and faced the group. "Me," he said.

"And who are you?" Dru said.

Constance put her hand on his shoulder. "He's Nicolas Roy." She took a breath. "He's my son."

The crew stared at her and Nicolas, clearly not sure what to make of the revelation. She'd feel the same way if she were in their shoes.

"Nick," she said. "These are my friends."

"Nice to meet you," the boy said. He surveyed the group and spotted Michael. "Hi, Mr. Whittaker."

"Hello," Michael said after a stunned pause.

Constance wondered how Nicolas knew Michael and what part Michael played in her life in the other world.

"I'm here to help you and Mom, Mr. Whittaker," he said. "I'm going to fly the Orb."

The inhabitants exchanged looks of skepticism.

"Show them," Kylos said and gestured to the console.

Nicolas looked at Constance. "Go ahead," she said.

The boy bit his lip. Now that the moment was upon him, his confidence seemed to wane.

"There isn't much time," Kylos said. "Don't be afraid."

The boy took a deep breath and shuffled forward. Constance helped him climb into the chair. Everyone watched and waited. Nicolas stared at the machine, uncertain.

Kylos leaned close to Nicolas. "It's just like the one Dr. Malic has at Wallops," he whispered and stepped away.

Nicolas extended a hand above one of the screens. Constance held her breath. She had been so convinced that he had the answer to their survival that she hadn't considered what they would do if he failed. The boy lowered his hand onto the panel. A spark from the panel struck his palm.

"Ouch," he said, yanking his hand back.

Nicolas looked at her with disappointment. She felt the weight of the others' dashed hopes.

"Try again," she said in a reassuring tone.

He hesitated and then placed a palm on the panel. This time there was no spark. Constance's heart sank. The ship had responded to Nicolas the same way it had responded to her. Then she heard it—a low hum—and one by one the monitors flickered to life. There were sighs of relief and cheers as the monitors displayed schematics of the Orb and oxygen, gravity, and temperature readings.

Michael joined Constance and watched Nicolas moving his hands on the panels. "How is this possible?" he said.

Constance squinted at the panels below Nicolas's hands. Had a panel just moved?

"It feels cool," Nicolas said as if hearing her question. "Kinda like water."

"Do you see that?" she said.

Michael nodded. The panels changed from a solid to a gel and flowed over and around Nicolas's fingers and hands, responding to his touch like a living organism.

"We've lost H ring," Garcia said, pointing at an image on one of the monitors on the wall above the controller.

"Looks like other rings have maintained integrity and gravity is restored," Muhammad said.

"The menagerie is showing life signs," Dru said. "The animals are okay."

Hashim squinted at yet another screen. "I think we'll be able to access the central axle and get it moving," he said.

"Good news for Lina," Garcia said.

"What's that?" Michael said over Constance's shoulder.

Files with pictures of the ten crew members who had died under mysterious circumstances flashed across a screen. Constance caught snippets of vital signs, medical data, and the words leukemia, contusions, tumor, bleeding, and cancer. Grace's image and information was there, too, but the information was moving too fast to read.

The chatter increased as the crew learned more from the schematics and readouts. Everyone crammed around the controller, brainstorming repairs and planning for how they might get the Orb operating again. Nicolas sat in the midst of the activity like a maestro, exploring his ability to manipulate the console. They were a long way from their new home, and it would take more than accessing the ship's database to make the trip, but now they had a chance.

She searched for Kylos, but there was no sign of him. She checked to be sure Nicolas was okay and exited into the corridor. The hall was empty. It was as Kylos had said. It was time for them to help themselves.

CHAPTER 37

The trip from the Wallops infirmary to Grace's house was a somber one. They had been aware of Malic's illness, and yet it was hard to accept that he was really gone. Dr. Belkin's team had spent nearly a half hour trying to resuscitate Malic, but it was no use. The cancer had finally won.

Constance stole a look at Grace in the back seat, staring at the stars. What must she be feeling? The man she had loved had returned to her ... only to be lost again. Grace had been stoic when saying goodbye to Malic. Constance wasn't sure she could have been as strong if she had been in a similar situation.

She turned her attention to Michael in the driver's seat next to her. After they had left Malic, Michael insisted he retrieve the automaton from the FSI conference room. Constance and Grace had expressed concern for Michael's safety, but he had argued that both Nicolas and Malic would have wanted him to regain custody of the machine. Constance suspected that rescuing the automaton gave Michael a sense of control and was his way of dealing with Malic's death. Fortunately, the Curators had abandoned the facility, and he had recovered the machine without incident. The horse sat strapped in the back next to Grace.

No one spoke as they drove over the channel and made their way to Grace's house to find Malic's mysterious box. Constance recalled Nicolas steering the boat to Wallops. Had it been her son's destiny to pilot the Orb through the universe? Was that what he was doing now? What if he never returned? She sighed heavily, and the window fogged.

Michael touched her hand, and she bit back tears. She had to be strong for Nicolas and Grace. He turned onto Main Street, drove past Sundial Books, and, minutes later, pulled up to the trailer and cut the engine. Constance and Michael followed Grace up the path.

"Would anyone like tea … or maybe something stronger?" Grace said, entering and holding the door for them.

Grace's cat rubbed against their legs and meowed.

"Tea would be great," Constance said. "I can put on the water."

"And I can feed Schrodi," Michael said.

"Thank you," Grace said. "If you two don't mind, I'll go look for the box," she said and disappeared into another room.

Constance filled a kettle while Michael found a can of food, scraped it into a bowl, and set it on the floor for the cat. They heard the sound of objects being moved around down the hall.

"You think I should go help her?" Michael said.

Constance shook her head. "Something tells me she wants to do it alone."

The kettle whistled. Constance found tea in a container on the counter, filled a pot, and carried it to the table where Michael had placed the automaton next to *A Map to the Galaxy*. She set mugs on the table and sat. Michael joined her.

"I'll be out in a second," Grace said from the other room.

"No hurry," Michael said.

Constance considered her father's book. If she looked through the pages, would she get a sense of her son, where he was, or how he was doing? Malic's entanglement had given her visions and opened her eyes to possibilities that days ago she would not have believed. If she closed her eyes now, could she see Nicolas? Tell him to return home where he belonged?

"Found it," Grace said, entering with a wooden box.

She set the object on the table. It was slightly larger than a cigar box and made of a dark wood with a brown and beige speckled horse galloping over a landscape inlaid on the top.

"This is the box Malic wanted me to have?" Constance said.

"It arrived two days after your mother … after the experiment. There was a note from Edward asking me to keep it safe. We weren't speaking at that point, so I tucked it away. I had forgotten I had it."

"May I?" Michael said. Constance nodded. He examined the outside and attempted to lift the lid. "It's locked. Do you have the key?"

"It didn't come with one," Grace said.

Michael held it to the light. "Maybe we could crack it open. The lock looks simple enough."

"With Edward nothing is—was—simple," Grace said.

"Besides, we might destroy what's inside," Constance said. "We don't know how fragile the contents are."

Constance took the box and rubbed her fingers over the horse, around the sides, and over the oddly shaped hole. It would require an unusual key.

"Why would Malic give you a box with no key?" Michael said to Grace.

"Because it wasn't for me. It was for Constance. Edward must have believed she could open it."

"Malic must have given you a key," Michael said.

"But he didn't," Constance said.

She wished Nicolas was with her. They had always been

good at solving puzzles together. She absently gazed at the automaton on the table, and then her eyes widened. Could it be? She pulled open the drawer under the automaton and removed its key.

"Is that it?" Michael said in surprise.

She rolled the key in her fingers. It felt like the right size. "There's only one way to find out," she said.

She slid the key into the hole on the box and heard the soft sound of tumblers clicking. She glanced at Grace and Michael leaning forward in their seats and lifted the lid. Inside was another VHS tape. Constance removed the tape and examined the spine.

"August twenty-third," she said. "That's two days after the message from my parents."

"It's the experiment," Grace said.

"The tape Malic said didn't exist," Michael said.

"He lied," Constance said.

"He was trying to save you," Grace said. "You don't need to watch it now." She attempted to take the tape from Constance.

"No," Constance said, clutching the tape. "I want to see it."

Graced touched her arm. "Haven't you been through enough today?"

In fact, it was one of the worst days of Constance's life. But so was the day that her father had told her her mother was gone and didn't tell her how or why.

"Grace is right," Michael said. "This could wait."

"I've waited my entire life to find out what happened to my mother," she said. "I think that's long enough."

CHAPTER 38

Constance and Michael studied Nicolas from the corridor as he manipulated the ship's controls. The crew hovered nearby and asked Nicolas to pull up charts and diagrams, enlarge images, and locate repair logs. With every request, the boy seemed to shrink deeper into the chair.

"We're betting on him to save our lives," Michael said. "You know he's just a child."

"He can do it," Constance said, but she, too, was worried about the pressure that was being placed on the boy.

The crew's conversation grew louder as they deciphered data and debated strategies. Nicolas removed his hands from the panels, grabbed his knees, and tucked his legs in front of him.

"He can get the console to work," Michael said. "But does he know how to steer us to the planet? Hashim's best guess is that Kylos gave us another hour."

Nicolas covered his ears and lowered his head onto his knees.

"We should go talk to him," Constance said.

"We?" he said. "You're his mother."

The words stunned her a moment. Michael was right. She

was his mother—at least genetically speaking. "What should I say?" she said.

"Trust your instincts," Michael said and nudged her forward.

As she wormed her way through the crew, she tried to think of what might comfort a boy. She didn't have any experience with children. She tapped Nicolas on the shoulder. "You look like you need a break from that chair," she said.

The boy shrugged. She helped him down. He drifted away to the shuttered window. She looked at Michael. He motioned for her to go to Nicolas.

"I thought I would be able to see space when I got to the Orb," he said.

"I could take you to another window if you'd like."

"Maybe later."

"Are you hungry?" she said. "I could get someone to bring you something."

Nicolas shook his head and looked at his feet.

"What about something to drink?" she tried again.

No response.

Constance was trying to be understanding about his age, but she needed the boy back on the console. "I'm not good at reading minds," she said. "Maybe if you just tell me—"

"I want my mother," he blurted out, eyes filled with tears.

Everyone stopped talking and stared. He looked at the adults, confused and embarrassed, and then sprinted from the room.

"Nicolas, wait," Constance said and exited to the corridor. "Tell the crew not to panic," she said to Michael and then jogged after the boy.

Nicolas turned into the stairwell. She picked up speed. The alignment stall could be dangerous for a child. She took the steps two at a time and gained on him.

"Nicolas, stop," she said. "You could get hurt."

She lunged to the final step and grabbed him by the

shoulders.

"You only care about me flying the Orb," he said, his voice shaking.

"That's not true. I care about you a great deal. More than I could have imagined," Constance said.

He sniffled. "Really?"

"Yes, really," she said and meant it.

He bit his lip.

How could she comfort the boy so he would return to the control room? *Think, Constance. What would a mother do?* Suddenly her skin tingled, and she saw Nicolas near water, perhaps a beach, watching something fuzzy in the near distance. She blinked, and the fuzzy object came into focus. It was a pony grazing in a marsh. She blinked again, and the image was gone. She didn't know how or why, but she was certain she had just had a glimpse into Nicolas's world.

"I think I know what might make us feel better," she said. "Care to join me?"

The boy nodded and took her hand. She helped him navigate the shaft and ladder connecting the stairwell to the central axle.

"This is like an elevator," the boy said after they had jumped into the dumbwaiter.

He leaned out the opening to watch their progress. She grabbed him as the landing of one of the rings passed by. "Careful," she said. "This elevator doesn't have doors."

Nicolas squeezed her hand tighter. The opening for the menagerie ring approached.

"When I give you the signal, we're going to jump," she said.

"Say tick, tack, go," Nicolas instructed.

Constance suppressed a grin. The landing came into view and she said, "Tick, tack, go."

They leaped from the elevator. Nicolas's eyes widened as they shifted in the alignment stall. They descended the stairwell and made their way down the corridor to the menagerie. Constance hesitated. She hadn't been inside since Grace's death. She shook the unhappy thought from her mind and opened the door.

A gust of air hit them as they entered. Nature sounds greeted them.

"What is this place?" Nicolas said as she led him down the hall.

"This," she said, "is where the animals live."

The boy stopped, stunned. "Animals live on the Orb?"

"Yes," she said. "And I have one friend in particular I'd like you to meet."

Constance grabbed the handle of the door next to her. She hoped Patches had fared well during the turbulence. She slowly slid the door open.

"It's a horse," Nicolas said with delight.

Patches paced, shook her head, and snorted.

Constance held her arm out to keep Nicolas from jumping into the stall. "Wait here until I see if she's okay."

Constance stepped into the straw. Patches bobbed her head. Constance touched the horse's rump, ran her hand along the body and withers, and caressed the neck. "Hi, girl," she said and rubbed the horse's nose.

Patches leaned affectionately into Constance and caught sight of Nicolas in the doorway. Constance felt the animal relax.

"Can I come in?" Nicolas said.

"Move slowly," she said. "You don't want to frighten her. Patches has been through a lot."

Nicolas took deliberate steps through the straw. "Hi, Patches," he said and touched the animal's neck. "I'm Nicolas."

Patches nudged Nicolas. He giggled.

"I can't believe the Orb has a horse," he said.

"The animals need a new home, like the people."

"What do you mean?"

"Well," she said, "everyone on the Orb is searching for a new home."

"Why? What's wrong with Earth?"

How could she explain that the Earth in her universe had been destroyed? She wasn't sure she understood it herself.

"Because the people like Kylos that brought us here think we need to find a new home in case something happens to our old one."

"Like an emergency plan?"

"I suppose."

"So where is the new home?"

"Have you ever looked at the night sky and studied the stars and planets?"

"Sure. I used to go with you … I mean Mom … I mean…"

"It's okay," she said. "You can call me Constance if it's easier." His confusion about her existence and their relationship was understandable. "What's she like—your mother?"

"A lot like you."

"No kidding," she said with a grin.

"But different," he added.

"Different how?"

"She worries more, mostly about me," he said.

I bet she does, Constance thought.

He stopped stroking the horse and cocked his head. "Do you know my father?"

She didn't know how to respond. How could she possibly know his father? Had Nicolas never met the man? What had happened in the other universe? She had a newfound appreciation for the sacrifices her other self must have made to raise a child on her own.

"It's okay," Nicolas said. "I thought maybe since you are here and back home, my father might be, too."

Constance tentatively put her arm around his shoulders.

"You're a remarkable young man, Nicolas Roy," she said, overcome with affection and pride.

He blushed. "Now you're just like Mom."

"Oh yeah?" Constance said in a teasing tone, but it was the greatest compliment he could give her. She could have sat in this happy moment forever, but she needed to get him back to the control room. "So, my young friend, you ready to take us to our new home?"

Nicolas shook his head.

"No?" Constance said with raised brows. "Why not?"

"I don't know where it is," he said.

"When you and your mother look at the stars, does she ever show you a constellation called Cygnus?"

"Sure."

"Well, our new planet is somewhere in the constellation Cygnus. We just need to find it."

The boy rubbed Patches' neck. "Cygnus," he said after a long pause. "That's far away."

"Yes."

"What will it be like going to the new planet?"

"I don't know."

"Will it hurt?"

"I don't know that either."

He stopped stroking the horse. "What if I can't fly the Orb?"

Their future and perhaps the future of humanity rested on the shoulders of this little boy.

"I know you're scared," she said. "I am, too. But you know what courage is? Courage is when you're afraid to do something, but you do it anyway. You've already shown me and the crew how brave you are by coming to the Orb." Constance held out her hand. "What do you say we finish what you came here to do and help us and the animals find a new home?"

Nicolas stroked Patches, gazed at the horse for a moment, nodded, and then took Constance's hand.

CHAPTER 39

G race rose from the dining table with Malic's tape and crossed to a television in the living room. Beneath the television were a stack of VHS tapes and a player. Constance eyed *As The World Turns* written on the tape spines with various dates.

"Don't judge," Grace said.

"I'm not," Michael said. "I used to watch with my grandmother when I was a kid."

"I think she meant me," Constance said, embarrassed.

Grace slipped the VHS tape into the player, cued it, and turned on the television. "You can watch alone if you'd like," she said, handing Constance the remote.

"No," Constance said. "I want you both here."

Constance and Michael sat on the sofa while Grace lowered herself into a nearby easy chair. Schrodi jumped into Grace's lap and purred. Constance hit PLAY. Young Malic appeared on screen.

"He looks so handsome," Grace said and squeezed the cat close.

"This is Edward Malic. I'm here with Drs. Nick and Barbara Roy."

Constance's father popped into view from behind the camera, waved, and then disappeared. The camera panned away from Malic. Barbara appeared on screen. Her mother looked as she had on the other tape, only this time she wore athletic-type pants and shirt and had her hair tied back. Barbara gave a short wave. The camera returned to Malic.

"It is no exaggeration to say that today is a day of monumental importance," Malic said. "If all goes according to our calculations, Dr. Barbara Roy will be the first human to make an incredible journey—a step that will pave the way for the human race to survive long after we've depleted Earth's resources. Despite the naysayers and government obstacles, today we endeavor to open up space itself. Soon the entire world will know the significance of what we accomplish here —how three researchers took on the task of securing humankind's future when nobody else had the foresight to do so." He looked off-screen at Barbara. "Are you ready, Dr. Roy?"

"I am."

"Be sure you record all of this," Malic said to Nick behind the camera.

Malic helped Barbara into a metal chamber and strapped her in. Constance's father came into view, kissed his wife, and then returned to recording. Barbara gave Malic a thumbs-up. He closed the chamber. Constance leaned closer and tried to make out her mother's face through the vessel glass. What was her mother thinking at this moment? Had her thoughts at any point turned to her daughter? Malic secured several locks. The camera framing widened and gave them a full view of the room.

"That's Wallops," Michael said.

Malic moved to the console. The camera zoomed in on images on the monitors.

"Those are schematics of the Orb," Grace said.

The diagrams were fully realized versions of the sketches

Constance's mother had drawn on the book cover. Each had a file number in the left corner—one, six, seven, and twelve—the code Malic had punched into the pad ... the numbers missing from the bookstore sign.

An alarm like the one she had heard on the rocket flight pad sounded. The camera pulled back to show the entire room. A clock counted down. Ten, nine, eight. Malic kept his hands on the console and his eyes on the vessel. Seven, six. Another alarm sounded—this one more piercing. The cat jumped from Grace's lap and scurried away. A console monitor turned red, and the words *Radiation Warning* flashed in black. Malic looked at the vessel with Barbara inside. The clocked counted three, two, one ... and then a loud boom, a blinding light, and the screen went black.

Constance stared at the static on the television, stunned. Michael took the remote. The machine clicked off. Her body trembled. She forced herself to stand. She stumbled to the back door, staggered outside, and gulped air. She had wondered what had happened to her mother, had feared the worst, but nothing had prepared her for what she had seen. The memory of Nicolas disappearing into the smoke of the rocket launch flashed through her mind, and she suddenly feared that he, too, was gone forever. She fell to her knees. The cool moisture from the grass seeped through her clothing and sent a chill through her body. She gazed at the night sky, numb. Nicolas wasn't coming back. She had been a fool to think otherwise.

The screen door opened and closed.

"Are you okay?" Michael said, kneeling beside her.

She stared blankly out at the water toward Wallops.

"Let's get you back inside," he said.

She shook her head. "Please, get me out of here."

He helped her to her feet. "Do you want to go to your motel?"

She nodded and allowed herself to be guided around the

side of Grace's home. Grace handed Constance her purse and squeezed her tight. Constance slid into the front seat of Michael's vehicle. He closed the door and whispered something to Grace before getting in the car and starting the engine. Grace waved as Michael drove away.

Constance closed her eyes. She felt the turns, the deceleration and acceleration, the vibration of the engine, and the warm vent air blowing across her cheek. She heard the turn signal, the tires rolling over irregularities in the pavement, the gravel crunching beneath the vehicle, and the engine click off.

"We're here," Michael said. She opened her eyes. "Do you still have a room?"

She shrugged.

"I'll be right back."

He returned with a key, opened the passenger door, and helped her from the car. They walked to the second floor and stopped at the room where she and Nicolas had stayed before.

"This is where…" she said, pointing at the room number.

"I asked if the room was still available," he said. "I thought maybe you'd like to stay where you had stayed with Nicolas."

He inserted the key and opened the door. Moonlight streamed in through the curtains.

"I'll turn on a light," he said.

"Leave it off."

Michael turned to leave. Constance clutched his arm to stop him, took his face in her hands, and kissed him. "Stay," she said. He looked away. She turned his face to hers. "I need you to stay."

She closed the door and led him to the bed. They kissed tentatively at first, and then with more passion. They undressed one another in the moonlight. Constance explored his body as if she had done so a million times before—every muscle and curve familiar and comforting. His fingers and lips danced over her skin, knowing just how to touch her. They fell onto the bed and moved in rhythm. Her body tingled, and she gave herself up to the pleasure. The visions she had had of their lovemaking became real, and her loneliness and the pain disappeared.

CHAPTER 40

The Orb wailed and quaked as Constance and Nicolas exited the menagerie. Panicked that the elevator might shut down again and cut them off from the rest of the ship or trap them like it had Lina, Constance sprinted with Nicolas up the stairwell, into the dumbwaiter, and the entire way back to the Curators' ring. She slowed once they were on the ring to allow Nicolas to catch his breath. The two jogged the darkened corridor to the control room.

"They're back," Lina said.

The crew greeted them with cheers and sighs of relief.

Michael wiped sweat from his brow. "We can't wait any longer," he said to Constance. "We have to do this now."

The temperature had risen significantly since she and Nicolas had departed, and the console panels and monitors were dark.

"We're ready," she said. She turned to Nicolas. "Right?"

Nicolas gave her a salute.

The crowd parted as she and Nicolas hurried to the console. She helped Nicolas into the chair.

"Anyone have a belt?" she said.

Garcia removed a woven belt from his pants. Constance yanked on both ends to test its strength, secured it around the boy's waist, and strapped him in.

"How are you feeling?" she said to Nicolas.

"Courageous."

She rubbed his head and took a position next to him. Her pulse quickened. What would be the consequence of moving the enormous ark? Every inhabitant had a memory of the trauma of the migration—a journey of millions of miles, a relatively short distance by space standards. What would happen as they attempted to travel light years? Should they secure themselves and brace for impact, slip into the migration chambers, or wait? Kylos hadn't provided information as to how to they might survive the journey. They were on their own, with one valuable tool.

Constance nodded to Nicolas. He touched the panels and, as before, the hard surface melted and flowed around his hands, and diagrams and charts appeared on the screens.

The Orb trembled.

"Come on," Lina said, eyeing the shaking walls.

"He's trying," Constance said, not wishing Nicolas to feel any additional pressure.

"The system is advanced," Hashim said.

"Are you saying you don't think the boy can fly this thing?" Michael said.

"On the contrary," Dru said. "The goal of advanced technology is to make it easier for the user. The interface should be simple for him to access."

Hashim nodded. "Kylos thought so," he said.

"Like we can trust him," Lina said.

"You can do this," Constance said to Nicolas. "We just need to find you a map."

"Like *A Map to the Galaxy*," Nicolas said.

She grinned. "Exactly."

Why not use her father's book as their guide? Its pictures and recommendations were hardwired in her brain. It was as if all those years studying its charts had been preparing her for this moment. She and the boy would pilot the ship together. She lowered her hands over his and felt the cool substance flow between her fingers. She concentrated on the charts that she had committed to memory—the constellations and planets and moons—and gently pressed Nicolas's fingers. Seconds later, the screens filled with images they hadn't seen before. Instead of schematics and readouts, they saw views of space.

"That's new," Muhammad said.

Constance moved Nicolas's hands clockwise and counterclockwise. The space images rotated under their direction. She pressed to the left, and the view shifted to the ship's portside. She pressed right, and it was starboard. Nicolas slanted his hands forward and back, and the perspective moved up and down. They sank their hands deeper into the panel and moved the perspective along the z-axis. The operation of the ship was intuitive and tactile—thought and touch translated into quadrants and coordinates.

Stars and constellations flashed across the screens in rapid succession until … there it was: Cygnus. She moved the boy's hands down to enlarge the star cluster. She mentally played connect-the-dots with the stars in Grace's painting and found the same image in the upper right-hand corner of the monitor. That's where they would find their planet.

"Can you hold it steady?" she said to the boy.

Nicolas nodded. She released his hands, retrieved Grace's necklace, and held it to her eye.

"That looks like Yoholo's necklace," someone said in a hush.

Constance adjusted the pendant until the holes lined up with the stars and planets on the monitor, and then she found it—no bigger than the head of a pin—Grace's planet. She placed a hand on the boy's hand to enlarge the display, but that was as close as they were going to get. Still, she had no doubt. She had found their new home.

"That's it," she said, pointing at the speck. "That's our planet."

"Where?" Muhammad said, squinting at the screen.

"I don't think we should move the Orb until we're sure," Lina said. "We could end up stuck there like we are here."

"I'm sure that's it," Constance said.

"That's good enough for me," Garcia said.

"Me, too," said Dru and Hashim in unison.

"We have to take the chance," Michael said. "If we stay here, we die."

"Michael's right," Muhammad said. "The hull can't take another rupture."

Lina threw up her arms. "Fine."

"Okay then," Constance said. "Time to get out of here."

The ship moaned and shook, sending the crew staggering. Constance snatched the back of the chair.

Michael grabbed her around the waist. "I'll hold you," he said. "You and Nicolas do your thing."

They moved their hands in the panel liquid until the speck of light that was their new home was centered on the screen.

"What do we do now?" the boy said.

Their destination was selected, but how were they going to maneuver the vessel?

"I imagine there's an initiation sequence," Dru said, as if reading Constance's mind.

"A password or code," Hashim said.

"Yes," Michael said. "But what code?"

Relax, Constance told herself and closed her eyes. Grainy pictures of the console flashed before her. An older man sat at the control with his hands on the panels. What was he doing? She squeezed her lids tight and watched what seemed like someone else's dream. The man pulled up the files one, six, seven, and twelve on the monitors. That was the sequence!

Constance opened her eyes and rotated Nicolas's hands. The Orb's schematics flashed on the screens. She pulled up the files one, six, seven, and twelve. A low pulsing moved through the ship. The lighting ebbed with the sound. The control room rumbled.

"This is it," Constance said.

"A countdown," Michael said.

"How do we know how much time we have left?" Dru said.

"Listen," Garcia said. "You hear that?" He thumped his hand to his thigh in time to the throbbing beat. "It's a tempo."

"He's right," Constance said.

"The intervals are getting shorter," Michael said.

Not only were the intervals getting shorter, but the frequency and decibels were increasing. With every flash, the color of the lights moved from the warmer yellows to the cooler blues. The tempo grew faster. Constance stopped hearing any sound but felt the ache of the high frequency in her eardrums. People covered their ears, trying to block out the pain.

Then came a rumbling vibration so strong, it rattled their teeth. Michael's grip tightened around her waist. He wrapped an arm around Nicolas's shoulders. The sounds of gears shifting and clicking into place gave Constance the impression they were inside an enormous wind-up toy. The Orb itself was changing.

She wanted to look out the window to see if her hypothesis was correct, but it was impossible with the shutters down. If the Orb was altering, it was unlikely any of the windows were now unprotected.

"Look," Michael said.

A previously dark monitor came to life. Everyone watched the image of the Orb on the screen as the rings moved toward the center and one another along the central axle. The ship compressed until it appeared to be a solid structure. The pain in her ears increased. The lights became a solid ice blue. The word "Execute" flashed over the image of the ship.

"Brace yourselves!" Constance called out.

The inhabitants wedged themselves against the wall and locked arms. Constance and Michael squeezed Nicolas tight. The migration had begun.

CHAPTER 41

Constance jerked awake. Where was she? Why was she so cold? She felt Michael's naked heat under the sheets, heard his deep breathing, and relaxed. She was in the motel room. They had made love.

She knew it was early. When she suffered from sleep difficulties, she always awoke at exactly 3:13. Witnessing Nicolas disappear with Kylos in a smoky rocket cloud had been overwhelming. She glanced at the bedside clock and was surprised to see it read 2:35. *Not even my insomnia is the same anymore*, she thought. She closed her eyes and attempted to visualize her body and mind becoming calm, but all she saw was Nicolas, hand in hand with Kylos as the wake of the rocket launch enveloped them.

She eased from bed, careful not to disturb Michael, slipped into his button-down shirt, wrapped it around her naked body, and tiptoed to the sliding door that led to the balcony. She scanned the marsh between the Chincoteague and Assateague islands, hoping to catch a glimpse of the ponies, but the world was dark and silent and still.

Her focus shifted from the marsh to her ghostly reflection

in the glass door. So much had changed in her life in the last few days. She saw that change in her tired and worried face. Her skin appeared to have lost its youthful glow and her hair its fiery auburn shine. She looked tougher but felt weaker. What would she do without Nicolas? How could she carry on?

Michael's breathing grew louder. He tossed in the bed, and then his breathing softened. Constance shifted her weight. Her reflection's lack of reciprocal movement froze her to the spot. She stared intently at the glass. The eyes, lips, and chin were hers, but it was if another person was looking back. Was this a trick of the light? She closed her eyes, silently counted to three, opened her eyes, and gasped.

The female Curator who had taken Nicolas was reflected in the glass and standing behind her. The woman gave her a smug grin. Constance spun around, certain she'd discover an empty room, and came face to face with her son's kidnapper.

"Hello again," the female said, cool and quiet.

How had she gained access to their room? Had she done it while they had been sleeping? Had she been waiting in the dark? "What are you doing here?" Constance said, her voice low.

The Curator hesitated, as if searching for the right words, and then said, "I'm stretching my legs."

Constance's brows furrowed. Was this a sick game? "You didn't answer my question," she said.

"What question is that?"

"I asked what you're doing here," Constance said. "Has something happened to my son?"

"What a foolish idea to think a child could save a ship like the Orb."

"What are you saying?"

The female stepped closer. Constance felt a cold breeze.

"The mission on the Orb has failed. Your son, Ms. Roy, is dead."

Constance's knees buckled. She willed herself to remain upright and steadied herself on the desk. She stared deep into the Curator's large eyes—emotionless and black. "You're lying," she said, the words so soft, she wasn't sure if she had uttered them.

The woman paused, processing Constance's response. "Indulge me. I'm rather new at this. How could you tell?"

Constance glared at her.

The Curator circled Constance. "Apparently, I still have much to learn from you. Let me reassure you. I intend to be a good pupil. We will have many lessons."

Michael stirred in bed.

The woman observed him with interest. "The human need for affection. That is also something you must help me to understand."

"Please," Constance said. "Is my son safe?"

"For now—as are you—but you won't always have Kylos to advocate on your behalf. He will come to see the folly of our mission."

"Constance?" Michael mumbled.

The Curator retreated into the dark entranceway.

"Wait," Constance said. "Will I see Nicolas again?"

A sliver of light from a crack in the bathroom door illuminated the Curator's face. "Whatever you think I am," she said, "I'm not a fortune teller."

"Hey," Michael said, stepping in front of Constance.

Constance leaned around Michael to stop the Curator, but she was already gone.

"Are you okay?"

"The woman…" Constance's voice trailed off. Why had the Curator come? Did she really know anything about Nicolas, or was the visit meant to be cruel? And what had she said about future lessons? The thought of seeing the woman again sickened her.

"What woman?" Michael said.

"Nothing," she said. "I couldn't sleep."

"It's early," he said, taking her hand. "Come back to bed."

She crossed to the bed, dropped his shirt, and returned to his arms ... but her thoughts remained on the female Curator's visit and Nicolas.

CHAPTER 42

C onstance and Nicolas had activated a tunnel in space
and time—a conduit from one part of the galaxy to
another. The migration was underway. The control room
morphed. Matter, gravity, temperature, and sound disappeared into a void, leaving Constance with a light-headed,
floating sensation. This migration was different from the one
that had brought her and the others to the Orb, perhaps
because this time they were sheltered inside the enormous
ship. Or were they?

Constance could no longer see Nicolas, Michael, or the
rest of the crew—only a bright, endless vista in all directions.
But she didn't feel alone. Others surrounded her. Were they
the Orb's inhabitants? Strangers? Misty faces appeared and
disappeared before her. Despite their ethereal quality, they
were reassuring. Then all became clear.

She was not looking at many people, but one person
multiple times ... and that person was her. Dozens and dozens
of reflections presented themselves, each existing as if behind
a thin, gauzy curtain. The expressions on the various
Constances gave her the impression that they were unaware
of each other's actuality, but she saw them all.

Constance drifted amid her ghostly counterparts. As she approached a doppelgänger, she had an instant understanding of that Constance's entire life history. Many lives were like hers before the migration to the Orb. In some worlds her parents had never died, while in others one or both had. Nicolas existed as she knew him or had brothers and sisters or had never been born. Michael appeared as a friend, colleague, or husband.

As her counterparts and their lives swirled around her, she wondered how much time had passed. Seconds? Decades? A century? All seemed possible. One Constance in particular caught her attention. The feeling of loss was overwhelming, and somehow she knew this was the Constance who had sacrificed Nicolas in order to save them. They owed much to this Constance. She sent thoughts of gratitude through the membrane, and for the briefest of moments the other Constance seemed to sense her, maybe even see her.

A force pulled her down. The control room walls and the other inhabitants reappeared. Nicolas was at the console, and Michael was beside her. She blinked and noted the others' bewildered expressions. The Orb was eerily still, like a ghost ship.

"Are we there?" Michael said. His voice was parched, as if he hadn't spoken in years.

All eyes turned to the monitors. They were dark.

"Let's go to the corridor," Muhammad said.

The crew stumbled from the room, anxious to see where the ship had taken them. Constance helped Nicolas from the chair and took his hand. They joined Michael and entered the hall. The inhabitants lined the passage, two faces pressed to every portal. Everyone stared in awe. "I can't believe it," someone said.

Constance and Michael found an empty window.

"I want to see," Nicolas said.

Michael lifted the boy, and the three peered out the portal.

They were no longer looking at Jupiter and its fiery Red Spot. They were now in orbit above a glorious golden planet with bright, billowy clouds that floated above equal parts land and blue ocean.

"Wow," Nicolas said, pressing his nose to the glass to get a better view of the planet below.

Constance wrapped her arm around Michael and clutched Nicolas's hand. The sight was like a beautiful dream … Grace's dream … Grace's planet.

CHAPTER 43

After recovering from the initial awe of witnessing their new planet, the inhabitants' attention turned to figuring out how to land the mighty Orb. They had journeyed to the farthest reaches of the galaxy. What if they failed to discover how to touch down on the planet's surface and died on the ship? Everything they had been through would have been for nothing. But their concerns were short-lived. Doors previously hidden began sliding into place to divide the ring into segments, and then each segment reoriented and thrusters pulsed.

"Fasten yourself to whatever you can!" Constance said to the crew as corridor doors closed and separated them.

Michael and Nicolas rushed to join her in a section seconds before its door closed. She motioned for Nicolas to sit on the floor, away from the window.

Michael sat next to Nicolas. "Come on, Roy," he said.

She stole a final look out the portal. Piece by piece, the ship dismantled. Each ring broke into pie slices. The Orb had transformed from one ark to dozens of lifeboats. Their unit disengaged with a jolt. She joined Michael on the floor with Nicolas between them.

Constance focused on their section's movement, the thrusters, and the stars and clouds that whirred by out the window. The lighting went dark, and the temperature dropped. She imagined that this had been by design—that the ship's creator had programmed cutting the lights and lowering the temperature to conserve power. She wrapped her arm around Nicolas to keep him warm.

They had been falling for nearly an hour when they broke through the clouds. The engines roared. Time to brace for landing. She and Michael locked arms around the boy and pressed their feet hard on the floor. She mentally counted down. Ten, nine, eight, seven. The thrusters surged. Six, five, four. Their unit hit land. Three, two. They slid along the floor. One. They slumped in a heap.

Their section expelled a final hiss, and then all was quiet. They pulled apart and stood.

"Everyone okay?" she said.

"The men are fine," Michael said, indicating Nicolas and himself.

"Are we there?" Nicolas said.

The three gazed out the window at the lush landscape. She had forgotten what it was like to look at anything other than Jupiter and the stars.

"We made it, Grace," Constance said.

Michael put his arm around her and nodded.

Nicolas tugged on Constance's shirt. "Can we go out?"

Would the atmosphere on this new planet support life or extinguish it? Grace and Kylos had believed humans could survive in this atmosphere and had gone to a lot of trouble to ensure they arrived safe and sound. That was good enough for her. Besides, what choice did they have? They couldn't stay in the capsule forever.

"Let's see if we can find an exit," she said and headed toward the door that had sealed them in. Air hissed into the compartment and brought her to a halt. "We're depressurizing," she said.

The hissing stopped, gears clicked, and the door lowered like a gangplank. Light flooded in. They squinted at the bright orange sky. The new sun was redder than the one in their solar system. Constance basked in its warmth and scanned the heavens. A gray moon was visible despite the brightness, and to the right of the moon was a smaller sister moon. The air was different than Earth's—thinner and warmer—but it tasted cleaner and purer. A lake or ocean stretched as far as the eye could see.

They stepped from the gangplank onto the gravel-and-sand terrain and stumbled as they adjusted to the planet's stronger gravity. It had been months since she had felt an uneven surface underfoot. Nicolas wandered toward the sandy shore, picked up a stone, studied it, and placed it in his pocket. The shiny Orb sections were scattered along the shore like pieces of beach glass. The rest of the crew had exited their pods and were also taking in the surroundings.

She tracked the land away from the shore. Leafy green algae grew among the rocks. Beyond that, the rocks disappeared and low-growing foliage covered the ground. Constance speculated it might be the early stages of a forest. The planet felt primitive, vibrant, and strong. This must be what Earth looked like at its beginning, she thought.

"So what do we do now?" Michael said.

She smiled. "Move in."

Constance and Michael set about coordinating the crew in preparation for spending their first night on their new home—whenever night fell on this new planet. The crew broke into teams. Lina organized the group testing the planet's water and soil; Dru recruited Nicolas and others to retrieve the plants and seeds from the Orb; Hashim oversaw the collection of vegetation samples; and Muhammad, Garcia, and the remaining crew worked on building a crude camp and an area for the animals.

Michael and Constance performed preliminary checks to see how the animals had survived the migration and were relieved to discover that other than being dazed, like the human travelers, the animals appeared to be fine. Constance ordered that they remain in their stalls and cages until Muhammad and Garcia's enclosures were completed.

She approached Muhammad at the fenced area. "How's it going?"

"We're ready when you are."

Constance searched for Nicolas and spotted him playing on the shore, building a sandcastle. "Nicolas," she said. "Want to give me a hand?"

Nicolas ran over and grabbed her with sandy hands. "This is a good planet," he said with such joy, she couldn't help but smile.

They joined Michael at the entrance to one of the sections of the menagerie.

"We're getting Patches," Nicolas said to Michael.

"So I understand," Michael said and handed Constance a harness made from strips from the Curators' tunics, which he had torn and tied together.

She and Nicolas stepped inside and made their way down the corridor. How different the menagerie looked all broken up and flooded with light. She found Patches' stall and opened the door.

"There she is," Nicolas said, hushed.

Patches bobbed her head and shook her mane. Constance sank into the straw, slipped the fabric harness around the mare's neck, and guided her to the stall exit. After a moment's hesitation, the horse stepped up onto the corridor floor.

Nicolas stroked the horse's neck as Constance walked her to and down the gangplank.

The mare snorted at the new planet's air and pawed at the ground.

"That's a horse that wants to be free," Michael said.

Constance slipped the harness from the horse's neck. "Welcome to your new home," she said and released her into the corral.

The horse inched forward, adjusting to the planet's gravity, and then took off and galloped in long, arcing curves around the pen, her mane blowing and her tail bouncing. Nicolas cheered. Soon the other animals were freed, and with every release the inhabitants grew more confident about their new home. Finally, the last portion of the menagerie was opened. A flock of starlings flew out and into the murmuration patterns for which they were famous. The birds soared in synchronized maneuvers—expanding and contracting without an apparent leader—and then the ribbon of black wings disappeared over a hill.

"You think they'll find a home?" Michael said.

"We did."

Nicolas tapped Constance's arm. "May I go see Patches?"

"Yes. But be careful. She's still adjusting to her surroundings."

"I'll go with him," Michael said.

The two entered the pen. She thought of the other Constance, the one who she had sensed behind the gauzy membrane during their journey to the planet. How had that Constance found the strength to give up her wonderful son so that the inhabitants had a chance at survival? Could she have done the same?

"You've done well," a familiar voice said from behind her.

"Kylos," she said and discovered him hidden near the capsule.

"It's good to see you again, Dr. Roy."

She scanned his face. "You're sincere," she said, puzzled.

He smiled.

Deep down she was glad to see him, too. She broke his gaze and watched Nicolas and Michael with the animals. "So does your presence mean we're out of danger?" she said.

"My colleagues are still divided. It is my contention that your successful arrival here proves humans have the ability to save themselves."

"What do those who don't agree with you think about our success?"

"That it proves that humans have the potential to become an intergalactic virus—an invasive species, if you will. For the time being I have convinced them to let you be and to observe your progress from a distance."

"In other words, don't blow it."

He cocked his head, processed her words, and chuckled like a shy child. "Yes. Don't blow it."

She suppressed a grin. It was the first time she'd heard a Curator laugh.

"My colleagues agreed not to interfere here, Dr. Roy, but with a condition."

Her smile disappeared. "What condition?"

"Nicolas must return to his mother. His stay with you was only temporary. My colleagues won't tolerate a boy with his skills out here so far from their reach."

She knew he belonged with his real mother but had dreaded this moment all the same. "I'd like to say goodbye," she said.

"It might be better if you don't. I don't wish to be cruel, but he's not yours."

The words stung. If what Kylos had said about the crew's infertility was true, she'd never have the opportunity to experience what the other Constance and Nicolas had. She would never know the special bond between parent and child. They would be the last—the only—generation to inhabit the planet.

"For Nicolas's safety, it's best he and I depart quickly.

You've made an enemy of Fifi, as you call her, and she has designs on the boy."

She grabbed Kylos by the arm to keep him from leaving. He looked at her hand, and she released him.

"Where are you going?" she said. "I mean after you return Nicolas?"

"To help the others," he said.

"Others?"

"You don't think yours is the only Orb, do you?" he said and walked away.

Another Orb? The ship parts marked with ORB-2 suddenly made sense. They must be the second ship. But where was the first? Was there an ORB-3 or ORB-4 or more? And, if so, were they coming here?

Kylos reached Nicolas. The boy looked at her, back at Kylos, and then ran at full speed up the hill and flew into her arms. Constance squeezed him tight, not wanting to let him go. *Maybe he can stay one more day*, she thought. She saw Kylos over her shoulder and thought of the other Constance. She had no right to keep him.

"You have to go," she said, pulling away. "Kylos and your mother are waiting."

Nicolas bit his lip. "I'm going to miss you," he said.

"I'm going to miss you, too." *More than you will ever know*, she thought. She squeezed his hands. Constance wanted to thank him for saving them and thank his mother for letting him, but she was afraid she'd break down.

"It's time to be courageous, isn't it?" he said.

She nodded. The boy gave her one long, final hug, ran to Kylos, gave her a brief wave, and then—in an instant—was gone. She gazed at the sky and silently wished Nicolas and Kylos a safe journey.

CHAPTER 44

Constance sat on the deserted beach of Assateague Island, clutched the astronaut figurine, and watched the waves of the Atlantic roll toward shore, break, and ripple to a stop at her feet. The stars and constellations were barely visible in the early-morning sky. The ocean wind made her shiver. She pulled Michael's coat around her and stole a look back at the parking lot. She felt bad about asking him to remain in the car, but she needed to be alone. Nicolas had been her whole world. Her entire body ached with grief.

Thunder clapped, and she felt a rush of cold air. Had Wallops launched another rocket? She searched the skies for a contrail. Perhaps a storm was on its way. She looked up the beach, expecting to find a cloud front, and saw a figure running toward her. Her heart skipped a beat. She stared without blinking, afraid that if she blinked, the ghostly vision of her son would disappear. He drew nearer, and her spirit soared.

Constance jumped to her feet and took off. The wind pushed against her. She pumped her arms harder and then, at last, Nicolas flew into her arms. She fell to her knees, kissed his cheeks, head, nose, and chin, and laughed through the tears.

He laughed, too, and giggled as she inspected him to be sure he was okay. He had returned safe and sound, just as Kylos had said.

Kylos. Where was he? She scanned the area and saw him observing them from up the beach. *Thank you*, she said silently. Kylos bowed.

"Mr. Whittaker," Nicolas said.

Michael jogged to them. He stared at Nicolas, stunned, and dropped to his knees beside her. "How did Nicolas…" he said.

"Kylos," she said. She pointed up the beach, but the Curator had vanished.

"Look what I have," Nicolas said. He reached into his pocket and removed a rock. "It's from the other planet. Wait till you hear about it."

Constance and Michael laughed as Nicolas launched into the story of his journey to the new planet. A ribbon of orange stretched over the horizon, announcing a new day. Constance had many questions, but they could wait. Nicolas was okay. And for now, the world was okay, too.

ACKNOWLEDGMENTS

We couldn't have written this book without the support and love of numerous people. Thanks to James O'Sullivan for his insightful feedback and detailed notes that made the book infinitely better; to Judith O'Sullivan for her enthusiasm and unflagging support of our careers; and to the rest of our families for your encouragement and love.

A huge thank you to Barb Goffman, writer and copyeditor extraordinaire, whose eagle eye and insightful notes helped clarify our story before we sent it out into the wild.

Heartfelt thanks to the delightful Jonathan and Jane Richstein, owners of Sundial Books on Chincoteague Island, for graciously allowing us to depict them and their wonderful bookstore in the novel and for encouraging us on a path that led to publication of this work.

Our deepest gratitude to our editor, Ron Sauder, for his sincere enthusiasm for the book, his fantastic title contribution, and for his spirit of collaboration and partnership.

Thank you to copyeditor Allister Thompson for taking care of all the little details.

Fond thanks to Ed Aymar, Joelle Charbonneau, Sherry Harris, Adam Meyer, and Alan Orloff, remarkable writers and generous human beings, who took time away from their own work to read ours.

Thanks to our writer friends and the Chessie Chapter of Sisters in Crime for your warmth and inspiration.

Finally, thanks to the hard-working bookstore owners, passionate librarians, devoted readers, and tireless bloggers for your love of writers and reading.

ABOUT THE AUTHORS

Paul Awad and Kathryn O'Sullivan are an award-winning husband and wife writing and filmmaking team. They have collaborated on feature and documentary films, screenplays, and web series.

Paul is a cinema professor and Kathryn is a theatre professor at Northern Virginia Community College. Kathryn is also the award-winning writer of the Colleen McCabe mystery series. They live in Reston, Virginia.

Visit their websites at www.paul-awad.com and www.kathrynosulivan.com.

Made in the USA
Middletown, DE
13 June 2022